We hope you enjoy thi
renew it by the due da

You can renew it at www.norfolk.gov.uk/libraries o
by using our free library app.

Otherwise you can phone 0344 800 8020 -
please have your library card and PIN ready.

You can sign up for email reminders too.

22/10/19

NORFOLK ITEM

30129 079 676 483

**NORFOLK COUNTY COUNCIL
LIBRARY AND INFORMATION SERVICE**

VILLAGE
by the FORD

BASED ON
A TRUE STORY

When reading, you will no doubt immediately suspect that this story, told with much humour and a touch of romance, is real. You would be correct! It is the unlikely but true adventure of a family who break away from conventional living and risk all, win or lose, in a far off and remote valley. The places, the granite bridge, the crystal clear stream, all are real; that stream is the bathroom for there is no alternative! You can find it on the map, dip your fingers in the water, walk along the valley. The people exist too and the names have not been changed – you may even meet some of them.

This may be every man's dream, but how many wives with three young children would dare? What are the chances of success - there is danger, lots of laughter but no crime or violence. Though conditions are primitive, life is great, exciting, so different – can it last?

i

To my wife, Janifer, who helped,
to our children, Christopher, Sharon and Stephen,
for the memories
and to the people of Relubbus.

Bound and printed in UK
Cornish Books
First Published 1998
Reprinted 1999.   Second impression 2003
Copyright © Gordon Channer 1998
IBSN 0-9537009-1-7

VILLAGE *by the* FORD

by

GORDON CHANNER

Valley of Dreams series

CORNISH BOOKS
5 Tregembo Hill
Penzance, Cornwall, TR20 9EP

Press Reviews
Village by the Ford

A seemingly crazy and impossible venture...but the story itself is a compelling one. THE CARAVAN CLUB MAGAZINE

Told with good humour in a collection of anecdotes of crises and triumphs. CHOICE MAGAZINE

an engaging and...amusing account...vividly evokes the family's adventures WESTERN MORNING NEWS

If you liked Nevil Shute's A Town like Alice, you will appreciate Village by the Ford. I couldn't put it down. TOURER MAGAZINE

This charming story...makes a good read. WEST BRITON

It is by turns funny and touching...recommended reading for all. MMM

A fascinating, readable, well-told tale THE CORNISHMAN

A gentle tale...Looking forward to the sequel RADIO CORNWALL

..and all the adventures that came their way PRACTICAL CARAVAN

Turned to reality his dream...the absolute limits of endurance CARAVAN MAGAZINE

...story of a young family's struggle CAMPING & CARAVANNING

This series has had 56 reviews including the Daily Telegraph

Contents

The Family at Relubbus

Gordon	Father
Jan	Mother
Chris	Age 8 (at start of book)
Sharon	Age 6
Stephen	Age three
Jim	Grandfather (Jan's father)
Audrey	Grandmother (Jan's mother)
Max	The big yellow excavator.

Period   Autumn 1968 –   June 1970

Sketches and photos – see end of book.

CHAPTER 1

Making the Break

The little green van halted quickly, it had no choice. The narrow potholed track, weed covered from lack of use, had suddenly petered out. Shrouded at intervals by overhanging vegetation, the rough stony surface ended abruptly after a granite bridge crossing the small river.

Half a mile back, the village where they left the tarmac road was more a hamlet, just a cluster of houses, and since then not a soul had been seen. Even the old cottage part way down the track appeared deserted. Straight ahead, some 300 yards distant, towering above a barrier of willows and gorse, a broad mound of ancient mine waste dominated the view. Having stood for perhaps a century, its sombre barrenness was still only partially softened by heathers dotted sporadically among the stones.

The vehicle's occupants, a man and a woman both in their early thirties, gazed up, glancing at each other questioningly. Was this the place? They reached for the door handles and stepped out, stretching, then leaning on the roof.

Dragging her eyes from the dark heaps of spoil, the woman, Jan, swung to survey the surrounding area and stopped, drawing in her breath sharply. Along the valley a scene of tranquil beauty held her temporarily spellbound. She gazed enthralled. The river sparkled, and even now in November most of the trees, perhaps bushes would be a better word for they stood in general no more than twice a man's height, still retained the greater proportion of their leaves. Dotted around, singly and in groups, close by and up the more distant valley slopes, their foliage was no longer bright green but yellowing, some almost brassy in the weak sunshine.

"Beautiful, yes – but so isolated." At the thought she turned further, dubiously eyeing the way they had come. Her escape route? A path back to reality?

And the stillness. Why were there no sounds?

Now the engine noise that had filled her ears through most of the night, into dawn and on until mid-morning had at last stopped, the quietness was... she didn't quite know what, but felt a certain unease as they stood, silent seconds slipping by. It would be easy to believe that time had stood still here, like the ancient realm of King Arthur, when people were few.

Her eyes turned northwards, across the top of the little van, to look at her companion questioningly. With unspoken understanding they stepped away from the vehicle, walked slowly back towards the small river and down the sloping bank, he leading, left hand held backwards to support her. Somehow changing sides on the short descent, they knelt together at the stream's edge, the water clear like crystal.

"Pure as a mountain stream," she thought, watching it flow smoothly from the bridge's shadow, "but so placid."

Depth varied from a few inches to maybe a couple of feet near the centre. Close by, a gravelly bottom supported tufts of red-topped grassy reed rising toward the surface, minute details magnified by the water's clarity. She turned at a murmur of sound. Downstream the river babbled quietly over exposed rocks where its bed dropped lower. A small smile touched her lips. The first sign of movement. The smile broadened in delight when a silvery trout jumped in the centre of the pool, the circle of ripples spreading towards them.

The man had seen the fish too, but he watched her. She was beautiful when she smiled, short brown hair uncombed after the journey, a fading summer tan on her face, heightened below, outlined against the V-neck of her white blouse. She stood five inches shorter than his five-foot ten, but kneeling beside the water their eyes were almost level, his grey blue, hers greeny brown, squinting slightly against the morning sun. She reached for his hand, they rose, turning to scan the chaotic tangle of gorse and willow. From their position on the valley floor, only a short length of river was visible, flowing roughly north towards Hayle. To both east and west the land rose gently, but nowhere a single sign of human habitation.

Gazing up towards the rising ground her doubts returned. What they planned was risky. Friends who knew their intentions had all expressed surprise, even disbelief. One or two had only half jokingly questioned her sanity! Their own parents showed no such tendency to soften criticism with humour.

But they must, she thought, do something! - Or should they? After all they were comfortable, even well off. She had a largish house, an old building partially renovated, the tastefully modernised kitchen was her delight. What about all her friends? Could she give them all up? And Gordon, close beside her, how would he fare? Most of all, what about the three children? They had talked it over of course and agreed, but she could still draw back. It was not yet too late! True the big car had been sold for a good price, replaced with a cheap little Mini van; every scrap of money would certainly be needed. However, even that was not an irreversible move. Standing silently, hand in hand, gazing at the wild Cornish valley before them, Jan recalled the words of a close friend, echoing her own recent thoughts.

"How," she had asked incredulously, "can you think of giving up your nice house and all the good things you've gathered together? You're surrounded by friends, you can't possibly go off to live in the wilds. It's crazy! *And in a caravan!*"

The picture of a head shaken slowly from side to side in puzzlement and her friend's last words still hung clearly in memory.

"What will you do for money? Think of the children! And why would you want to? Tell me that. Why?"

"Why? Because Gordon wants to," she told herself. And it was true, she knew that, and knew the reason; he needed the challenge. The more difficult, more isolated, more primitive, the greater his desire. A need to over-come, to build, to create something special, to leave a mark. But should she agree? Should she let him – go with him?

"It's more than that," she admitted, gazing with sightless eyes, lost in her thoughts. Thirteen years married, they were still deeply attracted to each other. No question of anyone else for either of them; but life had become so safe and assured, no longer a challenge. Love had not died, that remained good as ever, but the spark of life had somehow disappeared. Things were too set, too predictable, too secure.

4

She liked security, only... only what? Only she no longer felt entirely happy, no longer vibrant, full of life as she once had been. Neither of them were. The smooth daily repetition of a cosy lucrative existence lacked excitement. They could both see it stretching uneventfully into far-off retirement half a lifetime away. So it was necessary! Whatever parents and friends might say or think, it was necessary. But she remained apprehensive. Not afraid exactly, but torn, hesitant; was it right for the family, for the children?

A hand shook her shoulder. "You were miles away!" Gordon smiled at her. "Dreaming?"

She tossed her head quickly, clearing misty thoughts, covering confusion with a crisp response.

"Hidden secrets. Come on, we can't see far from here." She pointed, "Think we could climb up?"

Forcing a way across the valley floor he led up the steep incline, clambering towards the top. It was now obvious these old tailings from copper mining of a previous century were confined to just one side of the valley. It was nevertheless a mound of considerable size, a mini mountain sixty or more feet high, fading back into the natural rise of the ground. No track led to the top. At some past time stone had been removed for some purpose, leaving a sheer drop where a steep path might once have been.

As they climbed Jan drew level, not prepared always to trail along behind. Breathing heavily, forcing herself forward and beginning to take the lead, a rock in the loose surface twisted under her foot starting a minor avalanche of small stones. She staggered, threw both arms high in the air, vainly attempting to maintain balance, reaching as if to grasp some non-existent sky support. On the point of falling backwards, a strong hand grabbed the outstretched wrist. Feeling herself hauled bodily back from the brink into Gordon's waiting embrace, she looked up into his laughing face, her heart thumping wildly.

For several seconds neither spoke, comfortable in the closeness, not wanting to move. After a while she eased back, making a little kiss sign with her lips.

"Thanks." The whisper was barely audible.

"My pleasure. Always happy to display man's natural superiority."

"Chauvinist," she accused without much conviction, making no attempt to draw farther away.

Reaching a higher ledge they paused to look down, resting briefly to discuss the site's possibilities. Position seemed ideal. Away from roads, in a valley hidden from other people, hidden also to an unknown extent from wind. No traffic noise, they listened, no noise at all! Approach good, off a B road. Central, three miles from the southern coast and perhaps five from the Atlantic to the northwest. On the other hand, there were drawbacks. The waste heap must be moved. They looked down again and in both directions; the work involved seemed immense. Eighteen acres in total the form said, one part covered by waste, the rest so over-grown no one could tell!

"Living conditions won't be too easy." Gordon commented, and seeing her grimace of rebuke admitted more frankly, "OK, they'll be archaic."

She nodded knowingly. "That's better, remember I've read the details too. No electric, no telephone, no water except from the river. Without mains water we wouldn't even have a proper toilet. Archaic is right! Feudal might be nearer, straight from the middle ages."

Could a family of five, her husband Gordon, herself Janifer, always called Jan, and their children, Christopher eight, Sharon six, and Stephen only three, survive under such a regime, she wondered? Would the tiny amount of money left after buying this place be sufficient to live on, buy machinery and construct those buildings necessary to get the business started? Another thing, could she stand all this isolation after so many friends and social contacts?

Most of all, was it safe? What about floods, hidden shafts, or worse? There would be no one to call on in a crisis. Searching for answers she prepared to move on.

Gordon, leading again, pondered the sheer volume of work? His office career, promising and intensively mental, certainly never physical, had at least not left him fat and going to seed. He remained wiry, even thin but had those muscles forgotten how to work hard? Would they still have the stamina? The prospect of pitting himself against the elements, of moulding this remote, neglected place into something special entirely by the family's own efforts and against all the odds, had an almost irresistible pull. But what girl in her right mind would give up everything and follow her husband to such a life? Reaching the top they paused, looking back to the river, now a small meandering ribbon in the distance.

"Would this be a good place to raise children?" Jan scanned the wild panorama below from the new vantage point? "Possibly. Certainly they would learn self-reliance. It could be exciting. If successful, one thing was definite, life would never again be normal. Hard probably but fun, full of incidents, bound to be!"

This particular site offered possibilities far beyond any alternative remotely near their price band. Offered them she realised, just because of that remoteness and lack of any services. The estate agent's details read 'undeveloped caravan park'. *Undeveloped* was a masterpiece of understatement! The village of Relubbus, a roadside shop, a handful of half-hidden houses, and completely unsignposted, had eventually been found after driving through twice without noticing. Only enquiries at the little shop confirmed this actually was Relubbus.

"You must mean down the moor," the shopkeeper had said, "been on the market years, no one wants it, too much work."

"No one wants it?" The words echoed questioningly in her mind. Would it succeed? That remained the real question. She might be prepared to forgo a regular income, but no one could live forever on fresh air!

After a while they moved to the east, finding a new equally steep route down through the trees, turning to follow the river downstream for roughly half a mile. The site narrowed, perhaps two hundred yards across at the lower end. Virtually no part was level, and most stood choked with gorse, ivy, old willow bushes and copious brambles. Walking back, they stopped on a slightly raised area, but it offered little view past the tangled vegetation. Gordon half turned, pausing before he spoke.

"What do you think?"

The remark fell casually, vastly understating its vital importance. He waited tensely. The pause lengthened. She could never agree – not to give up her home, comfortable way of life, friends, everything! And what was on offer in return?

Her reply broke the continuing silence.

"You want it, I can tell that. No good pretending it doesn't matter. You really want me to agree, to abandon everything and live with you here, like..."

She stopped, unable to think of any comparison. "Well," she paused again, noting his clenched hands tighten but no change to his deadpan expression.

"Well – I think it's super! Let's buy it."

The breath he didn't know he was holding came out in a rush. This was the answer hoped for, talked about often at home in soft armchairs around the fire, but when it came to the real crunch, the raw reality, had he really expected agreement? More than agreement – encouragement. Buy it? Try to buy it, more like!

They looked at each other, stepping closer, arms enclosing, their lips meeting softly; two souls lost in a wilderness and in each other.

On the journey home, talk was of detail. The means, the way to proceed, what tools to take, which caravan to buy... and what equipment? Exciting. Miles sped by. Exeter, 100 miles away, slipped past while discussing yet again the caravan size, perhaps for the fifth time. Money, or rather lack of it, formed the key. They would search the local paper for something necessarily quite old and probably small, but sound enough to endure a long heavily loaded journey. It must carry not only everything needed for living, but tools and equipment for the work.

Relubbus had inspired them, not since their wedding had they felt so exhilarated, so pulsing with life, with the future. The challenge, the risk, heady stuff, stronger than wine, but... could they afford it? How much could they pay and leave any chance of succeeding?

One thing was clear. They did intend to make the

9

break. After months of tentative looking, Cornwall had tipped the balance. Once experienced, that valley and in a strange way the promise of uniquely primitive conditions to be overcome, made the mundaneness of their present lives almost unbearable.

They had to try! If not with this property then with another, but this was favourite. Sites in Wales were recalled where in October icicles formed inside the Mini van when forced to sleep in it one night, and others in Devon where the sea gradually encroached. None had the beauty of this Cornish valley. If only it could be afforded. This was the crux, a turning point; it called for more than a prudent offer. There are times in life for caution, and times for decisive action, even rash and risky action. A time to discard the securely comfortable but boring, in favour of the dangerous but blood-tinglingly exhilarating!

The following Monday, Gordon arranged to leave his job in favour of freelance assignments where he could work such hours and days as he chose, giving freedom for quick trips to inspect other possibilities. The house was put on the market, they had to know how much it would bring. When it sold the furniture would be stored with Frank and Ivy, Gordon's parents, in their loft. An offer was made for the site at Relubbus. Several caravans were viewed but none found suitable. A tow-bar was fitted to the Mini van. Action! It may not have been wise, but a deep restlessness drove them on.

The house sold quickly, but the offer for Relubbus was refused. The family moved in with Gordon's parents and looked at other sites, but none really appealed. They did however, locate and purchase cheaply a small second-hand ten-foot long Eccles Touring Caravan, storing it in the garden.

Gordon still worried that Jan might have second thoughts. He had watched her taking a last look round their old house during the furniture removal and seen flickers of doubt crossing her face. Would she weaken? It took some courage for any girl to do what she was doing!

A month flew by and the old year passed; 1969 dawned crisply cold but nothing that appealed had been found. Several other sites viewed were a great deal less risky, with proper services already available. All were certainly less work. However, no location yet seen offered the size or the scope for creating from scratch, presented by that Cornish valley. It preyed on their minds, alone extending the chance to model with their own hands a haven of peace and happiness, remote from towns and from crowding. They wanted somewhere that visitors could enjoy the countryside without destroying it, where birds, animals and even insects were more important than games rooms and entertainments. For that only Relubbus would do.

They discussed it often, comparing each alternative location viewed. Both realised only the complete lack of services and immense work required placed such a large project almost but not quite within their price grasp. Attempts to put it from their minds by stressing the bad points failed miserably; it was just those drawbacks, the risks, the unconventional living, that so stirred them.

Weeks later a letter arrived offering Relubbus at a reduced price, but still above what they could possibly afford. They wrote, very slightly increasing the previous offer, hoping but not really expecting a favourable response. Quite quickly a reply arrived.

"Our client is not prepared at this time to take a lower offer."

Gordon passed it to Jan. They looked glumly at each other, feeling beaten. They could offer no more! Dejectedly he reached again for the letter, re-reading it. The wording seemed strange, the *'at this time'* stood out. If not now, when?

Grasp the straw! An immediate response was drafted stating they never wanted to hear of Relubbus again and did the agents have sites available elsewhere.

A reply came by return. It accepted their previous offer! After all the formalities that would be required, they seemed destined to become the proud owners of that very, very undeveloped and remote, but wildly beautiful valley. There they hoped to survive and perhaps eventually prosper.

CHAPTER 2

Westward

The children had taken the first move to Gordon's mother's almost in their stride, it lay only a mile from their previous house. Christopher and Sharon remained at the same school, Sharon in her second year, while Stephen at three was hardly affected.

How would they take to Cornwall? The prospect, discussed with them often, reached a strange turning point with the arrival of the little tourer. Living in a caravan caught their imagination, they sat in it often, wrapped in an imaginary world of adventure, totally oblivious to likely future privations and hardships.

Weeks dragged by while the solicitors, as solicitors will, drew up and redrew contracts, sought answers to innumerable questions and made the statutory searches.

"When are we going?" the children asked daily, but eventually such questions ceased.

To their young minds the move had become one of those many things grown-ups talk about but never do. The long waiting period, though frustrating, was not totally wasted. There were things to prepare, plans to make. Gordon attended several auctions, usually with Jan, buying an old petrol-driven Haytor mower and various hand tools. They started packing the caravan, took another trip to Cornwall for preliminary meetings with the local authority, and still they waited.

During this time, some difference of opinion arose regarding a name for their new home.

"Wheal Virgin, the name of the old mine where the spoil originated." Gordon suggested.

Jan shook her head, "Who will realise Wheal is the Cornish word for a mine?" Her serious expression eased, "and you can forget about virgins!"

"What then?"

"River Valley. Why not? It's simple and easy to remember." A gesture as she spoke said, 'how obvious', the same hand reaching out to pat his arm, a sort of consolation for not being very bright. He half expected her to say "Good dog," but she merely leaned close to his ear, "I like simple things."

Appreciating her whispered comment, both the logic and the cleverly implied slight to his intelligence, his head inclined in a mock bow of acknowledgement.

"OK, River Valley."

Eventually of course the message came through, "Contracts have been exchanged. Completion will be on Friday, 20th June."

"That's seven more weeks away!" Jan exclaimed in dismay.

"I thought it would be earlier," Gordon replied, "but the seller doesn't mind if we move now the contracts are signed. I asked him when we met, unofficially of course. Bit risky perhaps, doing work before we actually own it, but time is important."

Neither of them had expected quite so long a delay. Jan nodded, obviously pleased, shrugging and spreading her fingers, palms upward in an age-old gesture.

"What's a little extra risk? You can't call this whole

affair the safest thing in the world!"

Two days later, Thursday the first day of May, a new month, a new life! Everything loaded and having said goodbye to Frank and Ivy, the family set out for London to visit Jan's parents. Jim and Audrey lived in Grove Park, between Camberwell and Dulwich. Staying overnight meant parking in the road outside the house, difficult to avoid with more equipment to load. Jan hoped neither vehicle nor caravan looked prosperous enough to draw a thief's attention.

On arrival, Gordon dashed off to a prearranged meeting and purchased a small Dumpy Level, complete with tripod. This instrument, similar to those surveyors everywhere are seen looking through, was essential for laying long drainage runs.

Friday, the day of final departure, Jan and her mother walked down to Peckham for last-minute supplies and spent much of the late morning cooking together. Following lunch the last items were somehow forced inside the caravan. It would be fair to say the weight carried was now excessive. Had both van and caravan been twice their actual size they would still have been overloaded. Gordon looked carefully at clearances between tyre and wheel arch, shrugged, and glancing skywards, offered a silent prayer that nothing would give way on the journey.

On top of the van, on its own roof rack, sat a canoe which they had tried to sell without success. Inside the caravan rested the mower, the lighter carpentry toolbox and a collection of useful things like bow-saws, garden forks, rakes, brooms, a scythe, together with bricklaying trowels and other assorted tools. The drawing-board was cumbersome but necessary for submission of plans

15

before any building work could commence. Between and around this collection lay food of various kinds donated by both sets of parents, all the family's clothes, utensils, a few of the children's favourite things, the crockery, cutlery, buckets and water-carriers. Even the bicycles had been fitted in – everything essential for the new life must be carried somehow!

The caravan was so full, not even tiny Stephen could enter the doorway. Heavier things, the bigger toolbox, the wheelbarrow, picks, shovels and numerous other items, were relegated to the Mini van, leaving just sufficient space in the back for the two older children to lie close together. One would rest beside the wheel-barrow, the other pressed tightly against the left wheel arch. It even became necessary to transfer the big drawing-board into the Mini van, leaning it diagonally so the children would lie in a narrow triangular tunnel, preventing piled up articles falling on their heads at corners. The entire stock of bedclothes spread beneath them promised a more comfortable ride than anyone else, but no room remained for young Stephen; he would sit throughout the journey on Jan's lap in the passenger seat. Fortunately no partition divided off the rear, so everyone could talk easily to each other. Christopher and Sharon could pull themselves up just far enough to peer over the seat tops and through the front window.

Towards evening, final preparations complete, the three generations ate together at a final meal, seven people easily seated round the big table.

"On the verge of departing civilisation," Jan thought, looking at the ample space, electric light overhead, the copious array of dishes and cutlery, then wondered for a moment how she would wash up without water on tap. "Even these chairs are the last proper ones we shall sit on for many a year."

The air was charged with excitement, suppressed in the four adults though they felt it as strongly, but uninhibited in the children. The young ones nibbled then abandoned their food, stood up, sat down again, looked through windows at the fading light, chattering irrepressibly, bubbling like the fizzy lemonade largely forgotten beside their plates. Stephen, not fully understanding the implications of the move was nevertheless caught up in the atmosphere, betraying his own exhilaration with a total inability to remain still, but saying little. The older pair were more vocal, impatient remarks flowing from their lips.

"How dark it's getting."

"Gosh is it that time already? Will we see to get comfortable in the van if it gets too dark?"

Finally in desperation Sharon demanded, "Mum! How can you eat so much?"

Her mother smiled, thinking "Because it may be some time before we eat well again!" but she said nothing.

Eventually, the meal over, they made their final departure, totally ignorant at the time that they would never again cross the portals of that house.

Jim and Audrey, with obvious reservations, were sorry and worried to see the children go. It could have been a tearful farewell but for Christopher and Sharon. Nothing could sadden their mood. They might be leaving their grandparents without hope of seeing them for some indefinite period, but such small sadness could never compete in their young minds with expectations for the future. Ahead lay the unknown, something none of their friends had ever done or were ever likely to do. Stephen continued to jump up and down, sensing and swept along by their high spirits.

While Jim and Audrey watched, Gordon closed the back doors of the little van after Christopher and Sharon had climbed and crawled into their small cavity. Then, stepping round, he swung into the driving seat. Jan was already seated, Stephen on her knee.

Shouting "Goodbye" and waving, the ensemble drew slowly away from the kerb of that tree-lined, outer London suburban avenue, which they were never to revisit. Two figures by the gatepost diminished steadily in the rear-view mirror.

The journey was destined to be slow. It would be an exaggeration to suggest the van was overtaken by faster cyclists, but they were the only things that failed to pass. Gordon fervently hoped not to meet any police cars, sure they would take the entire assembly straight to a weigh-bridge, providing they could find one strong enough, and charge him with a string of motoring offences. Fortunately they could not go fast enough to be dangerous!

At first the children chattered with scarcely a break, but as the engine droned slowly onward, conversation faded. Finally it died completely, to return in bursts as they passed from excitement back into sleep, suddenly to reawaken when the van's motion changed, rolling slowly to a stop at some road junction.

They had left at eleven o'clock, driving steadily through the night. Before midnight oncoming lights regularly illuminated the interior, periodically offering Jan a peep at the sleeping figures to her rear, but in the small hours these glimpses became increasingly infrequent.

All three children were fast asleep, the parents

chatted occasionally but more often sat quietly back, preoccupied in their own thoughts. Jan eased Stephen's weight on her lap, glancing over one shoulder again, hardly able now to make out the two sleeping figures vaguely visible in the reflected glow from their own headlamps. How would they react to the new life, she wondered? Christopher, the eldest, would take to the physical side well. He showed an interest in most practical tasks, had more common sense than one would expect in an eight year-old, though he was prone to exaggeration. *Hundreds* very easily became *thousands*. In spite of his youth, Gordon would certainly find him helpful.

Sharon would make new school friends faster, she always did. Her character was so easily likeable, open, generating trust and confidence, but she could quickly be riled up to an indignant state; both the boys and even Gordon at times, took unfair advantage of that. Especially she hated missing something the rest of the family knew. They often pretended to keep a secret from her, just to tease.

Stephen, the youngest, was less reliable, less obedient. Natural enough at not quite four, but he did possess an uncanny knack for finding trouble. Quiet as children go, little things he said indicated a quick brain hidden somewhere. Jan eased his sleeping form again on her lap; he stirred as the engine droned on, but did not waken.

Gordon glanced sideways at her, returning his eyes quickly to the dark road ahead. Jan was super, she held the family together. Nothing upset her, or very seldom. At odd times he and the children ganged up in an attempt to annoy her, but it was so difficult. Well aware of their efforts, she could often feign annoyance in fun during little verbal skirmishes. On those rare occasions when they did succeed in rousing her, she could be splendid, explosively dangerous and unpredictable but ready to laugh with them afterwards. Somehow, he thought, she brings out the best in us all, in me particularly, seldom pushing, patiently persuading, gently guiding without appearing to, though holding her own in the occasional argument.

Just how would Jan see his own strengths and shortcomings? Difficult to imagine. Persistence was probably his most important trait, one no doubt to be well tested over the coming months, but he might admit to being a little single-minded and to getting annoyed unnecessarily over small things. Less than perfect? Yes, a pretty safe bet. Perhaps he'd mellow with age?

He drove on, fancying something to nibble but there would be no food whatever on this journey, not even coffee; the caravan gas rings remained totally unapproachable. Jan had considered sandwiches but decided against. The children might not travel well; no one could be sure, they had never undertaken such a journey before. The total distance spanned over 300 miles, following the A30, then the A303, returning later to the A30 again. The Mini van however, could not remain unfed; still in darkness they drew in briefly to the blazing lights of an all-night service station for petrol.

The first faint greyish steaks of dawn appeared somewhere before Exeter and still the little van droned onward, slowly, slowly, eating up the miles towards Okehampton and beyond. Full daylight, a strong sun rising behind them, heralded their entry into Cornwall. They passed over the River Tamar then round that very tight hairpin, a characteristic of the A30 rising from the

Tamar valley *en route* to Bodmin Moor.

The children had woken now but were sleepy and talked little. Still on the A30, threading their way through the centre of Bodmin, all was well. Even Sharon, usually a bad traveller, was managing fine. Probably the excitement and expectations of a new life ahead took her attention from the van's motion. However in the middle of Fraddon, just after Indian Queens, somewhere near the midpoint in Cornwall, she called suddenly in a shaky voice.

"I'm going to be sick."

Gordon drew to the kerb, deceleration hampered by the heavy load but the stopping distance actually shortened due to their slow travelling speed. He rushed round, opening the rear doors just in time for Sharon, white as a sheet, to slide out and be instantly sick onto a drainage grid in the gutter. Five minutes walking up and down the pavement brought faint traces of colour to her cheeks and an assurance that she felt better. They would have stayed longer to make sure but the road narrowed at that point, a thin pavement backed by a granite wall to the left, tall houses at the road's edge looking down on them from the opposite side.

With everyone on board, the little van not so much accelerated away, rather it gathered speed like an athlete swimming through treacle.

"Typical of the contrariness of females!" Gordon suggested loudly above the engine's noise. "Out of hundreds of miles of uninhabited countryside, Sharon must choose a built up area to be ill in!"

Christopher and Stephen vigorously nodded agreement. Her immediate protest that she couldn't help it, the boys' comments and the argument that ensued, served to divert her mind from the van's renewed

21

motion as he hoped it would. No further stop hindered progress until they reached Relubbus at around mid-morning. Arriving in the little hamlet they slowed, sweeping right, rolling from tarmac onto narrow stone track. The children, now wide awake, craned forward eagerly seeking a first sight of the valley, clinging on tightly as the vehicle bumped and swayed over the uneven surface below.

Suddenly all three shot forward. The whole entourage shuddered as the towing van dropped into the first major pothole, tow-hitch grinding into stone below, gouging out a short trough and halting abruptly. Jan, retaining a hold on Stephen with difficulty, glanced rapidly behind, checking the children. Their faces held surprise but no pain.

"What happened?" She swung round to find Gordon regarding her, his expression resigned but unconcerned.

"We're just too heavy." He waved a hand at the road stretching ahead. "Touching on the bumps. If you walk with the children, we should manage. Might need a push in places."

The small track leading to the bridge was half a mile long, though visible for only a few hundred yards. As far as they could see, potholes stretched on without end.

The caravan eased forward. Its hitch, having risen a mere inch or so under reduced weight, cleared the obstruction and moved on, proceeding at slow walking speed. Occasionally the entire family pushed when an extra deep hole had the Mini van's wheel spinning in an effort to drag the caravan clear. At other times children ran in every direction, looking, investigating, in a state of euphoria, bouncing with curiosity and enthusiasm, especially so at points where river and road ran close with minimal intervening foliage.

Slowly, bumpily, the caravan progressed towards its objective, scraping noisily at intervals, rolling into and out of craters in the track surface. Jan couldn't help calling to mind nomadic caravans of the desert, slowly rising and falling, following the dunes of sand. When they paused after pushing from a particularly deep hole, she mentioned the thought to Gordon.

"Following the caravan, I feel like an Arabian wife, five paces behind the camel."

Flippantly he responded, "You're out of date. I've heard they walk in front now, in case of mines..."

"I know," she interrupted with a smile, "camels are more valuable than wives. Just you try treating this wife that way!"

The little party moved on past banks and verges, vegetation already brown from the sun but greener where reeds grew directly from the river's edge. A few taller trees, many bushy willows and lengths of Cornish stone hedges intermittently bordered the track. Still pushing at one or two points, they hurried forward as best conditions would allow. Far from abating, the children's excitement increased as each twist revealed expanding views of the valley ahead. Finally, reaching the bridge, the van crossed, rolled on a short distance and stopped. They had arrived!

Switching off the engine Gordon climbed out, limping, stiff-legged from his long stint at the wheel. Jan, catching up in a few paces, sighed happily and leant against the caravan side.

Energy undiminished by their capers on the trip up the road, and savouring continued freedom after the long journey, the children ran this way and that, before racing the short distance to the stream. Elated by this first sight of the new home and wild valley around, they slithered down the bank dangled hands in the water, clambered back up, across the bridge, sliding down on the farther side to hang dangerously far out and gaze underneath.

"Like letting them free in a chocolate factory," Jan commented quietly, watching. "They don't know what to do first!"

On an impulse, the youngsters raced back together from the river.

"Can we go anywhere?" Christopher asked.

"Yes, go ahead. Explore," Gordon paused, smiling, "but hang on while we decide the caravan's position."

The children in a group, looked at each other. Sharon, hand hidden from her parents' view, tentatively aimed a finger towards the stream. Christopher nodded and they galloped off again, Stephen in pursuit. Their preference lay precariously near the river's edge, right on the bank, main window pointing over the clear water.

Jan shook her head, ignoring the protests.

"Somewhere more private. Over there." She pointed to the south side of some low willow bushes, glancing at Gordon for approval. This was the home, her realm, only a convincing argument could alter the choice.

Stamping about in the long grass he located a level patch of ground and looked up. "Here?"

She nodded, turning to the children. Christopher shrugged, a realistic expression of resignation to greater authority, but Sharon resisted.

"Mum!" this one single word attesting to the total unfairness of parents. Little Stephen neither spoke nor gestured, no expression betraying his thoughts. The selected position lay some distance back from the river, it would take time to clear sufficiently for caravan, awning, and moving around space outside. None of the children offered further objections, no single subject able to retain their attention. Impatiently they kicked at bits of deadwood lying on the ground, looked hopefully towards their parents, eagerly awaiting any signal setting them free.

"OK. Go exploring. Stay close enough to hear when we call." Gordon grinned at them, waving one hand in an inviting arc covering the entire valley floor.

"Look after Stephen. Don't fall in the river!" Jan shouted after them, but they were already away. She couldn't avoid mixed feelings, watching, hearing happy voices retreating, dashing off into wild surroundings. They must be safe here, no one within miles who might harm or lead them astray, though they would probably catch themselves on the mass of brambles, and Stephen would almost certainly fall on the uneven ground. But this was their home now, she would have to restrain that protective instinct, permit them the freedom to enjoy, to probe, to discover.

Out came a scythe and the old Haytor mower. Their very first site-work had started! The prepared area expanded rapidly, quickly becoming large enough.

Jan shouted. She wanted the children back, not just for manoeuvring the caravan, though every little helped, but for two other reasons, neither obviously connected with positioning the new home. Firstly, in spite of a resolve not to restrict their freedom to play, her sense of anxiety increased as the period of absence extended. This was particularly true now, on the first day, and until the family became more familiar with the valley. At some deeper level, she sensed the importance of involving them fully, making the new life part of their creation too. Instinct told her if they helped from the start to overcome those problems that were bound to arise, it would stand them in good stead when later in life they met difficulties of their own.

Moving proved a struggle with the caravan still loaded but the distance was short. Briefly it did seem that unloading might be easier and indeed without the children's help could have been essential. Eventually, however, pulling and tugging they inched the caravan to its new resting place, door on the north side, leaving ample clear space to the sheltering willows.

Gordon carefully extracted several bigger, heavier objects, laying them on the ground well clear of the door. Then while Jan, with many little helping hands, removed the remaining lighter articles that would live outside the caravan, he backed the Mini van conveniently near for extracting bedclothes and other bulky items.

Unloaded but with much to tidy away, the family gathered inside for a well-earned coffee. Gordon looked at his watch. Two twenty.

"Fifteen hours since we started and not a drink or a bite to eat. Anyone thirsty?" He held up his cup towards Jan, still standing by the sink cutting bread. She understood immediately, lifting her own cup to clink against his, then took a swallow.

"To success!"

"That may have been the most important fifteen hours in our whole lives!" she thought, squeezing onto one edge of the bench seat to the left side of their little table, close to Sharon and Stephen. Gordon and Christopher sat opposite. A small sigh of contentment escaped as she watched the three children talking animatedly while drinking coffee and eating her quickly cut sandwiches. Would they always be so happy? Their first meal in the caravan, quite exhilarating she had to admit, meagre though it was; more so than meals at the house had ever been. "Shall I," she wondered, "get addicted to taking risks?"

The late elevenses (lunch might or might not follow later) could be taken at leisure. No hurry now. Plenty of hard work would follow, but today was for settling in. The children, unlike their parents, were in no mood to relax. Restless and energetic they dashed out again, having asked a barrage of new questions. What was next? How would they do this or that? One question after another, not waiting for answers, totally unable to sit for more than long enough to gulp the drink and leave, still clasping unfinished sandwiches.

After ten minutes during which they both leaned back into bench seats, chatting and savouring the new experience, Gordon rose from the table, talking as he went.

"We should be tired. I don't feel it, do you – mental stimulation perhaps? We'll be half-dead tomorrow!" Ignoring the step, he jumped from the caravan door to start erecting the awning and generally organise storage as best might be in the space available, calling the children to help and teaching them how. The awning, no front, just a roof and two sides that came free with the caravan, was mainly for storage. The chemical toilet would stand in one corner as inconspicuously as possible.

Many larger things, mower, wheelbarrow, bicycles, had no place under cover. They stood outside, destined to take whatever the weather threw at them. There just was no room. It proved difficult enough to store clothes and cooking necessities in one of the smallest caravans on the market, simultaneously leaving living and sleeping space for five, even if three were rather small.

By mid-afternoon some degree of order had emerged. Jan called "Coffee" from the doorway, standing clear as three children dashed to the entrance. Sharon, for once bringing up the rear having lost her normal second place, stopped suddenly before entering to stare in disbelief at the chemical toilet bucket standing exposed in the awning. She was amazed. Being so accustomed to entering a toilet and closing the door in a normal house, it had just never occurred to her that there was no room in the caravan.

"What will I do at night?" The words were tinged with dismay.

Jan turned to look sympathetically, seeing the deep concern on her daughter's young face. "Never mind the night, it's dark then, no one can see you. Worry about the daytime, anyone can look into the awning if they come walking upstream along the riverbank."

"But I can't sit out there in the dark on my own without a light!" Sharon's eyes grew rounder in alarm.

"A lamp would only illuminate you, not anyone watching. You'll sit there, wondering if there are eyes beyond the circle of light. Better to sit in the dark."

The young girl gave a little shudder.

"I'll wait 'til morning!" she promised.

Passing out the coffee, Jan explained. "Lunch will be at least another two hours while I finish sorting out. I'm having trouble with beds and water."

Sleeping arrangements were always going to cause a problem, particularly for the children. Christopher, the eldest would be OK having the top bunk to himself, but Jan worried how Sharon and little Stephen would sleep together, head to toe on the bottom bunk.

She glanced across to them now, a lingering thoughtful gaze. They noticed and looked back expectantly.

"Your beds. I know we've discussed it before, but I hope you really can manage two in a bunk?"

They agreed eagerly. Yes, of course they could, it would be fine, they were looking forward to it. No problem. The words were Sharon's, Stephen just nodded vigorously. Jan guessed the novelty would soon wear thin but there was no alternative, she smiled back with a small shrug of resignation, hoping for the best.

Drinking was the other problem. Amazing how much fresh water was taken for granted, but not here! The large carrier of drinking water brought along on the journey would obviously soon be exhausted. Washing and dish washing were no problem, the very clear river offered a constant supply of non-drinking water. Clothes too could be washed at the water's edge, third-world fashion. However, despite hearing on their previous visit that some local people drank river water, it seemed too risky. The children disagreed.

"The water looks great," Sharon protested.

Jan hesitated for a moment, then to illustrate the point, described in graphic detail a cow browsing along the bank somewhat upstream, flicking up its tail and making a series of great cow pats straight into the river just before the water-carrier was being filled.

"Would anyone like some in coffee? It might have an interesting flavour!" she suggested.

"Ugh," Sharon wrinkled her face in disgust, but the boys looked keen to try.

Gordon drained his cup with a grimace.

"Probably taste better than normal," he commented.

Jan threw out a hand, without any real force, attempting to contact the side of his face across the table, but he ducked catching her arm. The three children leaned backwards in surprise and concern, but relaxed, seeing the smile on Mum's face. They watched as Dad pulled the trapped wrist toward him, leaning forward to softly kiss the open palm.

Gently, almost reluctantly easing the arm away, Jan turned to Christopher and Sharon. "Dad will be busy, he won't have time for interruptions. We must handle water-carrying. You draw water from the river, take turns, I'll fetch drinking water; Stephen can come with me."

The lad could be of little help lifting the heavy container but would be company – and she preferred not to leave him alone. At least he could carry it empty. The nearest habitation lay in the village, so finishing her coffee and having seen Gordon lead the children back to work, Jan set forth to introduce herself at the little shop and if possible to beg a regular supply of drinking water, together with daily milk, bread and groceries. A second shop existed in the village, a post office they had not found on the previous visit, but Jan headed for the village grocery store owned by Samson Polglase and his wife Dorothy. They were friendly and helpful. Jan was welcome to the use of their outside tap, although they did show surprise that anyone should live *'down the moor'*.

This was to be Jan's worst chore! She found on that first journey, the state of the track and the surprisingly heavy weight of a carrier full of water, made the long half-mile walk back unduly arduous. Money was short, extremely short! At least calculations showed that it would be by the time everything was paid for. To save petrol she would use the van only for essentials, but whenever necessity sent her out in future, she vowed to take every water-carrying utensil available.

By evening both dwelling and storage were more organised. Shovels, with similar less vulnerable pieces had been pushed under the caravan to keep reasonably dry. The drawing-board, small tools and certain other equipment escaped the weather by remaining in the Mini van, and every caravan cupboard had been packed to capacity.

The awning, open fronted as it was and therefore only partially proof against the elements, took the surplus on the principle that some protection was preferable to none at all. Its grassy floor quickly became covered, just leaving room to use the open toilet and to enter the single caravan door. Usually awnings face south for sun, but the toilet would then be exposed to view from all the surrounding higher ground. Facing north offered better, but not complete concealment, the bucket remaining clearly visible from certain parts of the riverbank. It was unavoidable since no alternative shelter existed; the van and caravan stood alone in the valley, no other man-made structure, not even a barn, could be seen whichever way one looked.

It was not yet dark, but plenty late enough for the children. However, they were restive. Having slept through most of the journey on the previous night, the combined novelty of bunks and a new home disinclined them to sleep. Stephen fell for the second time from the lower berth, fortunately a distance of less than eighteen inches. He said nothing, not a howl or cry as he hit the floor with a bump, then climbed stoically back in. To avoid everyone's sleep being punctuated by further thumps in the night, something needed doing. Jan sighed, rose from the table, delved in a cupboard and after a struggle extricated a blanket stored with others in anticipation of winter. Tucking it under the children on both sides, almost like a twin ended sleeping bag, she stood, stretched and returned to the bench seat.

"Try not to wriggle out of that!"

The children continued to chat and giggle, Christopher's head stretching over the side to look down at the two below. Jan, sitting again at the table, made no attempt to discourage these high spirits. This night was special, unrepeatable – they would tire eventually.

It was strange to sit looking out as dusk approached, seeing shadows under various trees darken, listening to evening sounds through windows left open to relieve the worst of the heat. Lunch, served eventually at tea time, had been very makeshift; fried eggs with baked beans and a slice of bread. Tea had become supper, this meal not normally planned but served today in compensation for a missed breakfast. It consisted mainly of bread, enlivened by one thin slice each from the large rich fruitcake supplied by Ivy, Gordon's Mum. Jan hoped with care it would last the week. Seating five at the tiny table had not been easy, some alternative arrangement sat high on her list of future jobs.

When the children faded into sleep, neither parent attempted to rise, but continued to relax, talking idly. The gaslight hissed gently nearby as they awaited the coming of full night. The view darkened by degrees to complete blackness, a heavy pitch black with not the slightest flicker of grey or sign of a star, no pin-prick of light beyond the pane. It was strange to dwell on the fact that no matter which way one stared, no single soul would look back at the dim yellow light glowing in the caravan's small windows.

"The nearest person is totally hidden from our view, either in the village or in some remote farmhouse," Jan thought as she drew the tiny curtains making their little home more cosy but inhibiting partially the pleasant evening breeze. Even if she ventured outside, then shouted at the very top of her voice, nobody would hear. It surprised her to find she didn't care, rather liked the idea in fact. Too tired to read, she turned back to discuss quietly the next day's work, and the problems ahead.

Looking at their situation it boiled down to this. Success or failure hinged on the site being ready for next Spring, just eleven months away – and on finding sufficient paying customers for money to live through the following winter. For that they needed a water supply, toilet buildings and some sort of excavator and trailer. If normal prices were paid for the building work and the equipment essential to success, then there would certainly be no money left for food.

Economies had to be made somewhere! Standard materials were needed for the building; no compromise would be made there. Unavoidably they must undertake virtually every bit of the work themselves. That alone was exhilarating rather than daunting, but *time* was a big factor. Time and money, that was where the problems lay.

There was so very much to achieve before next season. Could they finish in time? Until some form of income flowed, they must live tight, work madly and spend as frugally as humanly possible on everything, including eating. The conclusions were not new, they had discussed them interminably before, but that was make-believe. Now was for real – inescapably for real! Possibilities of turning back were in the past, gone forever.

"The moving finger writes, and having writ..."

Thinking how appropriate that ancient verse was, Gordon rose, removing the collapsible table-top from between the two benches and replacing it lower down, resting on little rails fixed to the bench edges, thus forming a base for the double bed. Putting the back cushions from the bench seats on top of this low table made a level but somewhat bumpy mattress.

A little later he reached up from the bed and twisted a plastic knob. The hiss of gas died with the light, its incandescent white mantle quickly fading to black.

Darkness and silence reigned.

On that first evening, with the children sleeping only feet away and able to hear every movement if they should wake, Jan worried for the first time over their lack of privacy, surprised it had not occurred to her before. It might she thought, inhibit certain physical activities which neither she, nor Gordon she felt sure, were prepared to forgo.

In practice they found that the long wait for darkness and making as little sound as possible on the bumpy, somewhat squeaky bed, added a certain eagerness. The comic situation together with Jan's occasional suppressed laughter, in some strange way enhanced the magic of that first night. It had *never* been better. They lay together happily exhausted.

CHAPTER 3

Early Days

Jan awoke sometime before six, unable initially to understand where she was or the cause of her awakening. It took several moments to realise Stephen had fallen on the floor again, and that everyone else in the caravan was awake as well.

"Damn!" she silently cursed in annoyance. "The blanket wrapped around them must have worked loose. I wanted to dress while everyone slept."

The thin faded curtains though still drawn, did little to prevent light entering, and in any case it streamed through the roof-light. The little room offered no privacy whatsoever, no way to strip off her nightdress and slip into clothes without four pairs of eyes following every movement. Anyway she wanted to wash and the water lay outside in a pail. Had that bucket been filled the evening before? She couldn't remember. If not, a trip across open ground to the river to replenish it was unavoidable.

Another thought struck; the toilet was out there too! Although still early, it must already be full daylight outside.

"Life in the raw," a small shiver ran through her body, "but what did I expect?"

Laying in the strange bed looking towards the

door and wondering what to do, the movement of a warm body behind caused her to turn. Gordon was watching with interest, an elbow on the cushions that served as a mattress, chin propped on one hand, half a lazy smile on his face, obviously waiting to see her dress. Snatching up the clothes piled neatly on the floor close by, she swung from the bed and made a dash for the door, ignoring Stephen, now struggling to a sitting position on the threadbare carpet. Reaching for the handle she hesitated, turned, and looked at each member of the family, a warning expression on her face.

"If I see one of those curtains so much as twitch, nobody gets breakfast!"

Gordon watched her go, admiring shapely hips and upper thigh where the thin material of her summer nightwear clung, then remembered the bed he lay in needed dismantling and bedclothes storing in lockers before the table could be rebuilt for breakfast.

But this was a problem. Due to a hot still night and because of their nocturnal activities, he had afterwards fallen asleep naked with Jan still in his arms. He recalled with pleasure her warm response and little ripples of suppressed laughter when the bed creaked. The memory brought its own reaction in his body! Not wishing to step out of bed at that moment displaying such emotions, he stretched out an arm, hooked the nearby trousers under the covers and slid into them.

The children hardly noticed. Sharon, with Stephen still on the floor, were arguing over who had taken more than their fair share of bunk.

Christopher leaned from the bed above and called down, attempting to stir things further. "*I* don't know what all the fuss is about, *I* had a super comfortable night, but then, *I* never make a fuss."

So intent were the other two on their own war of words, it took them several seconds to assimilate Christopher's comment. Suddenly it penetrated. They stopped, both heads turned upwards, their combined animosity redirected towards him.

"You should try sleeping two in a bunk." Sharon shouted indignantly. Stephen growled something short and unintelligible. Christopher grinned, exactly the reaction expected and aimed for!

Arguments terminated temporarily when Jan re-entered, fresh, sparkling and now fully attired having donned her day clothes with unusual speed, uneasy at dressing in the open air. Gordon finished erecting the table and left for his own wash while the children started to rise.

During the babble of conversation over breakfast, Christopher, directed a question at his mother.

"What were you giggling about last night?"

Jan froze. Her knife stopped in mid-stroke as she realised he had not after all been asleep the night before while she and Gordon were making love under somewhat difficult circumstances. Her intense stare and suddenly motionless state, stopped Sharon in mid-sentence. All eyes turned. Looking slightly guilty, Jan struggled momentarily for an answer, glancing towards Gordon for support. He turned to stare casually through the window, a smile badly concealed.

Not usually evading the children's questions, she looked back at Christopher, hesitated for a moment, then replied with an almost straight face.

"Giggling, what giggling?"

Changing the subject she raised the question of schooling, suggesting that Gordon visit the local head-master to arrange places, preferably without delay. The two older children looked at each other in alarm.

"It's too soon, Dad, you're bound to need a hand for a week or two until we get settled in." Christopher protested quickly.

"Yes!" Sharon supported him. "I'll help Mum arrange the caravan and look after Stephen."

Stephen turned, intense resentment heavily etched on his face, saying nothing but clenching his fists ready to deliver a blow.

"Don't you think your education is more important?" Jan interrupted, smiling at their reluctance.

"No, we're quite clever, it won't matter for just a week or two." Sharon insisted.

Gordon, sitting drinking coffee, looked up at this unexpected teamwork, wondering if a small delay might encourage such infrequent agreement.

"Quite right," he muttered quietly so only Jan could hear, "can't stand intelligent women!" and had foresight enough to dodge the elbow that would otherwise have thudded into his ribs.

Ignoring him, she continued, "It's more important than you think. You may already be behind compared to children at the local school. Dad will go *today* to make the arrangements," and turned to Gordon with heavy stress and narrowed eyes, "Won't you, Dad!"

St Hilary parish had one school, about a mile from the village, approximately a mile and a half from the caravan. It had only two classrooms, a severe test of any teacher's skill. Each class had pupils of greatly differing ages, making whole class lessons impossible without boring the older pupils or leaving the younger ones behind. First opened some ninety years previously, built from local stone with traditional high windows and steep slate roof, it had escaped modernisation to the all glass-and-wood classrooms now so popular in schools. The headmaster turned out instead to be a headmistress, efficient, likeable and keen to expand class numbers. Christopher and Sharon were enrolled, due to start the following day, both in the junior class even though Christopher was two years ahead.

On returning, this information evoked dismay, with cries of, "Do we have to?" and other signs of great enthusiasm. Stephen smiled with malevolent satisfaction at Sharon, not having forgotten her offer to *'Look after him!'*

Work resumed extending the cleared area, a task destined to become only too familiar during coming months. Jan wished an immediate start had been possible on erecting the first toilet building, offering the luxury of extra storage space. She wanted somewhere to put the contents of the awning and everything still stored in the Mini van, including the big drawing-board and frame. Even without a water supply, a building would at least provide a private place to use the chemical toilet, avoiding possible daylight embarrassment. However, it was not to be. Although permission for these buildings had already been granted, the design was, in Gordon's opinion, ugly and impractical, with flat roofs above which water tanks must necessarily be mounted.

He wanted something better, more attractive and functionally sound, a design not only ahead of its time, but able the stand the test of future years. Certainly a pitched and tiled roof hiding the tanks and pipework, but he wanted a far better internal layout as well. To make the changes, various County and District council requirements must be discovered in a series of meetings, before drawing up and submitting revised plans. Delay in building was inevitable but Jan still hoped to see the roof on by winter.

The children helped on and off, raking up and making a pile of the vegetation which Gordon, sweating profusely, was cutting. The hot May sun shone relentlessly out of an almost cloudless sky, azure blue above, fading over the more distant hills southward along the valley. Working in co-operation the three children had no trouble keeping pace, their task partly work, partly a game. Having caught up sufficiently to be in danger from the sharply pointed end of the constantly swinging scythe, the young trio raced off to play again.

Long vegetation consisting of coarser grasses like cocksfoot, lay intermixed with wild flowers, particularly hogweed, campion and dock. Copious quantities of sorrel where the grasses grew shorter, indicated acid soil conditions. Some people eat sorrel with salad Gordon mused as he swung the scythe back and forth; it could well come in useful if they failed to be ready for the following season. Without paying visitors there would be no money for food! The idea stirred him to renewed efforts.

Looking twenty yards or so ahead, quite extensive patches of taller, heavier growth promised even harder work to come. Most appeared to be woody-stemmed gorse, a prickly bush with little yellow flowers and spiky leaves or perhaps needles. Naturalists allege that no matter what time of the year, a gorse flower can always be found. Pretty well true, the odd little yellow blip usually present even in winter, but most people only remember that great blaze of colour in early spring, a show now fading.

"Still, no matter how colourful," Gordon thought,

"it has to come out, roots and all."

He had already encountered a few growing in isolation nearer the caravan. Fortunately, with a pick and sufficient application of force these shallow roots could mostly be levered out. Where gorse grew densely, removal necessitated exposing bare ground beneath, but green shoots would quickly re-colonise even without spreading extra seed. In such a riot of grasses as existed on the valley floor, ungerminated seeds must surely have penetrated everywhere. Weed seeds too, he realised, but they would mow up green just the same and the quality of turf could be improved later.

On this first full day in Cornwall, Jan stayed inside striving to improve the internal living arrangements. She called "Teatime!" earlier than expected but a most welcome break nevertheless. Gordon straightened his back, rubbed a tired arm across sweating brow and plodded heavily towards the caravan, feeling the effects of the sudden change, the very physical demands of the day. The three children raced ahead, undiminished in energy; he caught them outside the awning, washing their hands in the bucket. They shook the water off and clambered inside but found no sign of a meal on the table.

"No food?" Stephen spoke before anyone else, his comment typically short.

"That's right. No food. Not until someone fixes my radio." Jan looking pointedly at Gordon whose head had appeared round the doorway behind the children. "Keeps breaking up, can't hear what people say. I don't mind having no TV and no one to talk to, but I'm not being cut off entirely from this planet while I cook."

"We could have tea first, Dad can fix it for you after," suggested Sharon hopefully.

"Some chance! He'll just slope off to work again. Until it's fixed, I'm on strike. Not just tea, everything!" She stared back at Gordon again, emphasising the last word.

He looked up sharply, suddenly all attention. This was serious! Fiddling to adjust stations for several minutes without success, he disappeared through the door, his tiredness only partly cast aside for the steps were used rather than the usual leap from the top. Extracting a length of wire from the toolbox in the Mini van, he returned to send Sharon outside, passing the wire through a window into her waiting hand.

"Hold on. I'll attach it to the set then come round and fix your end."

Immediately wire touched aerial, the programme sounded loud and clear. Twisting it on securely, he left the caravan to take the other end from Sharon, tying it to a broom handle.

"You've lost it." Jan's voice floated through the open window.

Attaching the wire to one thing after another, using almost everything in sight, proved no better. Nothing worked unless the wire end was in contact with skin. Bodies apparently made good aerials. Through the open window he glimpsed Christopher's grin, hearing his son's murmured suggestion. "Leave him outside holding it."

"Yes, until after tea." Sharon urged; impatience for food not her only motive for agreeing.

Stephen nodded vigorously but said nothing. All were grinning, well aware they could be heard through the open window; stage whispers, junior version.

Jan hesitated, glancing over one shoulder then smiling back at them, part of their conspiracy but not quite prepared to go along with it. "No. Then I'll have no radio tomorrow... and we can't leave him out there indefinitely."

"Why not?" Sharon's voice again.

Gordon leaned in the window, aware they knew that he was waiting, seeing surreptitious glances and little sniggers as they pretended not to notice. Unseen from inside he lifted an arm, then banged the flat of one hand sharply and with force on the caravan side. The echoing boom and jolt abruptly cut all discussion, Sharon jerking stiffly upright in alarm.

"Pass me a teaspoon."

"Why?" Jan immediately suspicious, rose from her seat. Having made such an issue of the matter, she was not about to give way. "You'll get nothing to eat with it before this is fixed!"

"Just give me one and I'll show you." He smiled at her, the smile and tone of someone humouring an imbecile.

"I'll certainly give you one if this doesn't start working soon," she whispered, smiling back and stepping over to pass a spoon.

Taking it, he coiled the wire end tightly round the handle, tossed it onto the caravan roof, then walked round to the doorway. The radio worked perfectly.

Meetings started with various planning authorities, first the District Council at Penwith, then the County Council at Truro. Each new visit necessitated modifying existing drawings or producing new ones before the next meeting. The drawing-board, cumbersome in such a small caravan, occupied most remaining available space. Even with the table dismantled, the stand legs could not be completely spread, making it slightly unstable. Life in the home became even more difficult, but Jan brushed it aside "Better get used to it. I want those drawings finished so building can start!"

The Planning Officer, Building Regulation Officer, Highway Authority, Public Health Department, Site Licence Department, each one needed to be satisfied. Gordon attended the meetings alone.

"Design is your job." Jan insisted, though normally every change was discussed together. After a week, as he returned from yet another meeting, she objected, "This will take forever!" flatly despondent at the diversity of approval required and convinced the council were being obstructive.

In fact most people had tried to be helpful, some going to considerable trouble, maybe feeling sorry for a family living under such conditions. Nevertheless, negotiations not only delayed building commencement, the time taken at meetings and with redrawing began to set even the clearing work seriously behind schedule.

However, the seemingly endless discussions, while frustrating, actually resulted in many improvements to the design. Though it seldom seemed so at the time, perhaps Gordon received such good treatment just because he listened to advice, even sought it on occasion, and modified the plans to take advantage of various officers' local knowledge and greater experience in the area.

Not only the toilet buildings needed consideration. Although Relubbus had existed as a village at least since the 1600's it had no name-signs and was hard to locate. This they knew well from their own first visit. There was little point in sweating away at preparation work if potential customers had the same difficulty finding the entrance. County Highways, responsible for marking the extent and location of every village, were asked if something could be done. They promised to schedule suitable signs for the next batch manufactured, to be erected well before the following tourist season, and helped also with direction signs to the site.

Life now consisted totally of clearing vegetation and drawing plans! At any rate, it seemed to. Except when time was short for the next meeting, the plans were worked on during wet days. If, as often happened, no rain fell for several weeks, then most drawing was done in the evenings, after energy for the more physical clearing work had been exhausted. With the drawing-board in use, life in the caravan suffered, meals were chaotic, even sitting comfortably presented difficulties, but progress was being made.

Young Stephen's freedom rapidly expanded, mainly from necessity. With his brother and sister at school and both parents working hard, often to the point of exhaustion, keeping him under continuous observation proved barely possible. Mostly however, his increasingly unsupervised play resulted from a growing awareness of the inherent safety of the valley. Traffic hazards were non-existent. No strange car had yet braved the potholed lane, and even pedestrians on the footpath were seen only once in a handful of days.

He took to the life with gusto, hiding in uncleared areas not too far from the caravan, throwing little stones in the water, watching pieces of reed race each other down stream or pretending to help with the work. Stephen never actually fell in the river although there was an occasional wet foot; in most places it ran so shallow that falling in wouldn't have really mattered anyway. Being alone suited his quiet nature; he never seemed bored, never needed or expected constant attention.

Having watched the drawing-board in use, he liked to sit with a paper and pencil, drawing his own pictures, sometimes houses but more often caravans. Jan showed an abandoned drawing to Gordon when Stephen, on a whim, suddenly rushed off towards the river.

"Look, caravans again. He's already forgetting about houses. Even after this short time caravans are becoming normal. The young are very adaptable."

For Gordon, work stretched out unendingly. Although the next season seemed far off, so much lay ahead that, as the days slipped by he felt a constant need to work faster, regretting it left him little time to play with the children. He had watched them anxiously at first, worried the difficult conditions might affect any of them badly. As he saw young Stephen playing, joining in with Sharon and Christopher when not at school, it was obvious that the new environment suited them and they delighted in it. Jan had guessed rightly when she forecast it would induce more self-reliance. Whether from lack of television, the cramped conditions, or just the wild surroundings, the family had never been closer or happier.

And Jan, when he thought of her, which he did frequently, he felt a deep stirring. She was radiant: complexion, spirit, everything, overcoming all difficulties, even revelling in them. Life was better now than it had ever been in spite of all the pressure of what must, absolutely must, be completed by the following spring and the ever-present possibility of total failure.

Into this great, if strenuous, life, both hardships and lighter moments intruded. Sometimes the two combined. One such instance resulted from necessity. Having no facilities for a bath presented a hygiene problem, particularly with hot weather and a surfeit of sweaty dusty work! First step in the solution involved heating water on a gas ring, sufficient to half fill a plastic pail. Telling the children to undress and wrap themselves in big towels, Jan, wearing her black one-piece bathing costume, picked up the bucket.

"Are you ready?" she glanced at them to check before opening the door, then carrying the hot water led the way. The little group followed in line, bare feet dodging thistles and gorse.

"Like ducklings follow the mother duck," Gordon grinned, trailing in the rear with two extra towels.

Jan stepped into the river, hesitating a second, the clear fast-flowing water still relatively cold even in early summer. Having planted both feet firmly on the sandy gravelly bed that shifted under her toes, she beckoned. Discarding his towel on the bank, Stephen stepped naked into the stream, standing there as his mother, with a sponge full of hot soapy water, washed the small figure down thoroughly. Gordon sat above on the bank ready to shout a warning in the unlikely event that anyone should approach down the track.

When satisfied, Jan pointed to the deepest part of the river, indicating he should lie down, letting the current wash away the suds. Stephen submerged without comment, no sound passing his lips, unusual for a three-year-old, then scrambled up the bank, re-wrapped the towel round his dripping body and marched off towards the caravan.

Sharon dropped her towel and entered the water to stop with a frantic gasp, "It's cold!" Further screams and shouts of protest accompanied her soap-removing dunking.

Finally Christopher, last of the three, clambered up the bank re-wrapping his towel and trotted off to join the others dressing in the caravan.

Jan, confident that even young Stephen could cope, let them go unattended while she stripped off her own costume to bathe. Gordon waiting his turn remained on the bank, glancing along the track occasionally, but mainly looking down in her direction.

She had looked real good in her black costume, long legs, bulges in all the right places – but when she took it off! His eyes would scarcely return to the road. That pale smooth skin, water and soap glistening on her bust, the movement of her body as she reached round to wash her back with one hand, the other stretched above her head steadying herself on the arch of the bridge, facing towards him but leaning slightly backward...

"Concentrate!" he told himself. "Watch the road!"

The whole operation was over too soon. He couldn't look away as she lay down in the cool current, rolling right over to remove the suds, then rose again giving a shiver, shaking as if to remove the surplus water with a quick twist of her wet body.

Climbing the bank to collect the towel he held, she looked up, seeing his eyes.

"Don't you dare!" she reached for the towel.

He noticed little ribbons of water still running over her completely naked slightly goose pimpled skin, dripping off her breasts, running down below the waist, over the satiny smooth abdomen, descending in trickles down long legs, the skin beneath changing from creamy white to sun-tanned on its descent.

She snatched the towel and draped it quickly over her body where it clung limply, concealing the wet flesh but not the shape beneath.

Stripping off shirt and trousers, he stepped into the

flow, plunging straight in. Washing could come later, right now he needed something to cool his blood and that cold water was very effective!

Word soon got around, no doubt the children talked at school. Some of the villagers thought it unbelievable that anyone would strip and bathe in the river, a few threatened to make sure by hiking out to visit on bath-night.

Several weeks passed, with Jan raking up and carting away in between cooking, while Gordon struggled on, cutting brambles, gorse and other undergrowth. He used alternately scythe, then sickle, and occasionally the pick; changing from right to left hand in turn to ease aching muscles and sore hands. Even young Stephen carried odd stones to a little pile. Sharon and Christopher helped too when not at school. The family adopted a motto, or rather Dad imposed it, "Everyone eats – everyone works!"

But unfortunately, they were not the only workers on the site. Other smaller less good-tempered labourers contested possession of the land. Industriously taking advantage of all the diverse profusion of wild flowers mixed in with the tangle of other vegetation, collecting nectar and pollen untiringly, were the inhabitants of several hives. A dozen of these familiar white wooden boxes with their sloping roofs and wide steps to receive the landing bees, were already in position when the family arrived on site. Only four or five were occupied – no one ventured near enough to make absolutely sure of the number. The beekeeper had promised to move them once he could locate a suitable new pasture.

"Be careful," he warned, "don't go near them. These are an Italian strain." Seeing a puzzled expression on Jan's face, he continued, pointing with one finger to stress the words, "Italian bees can be very vicious."

As he disappeared, walking up the track, Jan raised her eyebrows questioningly.

"Why should Italian bees be more prone to sting than English ones?" She smiled as a thought occurred. "Their version of pinching your bottom?"

Suppressing a smile, Gordon exhaled a fake sigh and shook his head sorrowfully.

"Can't stand clever women. Anyway it's Italian men that pinch your bottom. Worker bees are all female." He paused before adding, "No wonder they're unpredictable!"

Both stood smiling broadly at each other, relaxed by the small verbal duel. A hand reached out, touched and squeezed. Suddenly they were together; lips, bodies, minds, all in unison. No physical needs, just desire to be close. Life was great!

During the weeks that followed they well understood what the beekeeper meant! The little winged terrors were constantly stinging anyone in their flight path. Even just outside the caravan, more than fifty yards across the river from the nearest hive, no one was safe. These attacks were not constant, not even every day, but each was sudden and unpredictable. Only Stephen had escaped unscathed.

One sting caused Gordon's hand to swell, stretching the skin tight and hot. It became inflexible and difficult to use for two days but he pressed on ignoring it, unable to afford a delay. The keeper promised again to relocate his troublesome workers soon, and in the meantime explained how to kill a swarm quickly in emergency on the understanding that no one else would be told.

"If in trouble don't ask me, consult your local beekeeper," Gordon thought. Fortunately all attacks were of an individual nature, no angry swarming occurred, so the remedy thoughtfully advised at the risk of losing his own bees remained a reassuring but unused last resort.

Besides the family, several local people walking down the rough track, probably to observe those strange newcomers in the valley, were also attacked and stung. Ron the postman, who passed by not to deliver mail, but as a shortcut to visit a farm, was chased several hundred yards.

"I've never seen him move that fast before," Jan smiled in surprise and amusement, watching the rapidly disappearing figure.

One young lady suffered a simultaneous assault from two bees while crossing the bridge, both insects trapped in her long windblown hair. She uttered a piercing scream. Gordon, some distance away levering out roots with a pick, jerked upright in alarm, worried momentarily for Jan but instinctively knowing this voice belonged to another. He sighted the girl on the bridge, she was a stranger! A feeling of relief, followed by slight guilt at being pleased it was someone else, passed through his mind in that second. The scream faded and she stood petrified, frozen with fear. He too had been temporarily rooted to the spot but as the girl came back to life, arms flapping uselessly around her head, he dashed forward. Bitter experience had taught that these insects were very determined. While in the hair they seemed relatively harmless, but once disentangled, never flew away or gave up. Far from it, these bees invariably zoomed back for another attempt, planting a sting smartly into the first visible piece of exposed flesh.

The best defence was to slide one comb beneath the bee in the hair, and squash it upwards onto another comb. A pity to kill it, but death would come anyway as the sting remains implanted in flesh, torn from the bee's body, still pumping venom into the wound. Many people think it unduly stupid that bees should commit suicide in this way. Jan had read somewhere that a bee did not expect to lose its rear end, and certainly did not do so when stinging another insect in defence of its hive. Soft human flesh presented this special problem.

Seeing the girl in a panic and being struck with a sudden bout of gallantry, Gordon rushed to the caravan, snatched the two combs that were always left ready near the window, and ran recklessly to the rescue.

"Keep still! Bend your head towards me." The urgency in his voice penetrated the young lady's fear.

Her frantically waving arms and shaking head steadied temporarily as she complied. The two were buzzing away, well tangled in the copious hair, but struggling to find a way out.

Gordon slid a comb quickly beneath the first, and scrunch! The enemy was slain. But alas, at the same instant the other bee escaped the entangling tresses. True to form, it zoomed in a big circle, ready to charge in for the kill.

Could he save her?

Of course he could! The darn thing stung him instead, right on the ear. In the next few hours it was to swell to what seemed double its original size. Never mind. The damsel was rescued. She beat a hasty retreat, running headlong back in the direction of the village, leaving a bold would-be knight to ponder the price of noble deeds.

CHAPTER 4

Max

Removing the major vegetation section by section, left a none too closely cropped, uneven carpet of grass and weeds in many hues of green. All tended to brown in the sun, many quickly pushing up new shoots, intent on re-establishing themselves. The beard was gone but an untidy stubble remained. Luckily the ground beneath lay for the most part level, probably having been cultivated at some past time. The Haytor mower would finish this task, its thirty-inch rotary blades powered by a petrol engine but forward motion coming from muscle power alone. It proved hazardous in use!

Among the remaining ragged growth, generally some three to five inches in height, lay small stones and dead wood dropped over the years from trees that had died and disappeared, usually old gorse scorched in occasional heath fires. This debris shot from beneath the mower skirt like missiles. Gordon's thick trousers provided little protection. Even the folded cardboard later stuffed inside his socks was hardly sufficient, cricket pads would have been better. Everyone not feeling suicidal learned to retire to a safe distance!

Cleared material piled up steadily. The children when not at school, could no longer throw cuttings on top and were forced to deposit them alongside increasing the heap's girth. They pressed for this first bonfire to be lit.

Counting this job easier, their father classified it for evenings when energy, or rather lack of it, prevented him dragging more roots from the soil.

"Tomorrow," he promised evasively for several days, in some way considering the task non-productive for it added nothing to the area cleared. However, late one afternoon with Christopher and Sharon home from school and tea already eaten, a rolled-up newspaper was lit and lowered into the bonfire.

No one realised just how fiercely a mixture of gorse and other vegetation dried crisp in the June sunshine, would burn. The flame touched and in that moment the entire pile roared to an inferno. Rivers of burning particles ascended skyward, heading directly towards the none-to-distant caravan. Small though it was, they had no other home! It contained everything – food, bedding, even their clothes except those they stood in!

Christopher, entirely on his own initiative, rushed to the river with a bucket, dipping it in and racing back to the caravan ready to douse any fire that took hold. Jan snatched the blanket which at night wrapped the two younger children together in bed.

"Wet this thoroughly in the river, we'll put it over the awning!" she called, tossing it to him.

He rushed off as Gordon threw the bucket of water over the awning, wetting it down for temporary protection then raced off for a refill, grabbing the five-gallon water-carrier in his other hand. Sharon followed carrying two smaller containers, Stephen struggling with a saucepan.

Climbing in the Mini van, spinning wheels on the dry ground, Jan drove recklessly across the bridge to safety. Sliding to a halt and jumping clear, she looked towards their home and saw the rooflight still raised, forgotten when she had rushed to close the windows. Sprinting back across the bridge, she leapt up the steps, more warrior than lady, twisting the wing-nuts and pulling the skylight closed. Hunting hurriedly for hidden sparks, her glance fell upon the cooker, eyes widening; the involuntary indrawn breath checked her only a moment before she spun to the door opening.

"Gas bottles!"

Hearing the shout, Gordon bounded to the front, almost falling at the hitch, stumbling in his haste to twist the bottle valves closed then diving for the other blanket, the one kept next to the outside loo as a shield from passers by. Tucked tightly in around the blue steel cylinders, a thorough dowsing saturated the material.

Chris arrived back half carrying, half dragging his sodden blanket from the river. The two parents took it, somehow throwing the heavy material onto the awning roof, striving to untangle and spread the folds, stretching it out to prevent embers taking hold directly on the most vulnerable surface. Sparks could still attack the sides or even swirl up inside with a backward eddy of air, one landed on Jan's hand as she pulled at a corner – she brushed it away.

Racing back from the river again, three children ringed the caravan, ready to throw water on any fire that started, signalling to each other, arranging themselves without direction, choking sometimes in gusts of hot fumes. Fortunately, most smoke flew headlong over the caravan at a greater height, the intensity of the heat raising it quicker than the wind could force it sideways.

In the initial minutes, feelings close to panic moved everyone at speed; such vigour seldom seen towards evening when energy levels were dropping. Those first tasks were done now, but the bonfire itself had started to spread, burning through desperately dry grasses, the heat forcing Gordon back when he dashed forward to stamp out the leading edge. The blaze was moving, driving downwind where the heat was most intense, far too intense to allow any real counter-measures. In this direction too, lay the caravan!

They stood recovering breath, alert for flying embers, helpless at the moment to intervene – the fire travelling on unchecked. It moved with no great speed for the grass in this area had already been cut short, but none the less burned relentlessly on towards their home! As the foremost flames gained distance from the source, they eventually emerged from the protective barrier of heat to a zone that, although still scorching, might just be bearable for short periods. Leaving Sharon and Stephen to watch the caravan, Jan and Christopher ran to and from the river with water. Having tipped the first one over himself, Gordon took each new bucket as it arrived then holding his breath against the searing air and smoke, dashed in to douse the leading edge,

No fire could burn for long with such intensity. Rapidly the supply of combustible material crumbled, and flames grew less spectacular. Within fifteen minutes the family knew they were safe, though glowing particles wafting through the air would keep them on guard for another hour. That evening they sat recovering and relaxing around the small table, chatting together over this shared experience, congratulating each other on a disaster averted.

The following morning an unpleasant scorched patch, very noticeable from the entrance, marked a large elliptical shadow on the ground and the air close by still smelt of fire. Without doubt this scar would create a bad first impression on any visitor. It clearly indicated the folly of not choosing a more remote site for the bonfire. Unfortunately no more distant location could at the time be reached without great difficulty. Perhaps it would grow over before next spring?

Work remained unchanged but the pattern on the ground altered. A cleared corridor gradually elongated, arrow fashion, pointing toward the farthest corner of the two-acre paddock in which the caravan stood. The next bonfire would be built well away, and the wind direction must not be northeast when the fire was ignited!

The work was hard, the hours long, life alone by the river a world apart from their previous existence, perhaps most of all for Gordon. It contrasted strongly with his former occupation, not just physically but the solitary nature of each day. No longer had he an office full of colleagues or unending rounds of meetings, discussions and phone calls. There *was* no phone, nor any immediate prospect of getting one. Jan's company was always enjoyable but much of the time he worked completely alone, stripped to the waist, a tan gradually replacing the sunburn that had caught him unawares back on their second day on the site. He was fitter now than in the first week, muscle adapting more quickly than the mind. This loneliness didn't really bother him, not in the sense of causing unhappiness. It was just strange, the total absence of people so different, not even any outside noise as he worked on through long days. Odd thoughts that some catastrophe had depopulated the planet were dispelled at the sight of a faint silver dot and white following streak outlined against the blue, as an unheard aircraft miles high winged its way somewhere.

His imagination had always been vivid, but toiling under the seemingly invariable sun, ideas and thoughts came and went without boundary or restraint. The mine waste, where had it all come from? There had to be a certain mystery about such heaps formed perhaps a century or more ago when this area led the world in its mining activity and advanced engineering techniques. The shadow of history lay heavy in parts of Cornwall, an era of the past, a civilisation lost like the ancient Incas?

Well, not quite, for it was still a thriving county but the relics of its heyday, when fortunes were made and lost in the depths of the earth, were to be seen everywhere in the west of the county. Even from the higher ground of their own valley the top of a brick chimney at the old Tregembo Engine House, perhaps a mile distance, still stood visible against the surrounding landscape. In those days ships plied back and forth to Wales, delivering copper ore for smelting, returning loaded with coal for the steam engines, and horse-drawn wagons laden with ore and coal constantly passed each other going to and from the ports. Such things can prey on the mind of a lonely worker, especially one whose brain, used to greater activity, recreates in imagination those days of old. He wondered what relics of the past would be found when that great heap of waste was later moved. Would one come across the bones of a long dead miner, or a hoard of the mine captain's treasure? He would have to wait and see, but just the idle thoughts seemed to make the work go faster.

A robin came to watch or, perhaps just inspect; the first bird to show any interest in their activities. While it came quite close to the caravan occasionally, Gordon felt sure the bird's interest followed much more his own efforts. Probably the clearing work exposed new sources of food. How strange that a bird whose territory could not previously have extended as far as the nearest habitation should so quickly discover the benefits of association with man. Was it instinctive, like the tick birds on rhinos? Although Robin did dive in quite close to take a morsel from the ground now and then, most of its time was spent just perching on any nearby piece of vegetation, usually a not yet cleared gorse stem. It gripped the wood, one leg above the other, head slightly tilted on one side, a bright eye watching every movement, flicking quickly to the ground and back again as if to say, "Go on then, turn up something juicy."

Some time after the second week on site Gordon started talking to Robin in detail, before that it had been just the odd word or short question. Now it was anything from the merits of worms as against berries, to a discussion of the latest political situation. No worries occurred that the bird would not comprehend, the more he chatted, the nearer Robin came and the longer it stayed. It seemed quite natural to talk to the bird, not even to think of it as a robin any more, rather a being, not a person exactly but a friendly companion whose presence was appreciated. He never felt it was eccentric, no feeling of "I'm potty." Certainly not; he was quite, absolutely, positively, normal. There was nothing whatever wrong in talking to a robin, only... he wouldn't mention it to Jan, she might not understand.

£975 – Jan looked again, drawing a big ink circle round the item, an excavator for sale in the 10 June *West Briton* small ads. She had scanned adverts in the two local papers, both published each Thursday, for the past three weeks. The situation had become serious. Some type of earth-moving machine was badly needed but the money asked always exceeded what the family finances could spare.

Putting a cheque-book in his pocket, Gordon headed for Okehampton more in hope than expectation, and filled with a certain anxiety. It was all very well to tell himself he must get one cheaper but supposing he couldn't? This worry, growing stronger as each week passed, intensified during the journey to become a major anxiety. Not often did one hope for something dilapidated, in really bad condition, but if this excavator looked decent and well cared for then it just had to be faced, he would never talk the price down to an affordable figure.

The farm selling the digger took some finding but eventually, after driving up a little track, the correct name appeared on a farm gate and the search ended. Walking about in the yard was a chap dressed in city clothes looking more like a stockbroker than a farmer, the suit more noticeable than the man. He guided them towards the rear of a deserted barn. There it stood! Exactly what was needed, bristling with buckets and levers, but certainly not in top condition.

"There it is." The Suit gestured with one hand.

"Oh," Gordon replied in a mournful downhearted voice. It was precisely what he'd hoped for; fairly rusty and obviously neglected, giving just a small chance of getting it down to an affordable price. Another opportunity might not arise soon enough to save them. Without a machine they could never be ready for the following season. He was elated but nervous, not daring to let either show, and waited a while as they walked towards the excavator before commenting.

"Was hoping it wouldn't be in such bad condition."

"Well, perhaps we haven't maintained it as well as all that, but it works. I'll show you."

The Suit climbed aboard, turned on the engine and looked pleased when it started first time. Gordon's face remained deadpan. He hoped his voice wouldn't betray the tension inside. This purchase was so important. The well-dressed farmer flicked a speck of dust off the knee of his trousers then reached for a lever. The front bucket rose into the air, then lowered again as he pushed the same lever forward.

"Can I see the back end working?" Gordon asked without enthusiasm. The Suit climbed gingerly over and up onto the rear seat, with its array of six levers.

"This one lifts the main jib," he reached for a short silver metal lever with a black knob on top, and pulled backwards. The rear bucket shuddered, rose uncertainly a couple of inches and stopped. Further efforts achieved nothing.

"Great" thought Gordon, shoving one hand in a pocket to stop it shaking, but uttered an even more mournful "Oh."

"Don't know why that won't work?" The Suit, looked puzzled. "Don't understand these machines really."

Ah! Gordon gave another silent cheer, he didn't know why either, never having seen that particular model closer than fifty paces in his life, but wasn't about to say so.

"Expect all the seals on the rams have perished, and that hydraulic pump sounds on its last legs. Could cost a fortune to put this one back in order," he pondered, appearing to mutter to himself but making sure to talk loudly enough for The Suit to hear. Then speaking directly, "These models need quite regular attention, you're probably too busy with crops on a farm this size, to look after it."

The well-dressed farmer readily agreed to that bit of flattery, overlooking the unlikely chance that any visitor would know the extent of his farm. He commenced to recite all the important calls on his time, even volunteering that this was the only reply to his advert.

Gordon was in a sweat to complete the purchase before the phone rang with another offer, but this excavator had to be cheaper to be affordable. Never be an enthusiastic buyer, Frank, his father, had always said. So he listened, forcing himself to wait.

"Well it must be worth £500," said The Suit at last.

"You might find someone to take it at that but have to be pretty lucky." He was pushing his own luck and knew it, at £500 it offered a good buy. Ah well, in for a penny...

"Think those big ends are going and that black smoke probably means a rebore – tyres are well worn too. Really looking for something that can be used right away." Frowning, he half turned, looking towards the gate.

"What would you offer then?" asked The Suit, looking anxious.

"Couldn't say more than £350, then I'll probably be out of pocket."

To his surprise The Suit agreed, and started to talk enthusiastically about the farm once more.

Being quite interested in, though not very knowledge-able about farming, Gordon half listened, worried that another buyer would appear or telephone. He couldn't concentrate, was gripped with an urgent need to get a bill of sale quickly, but without appearing in any way eager. What could he say? Pretend to be in a hurry, that's it! He looked at his watch.

"Well, must get off, another appointment, give you a cheque, you write me a bill of sale and I'll have the machine picked up in a couple of days."

The signature on the cheque was a shaky scrawl, but The Suit didn't notice. Gordon couldn't relax until the receipt rested safely in his pocket, and still had to maintain a straight face. How to get the heart-rate up without exercise! One small step towards success. But how much would new parts cost, and there were still the buildings and some sort of trailer. Never mind, at this price the excavator was definitely a success, the family might manage to eat for the rest of the year after all.

On the journey back to Relubbus he drove basking in the warmth of euphoria, impatient to impart the news to Jan and the children.

Work of one sort or another took up the greater part of every day. With the digger's arrival awaited, cutting back the wild vegetation continued. Jan cooked, looked after Stephen, walked to the village for water and still found strength periodically to clear up the various gorse stems and other undergrowth that had been dug from the ground. But the June days were long. After twelve hours work, many hours remained before darkness fell. Daylight was not in short supply, it was energy. Jan worked intermittently throughout the day. Christopher often helped after tea, taking over for perhaps an hour, catching up with what had been cleared while Jan prepared the meal. She watched him later from the window, working with the rake, then dragging a huge gorse bush to the bonfire.

"Not many boys of eight could manage that," she thought, sitting, gathering her own strength for a little longer, wondering if they were being unfair. But he appeared to enjoy the work. Ten minutes later, when slower movements indicated he was beginning to flag, Jan returned to continue the task, sending him off to rest, knowing that in five minutes the lad would recover and be out playing somewhere in the undergrowth.

But no one relieved Gordon. Only he possessed the physical strength to lever roots out of the ground and by seven o'clock he was exhausted. At about this time regularly, work stopped, abandoned for the day, and very often he pushed himself to last until then. Alone, or with whoever was still helping at the time, he plodded back to the caravan and sank into cushions on one of the bench seats beside the small table while Sharon made coffee. Caravan seats had never seemed so good. Life was good too. He looked at the steaming cup on the table, and at Jan sitting relaxed as a rag doll but much more pretty on the bench opposite, a smile of contentment on her lips. Little Sharon, still not quite seven, was putting away the coffee jar, the milk, and tidying up like a proper housewife. All was well. His work-weary muscles, totally drained of energy, felt torpid, almost drugged; he could just detect that warm glow creeping gently back into them. Through the side window, hardly needing to turn, they could see Christopher and Stephen racing sticks down the river, and slightly to the south, the increasing size of the cleared area. Yes! Life was good!

After a long break, half an hour or sometimes more – his recovery time – they would often take a leisurely stroll. The riverside looked splendid in late sunshine, its unspoiled beauty putting all the hard work into perspective. Just gazing at it helped to recharge their batteries, fire them with enthusiasm to press on next day. This bank was one of the few walks yet accessible with any ease. They would wander arm in arm, feelings a mixture of young lovers and monarchs of the glen, surveying the estate, or rather those bits of it so far visible. Back from the river it remained for the most part, a nearly impenetrable mass of gorse, willow and bramble. In places these had encroached almost to the river's edge and had needed cutting back in the first few weeks after their arrival.

Pausing as they strolled one evening, Jan wondered how many years it would take to reach and tame these areas. They moved on, reeds and rushes on the lower bank rustling with warblers – a green woodpecker, startled in its search for ants, flew up and off in a catenary of quick wing-flaps and shallow dives, as if following an invisible clothes line draped over many props, yellow rump exposed as it went. A fiery sun, low in the western sky, threw their shadows across the water causing small trout to dart from cover to cover, jumping occasionally for a fly above the surface.

Often they sat close together on that sunny bank, choosing a place where the grass grew short and no reeds interrupted the view of the river. Sometimes the children walked with them, but when they sat down, the youngsters, driven on by restless energy, raced away to climb trees or play other games elsewhere, the remote and still largely unexplored valley having become their very own fantasy playground.

Jan gazed unfocused at the flowers around their legs, mesmerised by the rippled water flowing ever seaward beneath her feet. Beyond the short wiry grasses where they sat, campion flowered in copious pink bunches. Wild flowers were at their best in June. Towards the bank bottom grew a tuft in the same colour but different, ragged robin, not seen that often, becoming quite rare these days. Yellow rattle sprouted all round, some just coming out, some almost over, now more rattle than yellow. Gordon picked one, held it to her ear and shook it.

"Now I know where the name comes from," she turned, smiling over one shoulder, then nestled back against him with a contented sigh.

It seemed an idyllic existence at these moments, when they forgot the hard work and that their diet consisted largely of bread, baked beans, potatoes and fried luncheon meat.

* * *

The enormous vehicle approached, moving slowly, its lumbering gargantuan engine hiding at first the extensive, low-slung, articulated platform behind. With Christopher and Sharon at school, the remaining family had just entered the caravan for mid-morning coffee when the noise preceding it sent all three scrambling outside. This was a first – no vehicle but their own had yet ventured down the track! Approaching the corner that swung onto the little bridge, the driver, his head now poking out from the high cab window, scanned the structure with a decidedly unhappy expression as he slowed, almost to a standstill. The old excavator, strongly roped on behind and now clearly visible, had Stephen jumping up and down with enthusiasm.

Only the prospect of reversing the long unwieldy vehicle half a mile back to the village persuaded the apprehensive driver to continue. With no parapets and the track turning at a sharp angle, he could easily find his rear trailer wheels crashing over the bridge edge, leaving him solidly anchored and unable to move! Inching ahead, one right front tyre hugging the outermost extremity of the concrete arch, he progressed slowly forward, stopping and climbing down from his high seat twice to peer at the precarious position of those rearmost wheels. At one point, part of the last left hand trailer tyre actually overhung the river flowing below. Eventually however, he made it! The assembly came to rest on the wide flat area just before the bushes near the little caravan, dwarfing it into insignificance.

The digger had arrived! Transportation cost another £20, but it was still much cheaper than any excavator had a right to be. Gordon sighed with satisfaction at the delivery but knew that even undertaking the full overhaul himself, half as much again would probably need spending to bring the machine back into working condition.

Jan grabbed Stephen as he ran towards the large rusty excavator that was now being backed off the lorry under its own power. Most things on the machine did function, although nothing worked smoothly or well, that faulty rear trench-digging arm temporarily fixed; strapped firmly into position for the journey. Delivery completed and paperwork signed, the vehicle executed an intricate series of movements to turn in the confined space before departing again, recrossing the bridge equally slowly and with great care. They watched it disappear, bouncing off potholes, followed by a cloud of dust.

As the engine's sound faded, Gordon turned proudly to explain the controls to Jan. Stephen, now released, raced round the digger, stopping every now and then to gaze and give a series of little jumps in the air, a movement typical of his excitement. He looked with wistful longing when the motor started for the purpose of moving the machine to a more convenient resting place. In response to the rapt gaze on his small face, Gordon climbed down from the driving seat, lifted Stephen into the big front bucket which would later be used for shifting soil, and having instructing him to hold on tightly, drove round in a big circle.

Later Christopher and Sharon arriving back from school, dashed straight to the big machine in curiosity and fascination. Stephen stood watching them.

"I rode in the bucket," the young boy boasted, but quietly, to no one in particular. He didn't say any more, didn't even reply to their barrage of questions but the expression on his face, the tilt of his chin – it was so superior. It goaded them more than anything spoken could have. For once he was top dog and he knew it!

Sharon could hardly contain herself, it was almost like a secret, Stephen had experienced the thrill of a ride but she had not! She was bursting with indignation. Her very expression said "It's not fair!" It never occurred to her to think that she too could do special things; things the boys never did, like cooking with Mum, at which she had become quite excellent for her age. Christopher looked all round the machine, examining it in detail, but there might have been just a touch of envy when he looked back at his younger brother, standing, one hand resting on the front bucket in a possessive manner.

Watching from the caravan doorway, Jan and Gordon looked at each other and smiled.

"Do you think I should start it up again and give them a trip?" Gordon asked, loud enough for all to hear.

Three little heads shot up expectantly, two of them eager but Stephen's expression ambivalent, torn between desire for another trip and reluctance to lose his special status as the only one yet to have ridden. At a signal they climbed into the big front bucket and as the engine restarted, clung on to be driven round the same circular route.

"Hold on tight!" Gordon yelled towards the end of the journey. He slowed the machine almost to a stop and leaned out through an opening in the cab, instructing Christopher to stand with one hand each side of Stephen. The engine noise increased as the machine moved closer to the caravan, its bucket rising slowly, high into the air. The children looked unsteadily round gazing towards the river from that elevated position, then down to Jan standing in the doorway below. Cautiously Christopher released one hand from the bucket rim to wave at her. Jan waved back.

Gordon's estimate of the work required on "Max" was definitely on the low side. They named the excavator Max (a Massey Ferguson 203 industrial tractor with wide front loader and rear trencher) to distinguish it from the Mini van. That, as anyone might naturally guess, was called "Min." In his youth he had enjoyed delving into car engines but never tackled anything remotely approaching this size, and certainly never diesel.

"An engine is an engine," he shrugged hopefully.

With the help of a manual, a parts list showing exploded views, and taking very careful note of how everything came apart, he was confident, well fairly confident, that the work would not be beyond him. Some years before they had taken the children to see the film *Those Magnificent Men in Their Flying*

Machines. Two famous catch-phrases of the German officer seemed most appropriate.

"We go by the book of instructions!" would certainly be true, for there was no one to ask advice from if the work went wrong.

The second expression slightly distorted in his mind. "There is nothing a British gentleman cannot do!" Reconsidering he corrected, "Boasting again! Well, I'm British anyway."

He stripped the top off the engine, decoked, renewed injectors, stripped down the many hydraulic rams, put in new rubbers all round, changed the kingpin bushes and renewed the power steering. Then the rest of the steering system was replaced with an almost new set off a crashed tractor which the local Farm Industries depot was fortunately breaking up at that time. But still more remained to be done. The pressure valves were changed, hydraulic pipes renewed and the cab stripped down then rebuilt again. Eventually he delved into the intricacies of the rear hydraulics, changed the pump, again for one off that crashed tractor and repainted the whole thing in proper Massey Ferguson yellow.

The nearest stockist of spare parts was at Par over forty miles away, so for each new bearing or filter or pressure-pipe needed, Jan drove off in the van on the eighty-mile round trip to collect them. They tried to work in a way that enabled the purchase of several parts at once to save journeys and petrol but even so the trips were frequent. In the first week as Jan drove off for the fourth time, she reckoned the van could probably find its own way without a driver. For a time after the digger's arrival, all other site tasks were temporarily abandoned. Finishing before rain had top priority, since no shelter existed and all repairs must be undertaken in the open air. So far as possible neither the engine nor hydraulic system would be left open overnight – just in case!

The children came regularly after returning from school, always expecting to see the job finished and showing increasing scorn each day when it still wasn't ready for work! Christopher often stayed to help until one evening he managed to get oil on his school clothes.

"It's impossible to remove grease without it showing, just washing it in the caravan sink!" Jan challenged fiercely, directing the words in Gordon's direction.

Christopher, glad to have escaped most of the blame, made a sympathetic face towards his father, being careful to wait until Jan turned away. Gordon, feeling somewhat more resilient, the mechanical repair work less physically demanding, winked back.

"I didn't realise she washed them at all, did you?" he asked conversationally.

Swinging back towards him, eyes blazing, Jan took a threatening step forward but seeing him flinch in anticipation of the blow, stopped with a broad smile of success.

Other little faults kept turning up on Max and were done bit by bit between use, usually when the part ceased to function. Cracks appeared in the chassis from time to time, probably due to previous misuse, working the machine with various bolts missing or loose from neglect. These cracks were invisible in the digger's original dirty state. The main reason for cleaning and painting was to reveal them before they spread farther. Without any electricity, welding on site was quite impractical, but fortunately a mile or so up the valley a small engineering workshop operated, mainly repairing agricultural tractors. Stanley Thomas, the owner, or more often his son Tommy, welded the various flaws, even cracks in inconveniently awkward positions.

Eventually all was fixed and Max ran for a whole day without the slightest fault. After all the attention it was probably the best looked after fifteen-year-old digger in England. Jan could handle Max too, and did much of the driving; it required less muscle than most other work. Walkers passing through the site were very infrequent, but Gordon noticed with amusement their surprise to see such a big lumbering machine being propelled by a fair maiden.

"No," he thought, "that's not quite right. Jan is certainly good looking, but you can't call a brunette mother of three a fair maiden!"

A week later when nothing further had gone wrong, he suggested at tea that a certain amount of praise must be due to the brilliant engineer who, in spite of never doing one before, had managed successfully to complete the overhaul.

Not a lot of compliments were forthcoming!

"'Bout time. What took so long?" Christopher asked.

Sharon muttered, "Probably break down again tomorrow."

Jan nodded encouragement, drawn-in cheeks indicating her struggle not to laugh.

"Not good for a chap's ego!" Gordon smiled back.

Jan allowed her own smile to surface. How well the new life suited them. She was pleased they felt secure enough to make fun at Dad's expense, and at his easy acceptance of it. He's better this week, more energy. He can be a bit short when he's very tired. She turned again to watch the children talking and joking while simultaneously stuffing food into hungry mouths.

"Must tell them some time about talking with their mouths full," she thought but made no attempt to do so. Sharon was growing up fast, Christopher too. They had matured a lot living in the caravan, and they were happy. "But Sharon will need a room separate from the boys in a few years and none of them will want to stay in the same room as their parents. Will we be able to provide?" Jan wondered. She hoped so.

With the digger and its multiplicity of control levers all functioning sweetly, clearing resumed in earnest, and Jan no longer dashed off constantly for spare parts. Meetings too were fewer, not only allowing more time, but to Jan's relief, the drawing-board appeared less often. Progress at least appeared to accelerate but permission still had not been received for the new plans so no building work could commence.

The excavator's main task at this time did not involve earth moving, although one or two banks of soil were levelled with the front bucket. Pulling the heavier vegetation, wrenching bush and roots together from their grip in the soil, had become its main occupation. Mechanisation made work not only faster, but considerably less strenuous, making possible a later end to the day's toil before lack of energy forced a halt. The mown area now expanded more rapidly, raising everyone's spirits.

CHAPTER 5

Scones and a Mower

At first Stephen had looked on avidly as the digger
worked, watching from a distance, going off to play,
and returning to watch some more. Obviously this
interest would wane, but aware of the risks Jan took
him aside and knelt down looking straight into the little
lad's eye.

"You must never go near the digger while it's
working!" she warned. "Big machinery is dangerous.
Dad can't hear anything when that engine is running;
he could crush you with a wheel or the bucket and not
even know it!"

Stephen looked back at her, a certain resistance in
his features but he said nothing, no word of dissension,
no nod of agreement, nor did he look away.

Jan sighed, glancing down for inspiration. She
noticed he followed her gaze. Sweeping with one palm
a pile of dust and sand from the parched ground, she
shaped it, placing a small pebble hardly bigger than
a pea on top and a tiny dead gorse twig across to
represent arms. Simple though it was, the small figure
could be taken for nothing other than a person. She
looked up at Stephen holding his gaze, then deliberately looked down again, reaching out to place her
palm on the figure and press downwards, lifting the

hand to reveal the flattened shape.

"Do you understand?" she asked, staring intently at the small lad.

His face changed, serious, no longer rebelling. The light sandy brown hair nodded slightly twice, no sound emerging. Jan waited but he didn't speak. After a long pause she reached out, pulling him to her in a hug. He resisted for a moment then clung to the warm body that had always represented comfort. After a while she held him away to speak again.

"I'm going to be driving that digger sometimes, helping Dad. You must never approach me while I'm driving. Wait and signal from a distance. I shall be watching and will come to you. Is that all right?"

Stephen nodded more freely.

"Off you go and play then." She turned him round, patted his bottom and he ran off, jumping every now and again in the air.

Jan began to share her time between Stephen and driving the digger.

"If I help you it will go faster, then you don't need to work yourself to exhaustion every night."

She saw Gordon's nod, made with a certain reserve, and immediately guessed his intention; not do as much work in less time, but do more in the same time. In spite of the help he would work just as late.

"Silly," she told herself, "to have expected otherwise. I must be slipping!"

She drove into position, allowing him to connect the chain to the front bucket. This chain passed around bunches of gorse stems which were pulled out bodily, roots and all, just by operating the lever to hoist the bucket into the air. Each time the chain was being threaded round a new batch of gorse gave her an odd minute of waiting; time to glance over and check where Stephen played alone. So long as he looked happy she could continue driving. Sometimes he would remain in the caravan, where excavators had now been added to his favourite drawing subjects. During one such afternoon Jan was driving back to check on him and at the same time to fill up from diesel kept behind the caravan in gallon cans. Gordon had straightened his back for a minute to watch her go.

Unusually, two people were walking beside the river. Jan caught the man and woman as they strode along the bank. The couple were just far enough away not to be bothered by the engine's heavy roar or by dust flying up from the wheels, but as Jan overtook them the man gave a fleeting glance towards the digger. He stopped suddenly, turning to stare, and promptly fell down the bank disappearing from view. Jan braked, jumped off and ran towards the point where he fell. Gordon arrived simultaneously.

The man was OK, if a little embarrassed. He had not actually fallen in, just slipped down the sloping bank, submerging one foot in the water.

"Are you all right?" Jan called. She was wearing a skirt that swung nicely from the hip, and though by no means short, showed quite a lot of well-tanned leg. Gordon knew the material tended to ride up when she sat on the digger, a fact that the open cab did nothing to hide; he had been enjoying it himself on and off all afternoon.

"Yes, I'm fine," the chap said a bit sheepishly, surreptitiously running his eyes up and down Jan's figure, "just slipped and lost my footing."

She smiled back at him.

"Hmph!" the woman snorted. She didn't smile at all, looked daggers at Jan, grabbed the man's arm and dragged him away. Jan stood watching them go, not moving until brought back to reality by a voice at her side.

"What's this then, a strike or just a go slow?" Gordon asked in amusement.

"Don't hurry me, I'm enjoying myself. It's not every day a girl gets a man to fall for her so literally."

Christopher, when not at school, also learned to operate the bucket. Although still too small for the foot pedals, he could now reach the two hand controls that operated the front bucket. Sitting perched on the edge of the seat, leaning his chest against the wheel and stretching out, he could just work the levers with his right hand fingertips. After Gordon fixed the chain round each batch of gorse, Christopher could pull the lever lifting the bucket, yanking stems complete with roots clear of the ground as Jan had done earlier. He then lowered the bucket allowing the chain to be undone. Not a bad achievement for a lad still aged eight. In compensation for not having new toys like most children, he played instead with the real thing! At intervals the uprooted stems were loaded onto the front bucket, using the digger like a big wheelbarrow to transport a mass of vegetation to the burning area in one go. Gordon drove the digger, placing it ready for Christopher to make the next pull, but using the chain, several such pulls could be achieved from each digger position, saving that all-important commodity, time.

Stephen never normally envied his bigger brother's skills, making it clear by expression or behaviour, seldom by words, that he thought himself every bit as good. However in this one respect he did begrudge Christopher's special ability.

Stephen was himself allowed to sit in the driving seat if the vehicle was not in use, and knew perfectly well that his own short arms just could not reach the control levers. But he resented it! Whether from envy, bravado, or from a sheer desire to be bolshie, when Christopher drove, Stephen edged his way nearer and nearer to the working machine. He looked belligerently back when Christopher waved him away, planting both feet firmly on the ground, face set, absolutely refusing to obey.

He didn't say, "You can't order me around." He had no need. The stance, the determined look, his very manner said it for him. Usually he stayed some ten digger lengths away, but with Christopher operating the levers, little Stephen gradually worked his way nearer, within two lengths or less of the machine.

Jan had not wanted to interfere, it might seem to enforce Christopher's authority and create resentment, but Stephen could be in range if the chain broke or slipped. Things were becoming hazardous. She called them together.

"Now listen. This is getting dangerous. Stephen, you must not go so close." Jan lectured in a kindly persuasive tone.

"Christopher is closer." Stephen responded quickly, almost before she finished speaking, his little chin rising in defiance, jaw set in rebellion.

"Christopher is driving. He has to be closer. He's helping Dad." Her reasonable tones had little effect. Stephen's face turned rigid with rage but not a murmur passed his lips. Attempting to preserve family harmony, Jan tried again.

"Look, the less expert a driver, the more danger there is. Christopher hasn't had much experience yet, so he's still liable to make a mistake. You should give people room according to how skilled they are. Now be good and stand at a suitable distance."

Stephen's expression remained unchanged, absolute defiance seething below the surface but again he said nothing. Suddenly the little lad turned and strode off, not stopping at his usual distance. They watched him walk on and on. Eventually he climbed onto a mound of earth at the other extremity of the field, turning to stare fixedly at the digger.

Without a single word Stephen had indicated clearly enough what he considered a suitable distance from his brother's driving! Jan looked at Christopher, wondering if he understood, seeing immediately that he had.

"At only three!" she thought. "What will he be like when he grows up?"

Usually both Sharon and Stephen would come with the "Tea ready" message. They came together for the bucket ride, jumping aboard to be lifted high in the air and driven to the caravan. Dad worked the foot pedals, Christopher often sitting on his lap steering. For a while Stephen had refused to get in if Christopher drove, on the grounds it wasn't safe to be near a novice driver, but after a while he forgot.

Sometimes, particularly if anything unusual had occurred or there was other news to impart, Christopher joined his brother and sister in the bucket, leaving Dad to steer. No doubt he would impart his news slowly, hinting at first, keeping them waiting, rousing Sharon's impatience to know. He would tell in the end of course – with some exaggeration. Gordon could see from their faces the younger two were pleased when Christopher joined them, though Sharon disguised her pleasure with an assertive nod, "Good. A proper driver today,"

The work, though strenuous, was never dull. For the children, fun could prevent it seeming like work at all.

Tea was an important meal, an enjoyable meal and certainly not due to the food, at least not normally, though there were exceptions. Tea's importance lay in being the only meal with everyone always present. Breakfast in most households had that honour but on the light summer mornings, Gordon was up and away long before the children rose, though he sometimes came back to breakfast with them. For lunch Christopher and Sharon ate at school except, of course, for the weekends. So tea had premier place, where the children spoke of classroom and friends, and asked after progress at home. The food, mostly plain and repetitive, had the very best of seasoning – hunger! It was rare to see anything left on a plate. Once in a while Jan rebelled against the restrictions imposed by her low budget, lack of an oven, and only two small gas rings. On one such occasion Gordon and the two boys arrived for tea to find the table empty.

"What's for tea?" Christopher asked, craning to see, but Sharon threw a teacloth over the mixing bowl she was using and stood in front of it, face alight, basking in her secret.

"Go back out and wash your hands, then sit down." Jan directed, giving nothing away.

Both boys, intrigued and suspicious, dipped their hands quickly in the bucket of cold river water on the bench outside, rubbed together and withdrew them in one movement. Flicking off the water, they dashed back to join Dad, climbing into the seats round the table, still rubbing damp hands on their trousers.

Both girls stood together at the stove waiting, Sharon gently beating a mixture in a bowl, shielding it with her body to hide the contents. Jan had heated a frying pan over one of the rings, a bluish smoky haze began to rise from the hot fat, dispersing quickly through the door and windows, all wide open to combat the sun's warmth.

Jan signalled, "Ladle some right in the middle."

A great sizzling indicated Sharon's compliance, but the contents remained concealed. Shortly Jan turned something over in the pan.

"Who wants the first one?"

Gordon suggested Christopher, but both the boys pointed back to Dad. Nasty suspicious natures children have! Before their father could think of a reply Jan flipped it onto his plate, while Sharon passed him a tin of Golden Syrup, saucer and spoon. Syrup was cheap energy, he ladled some on. It was, he realised, a girdle scone. Some people say griddle scones, just a small thick pancake, but it was delicious. The two boys watched him eating, looking for any hint of either pleasure or distaste, and noted immediately his approval.

"Watch!"

Jan flipped one high in the air, catching it in the pan. A little cheer echoed round. Meals were usually a happy affair in the close quarters of the caravan, small variations on the normal became treats, almost a party. Gordon suggested that a little more testing was needed and perhaps he should eat another – it met with instant disapproval. Stephen said nothing, just stood holding out his plate, all suspicions gone.

Sharon took over cooking while Jan joined the

others at table, swapping again to eat her own. Normal bread, butter and coffee rounded off the meal as they chatted together. The consensus of opinion was, "Yes, a great tea. Why not more often?"

Jan nodded. "OK, if you like. If we had an oven, I could bake all sorts. Perhaps Dad can make one?"

Helpful as Max was, there remained the problem of trimming the residual vegetation, somewhat trampled and tangled after gorse removal, making work with the scythe more difficult. Cutting with the Haytor mower now proved even more hazardous, for it whipped up dust-clouds from the dry disturbed ground, eliminating any chance of spotting small stones that flew out like missiles.

One morning, a local chap, Stanley Allen (Stanley seemed a popular name in Cornwall) walked down from the village, and striding straight to the caravan announced he had bought them a mower at a local farm auction. Jan looked surprised. No wonder. Nobody had asked if they needed a mower. Did they want it? More important, could they afford it?

"It's a big one. Cheap!" Stanley paused for effect, "Cost £5. Only it's over Lelant, you'll need someone to fetch it." Lelant was five miles away.

"Not a chance." Gordon passed him a note. "We'll fetch it ourselves and save money – and thanks."

Following the directions, they reached the sale field and located the mower, practically the only remaining item. One thing Stanley had somehow forgotten to mention – it was a horse-drawn model.

"I don't believe it!"

Jan looked incredulously from the window. As the van stopped, she squeezed out from under Stephen, leaving him on the seat, and raced over to look all round the curiosity. He stumbled after her, determined not to be left out. Gordon, pulling on the brake, quickly joined them. Funnily enough it was an Allen scythe, could have been named after Stanley, but of course it wasn't. A fifteen-foot wooden shaft stuck rigidly out in front, a seat rising high above, perched on the end of a single curved spar of springy steel. Long control handles projected vertically adjacent to this seat, and a six-foot cutting blade, which moved backwards and forwards like a giant version of the modern hedge-cutter, jutted out horizontally to the right side. Two big iron wheels without tyres, each roughly twice the diameter of those on a normal car, supported the whole assembly.

"You're never going to try towing that home!" Jan laughed, shaking her head at the hopeless task.

Transportation had indeed suddenly taken on a new dimension! A relic of some bygone age, no wonder it was cheap, but then Stanley himself was quite elderly; they were probably all the rage in his youth. However, there was no reason why it shouldn't work.

"Yes, I am. Stay here, I'll bring the van closer."

How to transport it? he wondered, easing the van from gravel onto grassy paddock and steering over just ahead of the shaft. Jan put Stephen back in the van, much to his disgust, while Gordon experimented with various levers, discovering the cutting blade could be lifted and fixed out of the way in a vertical position. Quite a relief, he didn't much fancy charging along country lanes, the six-foot blade sticking out chopping off everything in its path like a modern-day Boadicea.

The van's towing hitch would be ideal for attaching a rope to pull the mower. Propping rear doors open, they rested the long wooden shaft on the floor. How providential to have a van not a car. Unfortunately the vehicle was just too low, leaving the shaft sloping very slightly downhill. Only its tip rested on the floor, a totally unstable arrangement. By luck an unopened bag of cement lay behind the passenger seat. Not luck really, no other undercover place for storage existed. They had purchased it a day previously to cement some large granite slabs by the bridge into rough steps for easier access down to the river. Everything else normally stored in the van had been left, dumped in a temporary pile outside the caravan door. Positioning the cement bag centrally and laying the shaft on top, not only made that shaft almost horizontal, but by lifting the end clear of the van floor, allowed it to rotate. Turning corners would now be possible without the shaft hammering against the side of the van – or so Gordon thought!

Securing the rope they towed away, turning slowly, but within a few yards the shaft slewed sideways, to slip off the cement and smash heavily against the left hand wall just behind the passenger seat, its sound reverberating round the van's interior.

"Pity. Wonder what an insurance assessor would think of a great dent like that, made from the inside?"

"No idea." Jan frowned. "If we claim, you can fill in the form – you've more imagination. You'll need it, no one is going to believe the truth!"

Stopping the engine, he jumped out, running round to lug the shaft back into a central position again.

Watching from the passenger seat with Stephen still on her lap, Jan voiced concern. "How can you prevent it happening again? We can't stop every five minutes all the way home, it looks stupid enough anyway."

Gordon nodded, inspecting the arrangement again.

84

It did look peculiar. He shrugged, "You take over the wheel, I must sit astride the shaft throughout the journey to prevent it slipping sideways off the cement." There seemed no other way.

"I'm not driving with *that thing* hanging out behind!" She reached for the door handle. "Something's bound to go wrong. You drive, *I'll* sit on the shaft."

They set off at walking speed, the mower following ten feet behind, those iron wheels bumping and bouncing, some part of the mechanism chattering away.

"You're going too fast, I'm a mass of bruises already," Jan complained as they joined the tarmac road.

The journey passed very slowly, little faster than a pair of shire horses might at one time have pulled the machine. Stephen, at first excited, knelt backwards on his seat shouting something once, his words drowned by engine noise and the rattle of iron wheels. As the distance dragged slowly by he eventually sat down then fell asleep. Almost an hour passed covering four miles, swinging dangerously wide on the corners. Only a mile to go! Jan was worried that Christopher and Sharon would already be home from school. The bag of cement had burst, shrouding her rear end, the grey powder spreading gradually in little puffs to other parts of her body. They saw nobody apart from two cars passing in the opposite direction whose occupants seemed intent on straining their neck muscles as they watched in disbelief.

Jan protested, "I feel like some freak show, sitting here covered in cement, bouncing up and down, no wonder they stare at me."

"It may not be you." Gordon replied over one shoulder. "What do you think are their chances of ever again in their lifetime suddenly passing a horse-drawn mower that's maybe fifty years old already, projecting from the back of a Mini van?" He diplomatically failed to mention that catching sight of a leggy lady bouncing astride the horse-shaft, and covered in cement might be something they were even less likely to see again.

The last half mile, over their own potholed entrance road, proved the worst. Every bump caused further clouds of cement to engulf Jan. Fortunately it was dry. Stephen, woken again as the van bounced from one hole to another, stared at his mother, a demonic smile of glee crossing his face. Climbing stiffly from the van's rear when they drew to a halt, Jan moved away from the caravan before allowing Gordon to remove most of the dust with a small hand brush, turning her face into the wind to avoid inhaling the powder. As he finished she stretched her arms and legs carefully.

"Pity you can't remove bruises the same way."

"I could rub them gently with oil if you like?" he whispered, still standing close.

A smile came to her lips, "Oh yes? I thought you were exhausted. You're not working hard enough!"

Did he detect a glint of encouragement in her eye?

The mower proved a great success. Instead of a pair of horses, its long wooden shaft attached to Max, the excavator. It cut splendidly with Stanley, who volunteered to help, at the controls. Gordon drove Max while Stanley sat on the mower, calling instructions.

"Drive on!" he shouted stridently.

They entered the thick matted undergrowth, penetrating like a hot knife through butter until the blade encountered a thick gorse stem, missed when the others were pulled out. As the cutters jammed and the whole apparatus slewed on its spring, Gordon braked heavily, then quickly reversed the tractor. It demanded constant vigilance. Luckily Stanley, being experienced, sat well back in the seat. What a pity he only came for the one morning, to demonstrate the old machine's capabilities.

When he left, Jan tried. At the first obstruction she shot from the high seat to land with a loud "Ouch!" sitting several feet lower, astride the wooden shaft. After that she refused to go near it, driving the tractor instead, leaving Gordon to occupy the lofty perch. He copied Stanley's stance, sitting well back and hoping he too would not land on the shaft, fearing never to be the same man again.

***

Jan was restless. She loved the valley but somehow could just not settle. The strange mood had been building up for days. Why? She had thought the work would be enough, and they had worked! Clearing, clearing, clearing. For six weeks without intermission, without respite, with few alternative jobs to give variety – on and on relentlessly. How could it possibly be only six weeks? It would be mid-June, the longest day next Wednesday. Why couldn't that building permission come through? She needed a break, just a day away and so did Gordon, she knew he did, only he stubbornly wouldn't admit it. He needed a rest more than anyone. His muscles, unused to continuous manual work, had protested loud and long. Only her own comforting fingers could rub the stiffness out of his joints on some nights.

"And," she thought, "the solitude is getting to him. He enjoys working alone but a couple of times recently I've overheard him talking to that robin. It follows him around all day."

It was Friday, she had seen Christopher and Sharon off to school, washed up and tidied the caravan, and was about to hurry out and help with yet more clearing. She didn't go. Instead she sat uneasily at the table drinking another coffee, fighting the tension within her.

Through the week several attempts to arrange a short escape had failed, even slyly enlisting the children's aid without their actually realising it, had no effect. She had started with hints.

"I wonder what it's like to spend a day away?"

The following day the emphasis had changed.

"Wouldn't it be nice if..." she had supplied a whole series of possibilities to follow the if.

Now, on Friday, she was desperate; the need to get away tangible, it tore at her. She wanted the digger to fail just so she could shoot off to Par for parts – by afternoon the thought of sabotage to ensure the digger really did break down, had even entered her mind. She cornered Gordon as he arrived for tea, ignoring the children already sitting at the table.

"You need a rest!" her accusing finger dug in his chest. "A trip out, a little excursion, that's what you need. Don't argue!"

He opened his mouth to reply, temporarily taken aback by the unexpected onslaught, but she cut him off, poking his chest again.

"Away from the site, or you'll slope off to work like you always do."

The children, equally surprised by the outburst had swung round looking part expectant, part puzzled, first towards Jan then at Dad, awaiting his reply.

Though averse to anything that interfered with progress, surprise at her uncharacteristic behaviour made him pause, silencing the straight refusal on the tip of

88

his tongue. A break was well overdue, he knew that but he hated losing the time. Despite unflagging efforts and working all hours, progress seemed so slow. And what about cost?

"Can we afford it?" he asked.

She breathed in deeply. Not the outright refusal expected, but he might still wriggle free, using expense for an excuse.

"Yes, of course we can. It needn't cost more than eating at home. We do have to eat you know! I can always pack a lunch." Seeing his hesitation, her anxiety returned. She rushed on, "Tomorrow – it's Saturday. This weather doesn't look like it will ever change. Why not tomorrow?"

Gordon looked at the concern in her features as they faced each other, the children momentarily forgotten. This is important to her, he thought, sensing his wife's anxiety, seeing tension in her shoulders. She's right about the weather, it hasn't rained for weeks and I don't think it's going to now.

"OK, tomorrow. Where?"

He saw the muscles relax, a smile replaced the little frown, and she glanced towards the children in delight.

"Anywhere. The beach will do; the Mount, it's sandy. At three miles you can't say it will use much petrol." She had won; it didn't matter where, just down the road, the North Pole, the moon, just away – anyplace!

They woke at dawn, habit, but as Gordon made to rise Jan laid a gentle restraining arm on his shoulder guiding him back, whispering, "Not this morning," snuggling into his arms and drifting back to sleep.

Something was shaking her toe. The foot moved in a spasm of its own and the irritation stopped. She lay barely awake, trying to remember something. There it was again! A hand on her foot, shaking it. Drowsily she lifted her head to find Stephen at the end of the bed, reaching over the sleeping form of his father. Seeing the head rise he stopped, withdrawing the hand slowly, watching her but saying nothing. A mistake Jan realised, planning the trip with the children the night before and thinking with no work they could lie-in this morning instead of rising with the dawn. Absolutely pointless now to say, "Go back to bed."

Within a short time everyone had risen, washed and dressed. Christopher went to the river for water while Gordon stacked away the beds and Jan prepared breakfast.

Leisurely breakfasts were a luxury in themselves but the children soon became impatient. Jan smiled at them indulgently, feeling far more relaxed, tensions of the past week already dispersing. Leaning back into the bench seat she laid a hand limply on the table, looking back at the three eager faces.

"No good you trying to hurry me this morning, I've a picnic to pack and I'm definitely not leaving dirty washing up." She paused. "Sharon, fill the kettle with drinking water and light the gas again, then all of you..." her eyes ranged round the table resting finally on Dad as she repeated with emphasis, "*all* of you, go take yourselves off outside. I need at least half an hour."

Sharon was striking a match as Gordon, trapped in the corner seat, heaved himself up following the boys towards the doorway. A hand reached out, detaining him.

"Try to keep them amused, stop little heads poking in here every five minutes to see if I'm ready," Jan whispered, noticing the pleasure on Sharon's face at being allowed to overhear while lifting the full kettle back onto the gas. Nodding her head at Mum's glance of approval, Sharon left to join her brothers, shortly followed by Dad who leaped as usual from the caravan, ignoring the step.

"OK. I'm all yours. What shall we do?" he called to the children who had wandered towards the bridge.

They trooped off together, no special plan in mind. Christopher led, proudly showing secret paths, tortuous low ways, scrambling and wriggling under bushes into parts his father had previously thought impenetrable. They had developed some knowledge of the vegetation around them, maybe catching their parent's interest or perhaps the absence of more lurid attractions like television might have been responsible. Having learned new pathways from the children, he was pleased in exchange to reveal near the bottom of the site a sweet chestnut tree, suggesting they collect its nuts that autumn for use at Christmas.

Wandering back towards the caravan none of them seemed in any hurry. It was unusual, unprecedented, to have Dad in the mornings! He was not as much fun in the evenings, worn out, not at all inclined to follow a scrambling safari through and around the denser undergrowth. Gordon too enjoyed the role of a normal Dad for once, sometimes following, sometimes leading, seeing favourite hiding places, best climbing trees, answering endless questions and making odd points of his own. He mentioned a tree name and found they knew it already, and having picked up the common ones were competitively keen to display their knowledge.

Chatting in this manner the little band progressed towards the caravan. Stephen found two sycamore leaves, insisting they were different since one had a large black spot; totally disinclined to accept that disease caused the blemish. All three missed the spindle tree with its small semi-glossy green leaves and green stems, so named for its frequent use as spinning-wheel axles.

"Cheating!" Sharon claimed. "Trees have big trunks, this is only a bush. It shouldn't be allowed!"

The boys agreed, stopping, standing next to her, shoulder to shoulder.

Dad hesitated. What was this, teamwork? He looked down at the keen expressions; they wanted to win, to score a point. Is that why they argued so much, to score points off each other? Some married couples did that.

"OK. A bush." He shrugged, maybe it was.

On reaching the caravan, Jan cleverly served hot coffee, having watched their approach and judged the arrival nicely.

The family departed shortly after nine, all their worldly possessions left unattended for the first time since arrival, theft never a problem in the valley, not that much would have been worth stealing. The caravan door refused to lock but the chance that anyone at all would even pass by was slim.

Fifteen minutes later they lay stretched out on the sand. Cornwall was blessed with so many beaches that few ever became crowded. They could see two people in the distance and another couple at the water's edge, but holidaymakers seldom rise early; more would appear later. The tide, far out across the rippled sand but past the turn and beginning to rise, still left uncovered the way to St Michael's Mount. No longer an island at low tide, attachment to the mainland lay over a stone causeway. Jan had done her homework in advance, having somehow obtained a fistful of pamphlets, one on the Mount's history. The causeway was built in 1425 then home to an order of monks. The Mount passed to the St Aubyn family in the year 1647, they still lived there today. She couldn't recall the rest of those many pages on its distinguished past.

"We might do the castle tour some time. Even when the causeway is submerged, little rowing boats take you across to the island." she suggested, but showed no inclination to move, lying back in the sand again, draping a hand lazily across her eyes to shade the sun.

Gordon glanced up at the castle. How easy for today's visitors compared to the prodigious journeys on foot of past pilgrims. His gaze swung lazily toward the children, industriously building their own castle of sand before the tide would come in to wash it away.

"When can we start our building?" he wondered, pushing it quickly from his mind, remembering his promise to Jan not even to think about the site today, and fearing she would read his thoughts.

Stephen, tiring of the castle, dragged his father off to find shells. They were not so plentiful here, unlike the Atlantic coast, the search largely unsuccessful but providing sufficient excuse to play in waves washing up the shore. Fine sand underfoot near the Mount became coarser farther along the beach, turning to tiny pebbles, growing larger towards Penzance three miles off in a westward direction. These pebbles, large and small, were ground smoothly round from constant shifting in the tides.

All had brought costumes, the parents to swim, which they did, taking turns to watch as the children played at the edge. By about 10.30, perhaps twenty couples and families had spread widely along the beach. The sandcastle with its many turrets and dry moat still stood, but lay neglected. Jan walked off to return holding three small ice creams. She had said nothing on leaving, Gordon assumed to search for a toilet. Carrying the three cornets across the sands, she looked towards him, half expecting disapproval at the extravagance, but he nodded encouragement. The children were delighted, Christopher and Sharon dashing to meet her, vocally appreciative. Stephen, running to catch up, signalled his pleasure by facial expression alone. Jan watched them, pleased with the reaction, it added somehow to her own feeling of wellbeing, a contentment completely missing through the previous week. Surprising, she thought, what people miss by having everything they want whenever they want it.

Fortunately the children were already very brown from helping on the site. In the clear Cornish air it would not have been advisable to allow such long exposure to the hot midsummer sun without the protection of a good tan. The budget might stretch to an ice cream, but expensive sun creams had no place in their calculations!

The morning slid lazily by, children playing various games, Stephen being included to some extent in most. Christopher, always sensible, came for Mum when they wanted to go deeper but it was Dad who went, supporting them when they tried to swim. Towards midday Stephen tired and came to sit, asking for food.

Picnics vary – when laid out on a cloth spread across the sand this one was nothing special; but special too is relative. A variety of sandwiches, a few pieces of cake, one thermos of hot tea, another of cold orange cordial and a tin of peaches eaten with a shared spoon – for them a creditable spread. This, together with the sea fast approaching the position where they sat, made it special for the children. Jan watched their faces, alight with expectation as a bigger wave softened the sandcastle's outline, stopping inches from the cloth on which their picnic stood. They turned to her assuming a rapid retreat, but she sat unmoved. Their excitement increased, eyes returning to the sea, searching for the next big one.

"I knew risk-taking was addictive!" Jan reflected.

The children's spirit of joy contagiously affected everyone; laughing and having fun, forgetting for a while all the heavy work still to come.

The break had been good. Jan was pleased. Having moved eventually farther from the incoming tide, she lay on the sand, head on Gordon's lap and quietly watched him looking at the children near the water. He glanced down smiling affectionately to see her lips pucker in a small blown kiss. The hand resting on her shoulder squeezed softly in return. Watching his reaction, she suggested quietly and without emphasis, "We could do this more often you know. I could get to like it."

No expression of resistance appeared on his face. She thought he nodded but wasn't sure. Continuing in the same soft tone she warned coaxingly, "And you needn't think you're going to work this afternoon, because you're not."

Returning to the site at something after three, Gordon lay next to her outside the caravan on brown grass growing from soil baked hard by the sun. The children played, came back to the caravan, sometimes one or other, at times all together, only to speed off again on a sudden fancy. Open books lay nearby, largely unread as both relaxed, Jan dropping off once into a light sleep, head across his shoulder, to wake with a smile as the children came tearing back yet again.

"Do you realise," she sighed when the youngsters departed once more, "this is our first complete day off since arriving over six weeks ago?"

"Don't expect a whole day off every six weeks! My trouble is I spoil you!" Gordon warned solemnly, but with a gleam of love hardly concealed.

She gave a little pout, paused for a bit, then sighing with happiness, lazily responded.

"I know. But the day's not over yet. I'm sure there's still lots to enjoy." She yawned contentedly, stretched both arms in the air, letting one hand fall back gently onto his leg, outstretched fingers lightly touching the inside of his thigh.

Chapter 6

The Canoe

Negotiations had been taking place regarding not only the site buildings but also in connection with water and telephone. Water in particular proved difficult. Arguments over pipe size was causing delays. To carry the total volume required, including enough for all the permitted static caravans, the water authority eventually decided that a minimum pipe diameter of three inches would be needed. However they were sticking out for a six-inch size for their own convenience, in case they wanted to make a connection to St Erth, two miles down river.

"OK," Gordon had replied, "but *you* must pay the difference for the larger pipes. I don't mind laying them for you but we just can't afford the extra cost."

There the matter still rested. Pipes could not even be ordered until approval was forthcoming, and due to the high pressure of water in the valley, apparently Grade D pipes, the very strongest, would be needed.

The telephone too had some complications caused by doubts over what size of cable to use, with deep enquiries into how many lines would be required when the park reached full size. Meanwhile, those hours of clearing work continued, the longest day approaching – they dropped into bed at night and slept so soundly, morning seemed to come as heads touched the pillow.

* * *

Something touched her lips. It felt nice. Steeling herself to lie immobile, eyes still closed, she waited. The warm sensation moved across one cheek, softly nibbling an earlobe, then down under her chin and slowly out towards the shoulder. She knew exactly what it was, could feel the closeness of his warm naked body; had felt those lips so often before. How strange that they could still set her skin on fire. The warmth edged lower as a roughened hand, searching gently, slipped under the thin nightdress to rest on the bulge of her hip. It felt incredibly good. Forcing her eyes open, determined to resist while still able, she spoke quietly.

"You should be working!".

"Do you really want me to?"

"Yes... No!"

The words were whispered, the second one urgently, a hand reaching out for his shoulder, pulling him back as he made to move away then hesitating, whispered again reluctantly in his ear, "The children may wake?"

He sighed, kissing her once more before leaning backwards and stretching, then pulling himself up to a sitting position in the bed, moving the pillow against the caravan's side to form a back rest. "Do I have a dressing-gown?"

"In your Mum's loft."

"Not a lot of good three hundred miles away. A coat or something?"

"An old coat, yes, in the wardrobe right at the back. Thought you wouldn't need it until winter?" There was a question in her voice.

"Fancy a dip?" He reached to lift the curtain and peer outside, letting it fall back into position again.

"At this time in the morning? Must be mad! And

why aren't you working, it's gone six already."

"Can't possibly start work before breakfast."

"You always have!"

"Ah. Not fitting for a man of property." Gordon waved an arm regally in the air then reached with two fingers into a cupped hand, holding them to his nose and inhaling an imaginary pinch of snuff.

"Man of property? You mean..." Her smile broadened as he nodded confirmation.

"It's today. June 20, twelve o'clock is completion. We actually own the land from midday. Just a formality, I know. What will you do if anything goes wrong before twelve?"

"Don't!" A look of alarm crossed her face. Too much like tempting providence. Best left unsaid!

Leaning to brush her lips again, he swung over taking two steps to the tiny wardrobe, located the coat, grabbed a towel and was gone through the door. Little time passed before it re-opened.

"How cold *was* the water?" Jan asked, glancing at the clock. His dip had taken only five minutes, a good indication.

"Refreshing. Makes you feel great." Pulling in his waist, throwing shoulders back and breathing in deeply to expand his chest, he moved towards her. "I could be your Tarzan this morning."

"You look more like Flashy Gordon."

"You mean Flash Gordon."

"With a coat like that and nothing underneath – I know what I mean!"

* * *

"Look." whispered Jan, "What's he doing?"

99

Gordon turned from after-lunch coffee, following her gaze through the window. Grey cloud hung heavily in the sky, obscuring the sun for the first time in weeks, the coolness a relief but threatening rain later.

Walking towards the now almost cleared area to the south of the caravan stalked a sinister-looking figure in a battered trilby hat and dark raincoat. Every few paces he stopped to peer intently at the ground.

"Cheek!" Jan objected, and asked again, "What's he doing on *our* land?" Her voice grew louder and more galled. "He looked straight at the caravan when I first saw him, then turned away. I'm sure he saw me. He's deliberately ignoring us."

"We'll see about that!" Gordon rose quickly, slipping off the bench and round the corner of the table. He had jumped from the caravan door ready to dash across and give the stranger a few strong words, when he slowed, struck by a sudden thought. "I wonder if indignation is catching? I don't normally approach people so antagonistically." Grinning to himself at the long word that somehow came to mind, his mood improved, pace slowed, he took a deep breath and strode towards the stranger in a more relaxed frame of mind.

"Can I help you?"

The man in the hat looked up, hesitating. "No, I don't think so," he turned away to continue searching.

Not much caring to be left standing in his own backyard, Gordon replied quietly and a good deal more casually than he felt, "You're trespassing."

The uninvited visitor stopped sharply and turned, a look of surprise crossing his face, and perhaps a shade of embarrassment.

Much more satisfactory! Gordon smiled. Now they were face to face, the figure no longer looked sinister.

It seemed pointless to be unfriendly. "We purchased it in May. What are you searching for?"

The visitor's quest for purple marsh orchids conflicted absolutely with their own aim of a flat grass area for tourers; two seemingly incompatible ideals. However, a mutual interest in natural history and the orchid man's obvious knowledge of it, changed the atmosphere. Over the following weeks they became firm friends, Gordon appreciating the man's guidance and help in identifying particular items of local flora. The purple marsh orchid would, purely by chance, have remained safe anyway, growing abundantly on the sloping riverbanks that were to stay totally undisturbed. In places along the stream at the height of flowering in May and June the display had been prolific. Pointing to the considerable colour variation between plants growing side by side, this new friend suggested some hybrids, crosses with allied but different species might well be present here. The orchid season was already passing but had caused a meeting that, from a most unpromising start, might well prove invaluable.

It did rain later that evening, continuing well into the night. Heavy drops drummed on the roof, commencing with unexpected force as Christopher and Sharon prepared for bed, young Stephen already lying in the lower bunk. As the first wave hit the metal surfaces like a squall, the little caravan appeared to rock, causing everyone to look up. Darkness had not yet fallen when Sharon, shrugging on her nightdress, approached the door, first glancing over her shoulder apprehensively at Mum, then opening it slightly and peered out toward the exposed toilet. A sigh of relief escaped her lips at finding the rain, coming from the normal southwest direction, was not entering the open awning. She slipped out, glancing along the riverbank against the slight possibility that any fool would be walking there on such an evening.

Later, their single light extinguished, the family lay resting uneasily, listening. The rain slowly diminished, only to lash down anew as another squall struck the caravan, drumming again on aluminium roof and sides, swaying the small room on its rusty steadies below. The new wave came without warning, Gordon felt Jan hug closer, her grip tightening on his shoulders as it hit. The movement had a feeling akin to speeding across a humped back bridge, with the added concern that while bridges never blew over, caravans had certainly been known to! Thank goodness the awning lay downwind. Sleep came slowly that night to everyone except Stephen.

In the morning Jan rose, guessing it would be some time after five. She opened the caravan door to wash in the dim light from a pre-dawn sky, dark overhead, but already glowing clear and cloudless at the eastern horizon. Dipping a flannel in the bucket containing fresh water that Christopher had scooped from the river the evening before, she washed quickly, returning to dress as Gordon, already fully clothed, passed her in the doorway.

"I'll be back to wash and have breakfast with the children. Need to check rain hasn't affected the digger."

Then he was gone. Not a word about herself, no "How did you sleep?" or "Are you all right?" not even a "Good Morning," only the digger!

"Get your priorities right," she thought, smiling inwardly, looking at the bed still laid out, not put away nor the table erected as he usually did. "Always knew I came after that damn machine anyway!"

Minutes later, while stooping to stuff bedclothes into

lockers under bench seats before rebuilding the table, she heard a deep note some way off as Max's engine started. Nearly an hour until breakfast, half an hour before the children need be roused. Luxury! She rubbed one cheek against the soft material of her nightdress, before pulling it over her head and donning day clothes, unable to unwind fully unless dressed and ready for any unexpected emergency. Sinking back in the bench seat, she reached out without rising to draw the little curtains at the rear and side, then settled back again to relax, watching the sky gradually lighten.

Breakfast of eggs and fried bread simmered on the stove, bacon would have been nice but it lay beyond this week's resources. The children were dressed and seated at table when Gordon arrived back, leaping up three steps, already later than intended. No time to use the mug of hot water Jan had put by for shaving; he would do it afterwards.

The children looked in slight surprise at the dark stubble as he squeezed past to sit in the corner.

"Make way!"

Arms came off the table as Mum placed steaming plates in front of Dad, then Christopher.

"Ladies should be first, Mum!" Sharon's objection produced a smile between father and son.

"Smallest first." Stephen mumbled, nodding to himself with conviction.

Jan winked at him, leaning forward to whisper loudly, "I'm serving ugliest first today."

* * *

Mail was never brought to the door, at least not unless a big parcel arrived. It would have been unreasonable to expect it until the lane's condition improved. The postman deposited letters inside a box nailed to a tall wooden stake driven in the ground half a mile away at the site entrance, on a small plot that once contained a row of five miner's cottages. Many large granite stones from collapsed and demolished buildings still lay strewn on the land.

Returning from collecting more diesel for the digger, Jan had all but driven past, stopping on a sudden whim, a feeling, to look inside. Letters were rare but one rested snugly on the bottom when she lifted the lid. Now, back at the caravan, the kettle heating ready for coffee, she looked down again at the handwritten envelope with pleasure and a tinge of foreboding. It came from her parents, her mother's writing unmistakable. Jan remembered the last letter, carefully written, no outright condemnation, just sympathy oozing from every line. A hope, thinly veiled, that sense would prevail, that Gordon would seek a proper job and return her daughter to a normal, suitable life. Would this one follow the pattern? She had replied, of course, but adequately describing on paper the atmosphere of peace surrounding the valley and the children's delight in living there – that had stretched her literary powers. She had deliberately omitted any mention of work or the facilities. Had she succeeded? Would this letter, lying yet unopened, reveal continued misgivings?

She had lifted it tentatively already, only to lay it down and nervously adjust the gas under the kettle. Raising the envelope, easing a table knife under the flap, Jan sliced through the paper, extracting its contents quickly to scan the short message.

"Expect us both on Friday!"

She laid it aside, apprehensively looking round the

little caravan, seeing it critically as a stranger would. The cramped space, two in a bed, no privacy... and the cooking facilities – two gas rings and a sink with no running water and no drainer – whoever would call those cooking facilities?

Tolerance of their circumstances, acceptance that their home was not too far from normal, these ideas had grown as months flew by. She realised that now. Nobody else would see it that way, certainly not her mother.

Her heart sank lower; the loo... exposed in the awning for all to see! How would she explain that away? Cover it with a blanket! And washing; that bucket of water on the bench outside? Could she put them off coming? No. Friday was tomorrow! How long had the letter lain in the box? She remembered Stephen, still asleep in the Mini van – never mind, he would come in when he woke. Another thought struck her. What about baths? The children would tell, they would delight in it!

Footsteps sounded, approaching the caravan. Gordon was coming. Coffee. She had forgotten completely, must have turned the gas off instead of adjusting the flame. Striking a match and lighting the ring, she reached for the cups as he swung smiling through the doorway.

"A chap has to fetch his own coffee now?"

"Sorry, forgot." The response lacked sparkle.

"What's the matter?"

How had he sensed her mood so quickly? She took a deep breath, looked round the caravan and sadly back towards him, speaking simply in a flat voice.

"Jim and Audrey are coming tomorrow."

Jan's mother's name was Olive but she hated it and insisted on being called by her second name, Audrey. Gordon understood the sombre mood now. He remembered the suspicion, the disapproval with himself in particular; had felt it strongly when the family took their final departure from London. He knew they still half-suspected their daughter had been dragged away to a primitive life of poverty and drudgery, to become prematurely bent and wrinkled with age; a place where their grandchildren would live lives of hardship and misery.

Listlessly Jan reached across for the kettle, but he intercepted the movement, pulling her closer, kissing one cheek gently.

"Don't worry. We live this life for ourselves. It doesn't matter who disapproves."

She looked into his eyes, straightening her shoulders. "Yes!" With an affirmative nod of the head she smiled back, hugging him close, then whispered wistfully, "I hope they like it though."

Looking at Jan, awaiting her parents' arrival, Gordon knew they would see how wrong their assessment had been. She was vibrant, suntanned, happy – and as he knew, devastatingly beautiful! They would find Stephen healthy and happy too, but would wait until evening for Sharon and Christopher to walk back from school. Perhaps eventually they might fully comprehend how a family could lose so much materially, yet still find a better life.

Jim and Audrey understood in advance that staying on site would not be possible. The little caravan hardly had space to sleep its five regular occupants. Bed and breakfast had been hurriedly booked in St Hilary, the next village, but Jan insisted on providing lunch and tea. Eating would be in relays, or the children could use pillows on the floor. It was difficult seating even the immediate family around the small collapsible table;

Sharon and Stephen had to sit very close. No way could two extra adults be squeezed in unless the children sat elsewhere.

Jim and Audrey's thoughts on arrival were poorly hidden. In spite of the valley's beauty and the pleasure of seeing their daughter again, they were obviously terribly sorry for Jan, living under such conditions, and a little frosty towards Gordon for reducing her to these circumstances. However, returning from a brief look round, on which he conducted them during final food preparations, Gordon watched with great interest as they looked in amazement at Jan and the meal she placed before them. It was nothing expensive. By chance, chicken pieces had been on special that week. Jan boiled them first, finishing off to a golden colour by frying, adding a stir-fry mixture of such vegetables as she could buy cheaply, and French fried potatoes, again boiled and finished in the pan. Jim and Audrey were not to know that only happy coincidence provided a better than usual lunch that particular day. There would be sufficient for tomorrow but after that it was back to the more usual thin slices of luncheon meat and mash. Chicken didn't come on special offer every day, and without a fridge, buying ahead was out!

As they ate, four at the table, Stephen on his pillow on the floor, Gordon could almost see their minds reassessing the situation. Jan was healthily tanned and clearly happy, serving with ease a creditable meal from two rings. Moreover, that she could easily cope, even in the cramped conditions, with visitors, cooking, looking after Stephen, including some outside work – all was so obvious. Neither Jim nor Audrey could avoid seeing it, whatever their opinions on arrival.

They stayed just a few days, but during that short

period became completely enchanted by the valley, captivated to the unbelievable extent of discussing living there when Jim retired shortly. Even Gordon had risen a point or two in their estimation, although he worked on through their entire visit, seeing them mostly during meals. Jim even helped improve the steps beside the bridge that led down to the river, working single-handed in spite of his leg. Somehow the plot of land by the site entrance arose in conversation, and the need for someone to look after it. Audrey jumped at the chance, asking if a bungalow could be built there. With Jim's arthritis-troubled leg growing steadily worse, a bungalow offered the only practical solution.

"Possibly." Jan replied, reservation sounding in her voice, turning with raised eyebrows, passing the question to Gordon.

"It had permission previously; out of date now." He hesitated, struggling with the unforeseen turn of events. To encourage or discourage? "We could reapply; need a new design though, something special – every visitor will see it, their first impression as they enter the park." He glanced at Jan, catching the imperceptible nod of approval before turning back to Audrey with a caution.

"You understand the toilet buildings come first?" Nothing was more important. They must get paying visitors soon; funds were running low!

Audrey nodded.

Gordon continued before she could speak, "I can promise one thing. We'll build your bungalow before starting one for ourselves, but after next year's tourist season." It was an easy promise to make. Jim would have funds from the sale of his own house in London, certainly sufficient for building his bungalow. Earning money from the site to build anything for Jan and the children could take years! Or never?

Saturday and the time to leave had come. All five stood waving as Jim's car bumped slowly down the road. They had spent last evening in the caravan discussing bungalows while Gordon drew and redrew sketches of their ideal home. Audrey had already tentatively arranged that Jim put their house on the market when he retired. "We could live in a caravan until our bungalow is built," she suggested, and persuaded Jim to leave a signed blank cheque to purchase 'something suitable'. "With any luck we could be back permanently, perhaps even by Christmas. At least with a caravan here we can visit more often."

What a change of mind from their arrival. Gordon half-believed that they originally harboured notions of rescuing their daughter and the children, taking them back, away from the terrible life they had fallen into! As the car disappeared he sat down with Jan, coffee in hand, asking, "Will they really come or change their mind on the way home."

"Yes, they'll come; Mum's very keen. You've gone up in her opinion I think."

Together they discussed the actions required before Jim and Audrey's return. Obviously the toilet buildings still held top priority.

"But," Jan suggested, "preparing a spot for Jim's caravan will only take an hour, then if I find something suitable advertised, we can buy it."

Seeing Gordon's reluctance to be deflected from other work even for a short while, she continued hurriedly.

"Obviously we must choose one that the owner will deliver, if the place is ready he can park it on the spot so it won't need moving – save you time. The extra storage space could be useful for..."

Leaving the tempting thought hanging in the air, she shrugged, not pushing. The decision was his, to do or to leave, but as usual she had cleverly said just enough to let him have her way. Together they selected a conveniently level spot near where the water main would eventually reach. A small soakaway was quickly constructed for waste water, a shallow hole excavated with the digger to be filled later with small stones by the children, a temporary arrangement until completion of the large septic tank needed for the toilet buildings.

That evening the drawing-board reappeared, much to the children's dismay. Its presence exiled them or at least required relative immobility if they did enter, since the little van rocked with any sudden movement inside, stretching and creaking on those well-rusted supports. When someone jumped from bench to floor, Gordon's drawing-ink lines tended to become Chinese characters!

The sketches made with Jim and Audrey were quite quickly turned into proper drawings. Time must be made in the coming month to discuss them with various council officers.

As clearing operations extended to areas farther away from the caravan, erratic changes of ground level revealed a surface no longer constant, but rugged and fluctuating. Whereas the two acres so far prepared had been flat underneath, perhaps from some long forgotten cultivation, no similarly smooth contours appeared elsewhere. No quick clearing of undergrowth would produce a usable surface here! Dips, ruts, gullies, mounds and banks, all were partly obscured or hidden completely by old gorse intermixed with brambles and the occasional larger tree.

Gordon discussed with Jan these isolated trees.

"Levelling will be easier if I remove them all, but the easiest way may not be the best. It has to look attractive."

She nodded, "Less work is definitely tempting, but I don't think you'll take down any good trees however much work it saves. I know too well how you feel about plants and animals."

He thought about it, realising she was right, but a few would have to go; not all could be saved. Many were hollow, dangerously damaged from past gorse fires. New ones could be planted too, but new trees took a long while to grow! For now he'd save the existing ones, making a feature of them, use them to create numerous separate areas, each varying in size and shape. More could be added later when time was less pressing. Levels between areas could change too, that would help, but each section must be flat in itself; no sloping pitches.

The county council had wisely suggested that kinks should be added in the long road to the downstream end of the site, improving appearance and lowering vehicle speeds. That could be achieved nicely by working round existing trees and banks. So much for intentions. For a start, uprooting the gorse would remove a fire hazard as well as allowing the shape and best level of the next area to be determined. Here however, the gorse though widespread, grew only partly in clusters suitable for pulling with the machine, much appeared as separate stems which a chain would not grip. These of necessity, would be removed by hand.

The longest day had passed by, but daylight arrived early and disappeared late, work was hard and unending. Robin, still present, offered welcome company, not even the engine noise moving him far. When the machine stopped the bird approached close enough to reach out and touch. Now, with work farther from the caravan, Jan could help less and spent more time with Stephen. Gordon, alone for even longer periods, increasingly chatted to Robin; not continuously, companionable silences were fine, but at frequent intervals they talked, or rather Gordon talked, but he knew Robin understood. Moreover, a male blackbird appeared, not sitting on branches and making quick sorties for food like Robin, but shuffling in the undergrowth, scratching up old leaves, turning over sticks in search of a meal. He too became a companion to chat with, to ask opinions of, not exactly lightening the work but diverting the mind, making long hours pass faster.

Among the gear transported, roped to the roof-rack on that initial journey back in May, had been a canoe. Almost certainly the only entirely unnecessary item carried, they had tried to sell it and failing, didn't really know what to do other than bring the craft along. On rare occasions in late evening the canoe would be used by way of relaxation. Floating along was pleasant and almost energy-free, a vital requirement at the day's end!

Jan encouraged it, driving one of the children, Dad and the canoe, the half-mile up to the village. Anything special done for their young family had of necessity to be virtually cost-free; trips down the river, like rides in the digger bucket, met this requirement. By the old granite bridge in the centre of Relubbus, Gordon would lower the vessel into the water, steady it while his passenger embarked, then glide smoothly downstream to the caravan. These sorties were not competitive, mostly drifting with the current. Floating along the surface using the paddle only to select the best line was not only enjoyed by the children, but therapeutic for Dad on days when hours of hard work seemed to result in little progress.

Usually either Christopher or Stephen would be passenger, Sharon seldom asked to go. Though these trips were used to unwind, a relaxing contrast to the day's muscular work, the canoeists were quite interested to see how swiftly the flow would carry them. It became apparent that a straighter course was not necessarily quicker, since the current more often ran fastest round the outside of bends. However if Gordon did feel up to a few quick strokes then a straighter line, closely shaving the meandering curves, definitely had the edge. The boys enjoyed these mini excursions, pressing for more regular runs, but petrol costs and Dad's frequent total lack of energy in the evenings made such trips a rarity.

One morning when every setback and minor calamity possible seemed to have interrupted work, Gordon returned to the caravan instead of waiting for Jan to bring coffee. Nothing really crucial had occurred, just a series of small exasperating mishaps. In the relentless drive to achieve more each day, nothing – never mind how trivial – nothing was as irritating as time wasted. Even more so because these incidents were avoidable, his own carelessness!

Firstly, having expended considerable time working carefully round an unknown plant he wanted to preserve, an inadvertent stumble had snapped it off, triggering annoyance tinged with guilt; he had killed it.

Then a bunch of gorse stems, apparently close enough together to hoist out with the digger, were snapped off by clumsy operation of control levers, snatching on the chain rather than easing it steadily upwards. It was weeks since that had last happened. The stems broke part way up, leaving roots to be excavated by hand.

Finally, the engine died. Carelessness allowed the machine's fuel supply to run out. Nearly half an hour passed, topping up then bleeding air from the system, before it would run again. Such days were bound to happen, he knew that, but the pent-up frustration that nothing would go right persisted!

Jan sensed the tension immediately he stepped inside the caravan, disliking the way it made him, not exactly sullen, but unresponsive. It was she who made the suggestion.

"A canoe trip might improve your mood, I'll run you upstream then come back and put the kettle on for coffee."

He stared at her for a moment saying nothing, then turned and was gone through the door, striding to the van, swinging both the rear doors wide and climbing in holding the canoe instead of fixing it to the roof-rack.

Sensing the need for hurry, Jan intercepted Stephen, signalling him to stay, snatched the two big water-carriers, tossed them onto the passenger seat and drove off quickly, ignoring the track surface. On the journey Gordon said little, his mind turning morosely inward, breathing deeply, gripping the vessel as the van sped faster than usual over potholes, the bumps unnoticed – lost in his own black thoughts. No peaceful ride was planned.

"This canoe is going down that river as though it's jet-propelled," he told himself, lowering the boat into the stream.

He pushed off, dug in the double-ended oar and heaved forward with vicious thrusts at the water, shaving corners to the closest possible line. Not ever before had he attempted a daytime trip, while still fresh. Never had the canoe moved so fast! Every ounce of frustration with that morning's mishaps poured into muscle sinews, burning up tension in a frenzy of sustained effort. Approaching the last bend before the caravan, heart racing, sweat trickling down his back, far from easing up he pulled the paddles ever more fiercely through the water, shaving the final corner closer than a cat's whisker.

Without warning the front end caught! Momentum dug the prow deep into soft wet soil, throwing his weight forward. The tail swung round in an instant, broadside across the river, wedging on the other bank. At this point the river ran unusually narrow and nearly three feet deep. A difference of several inches immediately appeared between the upstream and downstream water levels. Struggle as he might there was no shifting the vessel back against the weight of water. Pushing vainly, paddle against bed, produced no result. Abruptly the oar slipped and before he could recover the canoe rolled.

With arms flailing frantically, fighting hopelessly against gravity, he crashed to the river, his head forced beneath the surface until one shoulder rested heavily against a gravelly riverbed. He could feel the force of water moving small stones all around, see lines of rising bubbles rushing away on the current, light playing on the choppy surface above, but his feet were still in the canoe and it would not budge. Reaching out with one hand Gordon drove fingers deeply into silt and gravel of the bed, grasping for some purchase to pull himself free, his other hand pushing frantically on the fibreglass side. Suddenly, like a cork, he burst through the surface gasping air into starved lungs.

Perhaps survival was a greater mark of success than speed; or was it shock he wondered which gave that tingle of well-being even after, or perhaps especially after, such a near disaster. No doubt he would tingle yet more under Jan's wrath when she saw the state of him – drying clothes in a ten-foot caravan figured very low on her list of favourite occupations. Wrenching the boat free he dragged it up the bank, draining the water and heading for the caravan.

Stephen, elated with surprise and excitement at the sight, pointed to the bedraggled figure plodding back lugging the canoe, water dripping from every garment, hair a wet flattened tangle. Jan, her attention drawn to Gordon's approach, abandoned the water-carriers she was unloading from the van, grabbed Stephen's hand, quickly entered the caravan and slipped the bolt locking the door. Sticking her head through an open window, she shouted.

"You needn't think you're coming inside dripping like that!"

A towel and dry clothes flew out to land on the grass, leaving him no option but to strip, towel down and re-dress, watched from the window by two laughing faces, giggles of mirth clearly audible. Only then did the door get unlocked and coffee served! Good job it was summer. Stephen could hardly wait to tell Christopher and Sharon later when they came home from school. He would do it in few words, then infuriate them by refusing to say more.

Inside the caravan sipping hot coffee, Gordon rested back in the cushions, feeling better and wondering why? On impulse he addressed Jan sitting opposite.

"That's the absolute worst canoe trip I ever made, but the sombre mood is gone. I feel great! Adrenaline intoxication perhaps?"

She smiled, shrugged, leaned closer and whispered back, "Cold water may expand your spirit but I couldn't help noticing, it certainly shrinks other parts."

Some time later quite by accident when chatting to the fisheries officer, they discovered that the River Authority objected to canoes.

"Brown trout, quite numerous in the Hayle, lay their eggs in shallow holes excavated in the gravel bed, covering them again after laying," the officer explained. "These nests, we call them redds, often occur where the bed rises nearest the surface to receive maximum oxygen. Unfortunately this leads canoes to damage the redds, keels tending to touch bottom at these same shallow places. We also know that transmission of various fungal fish diseases is attributable to canoes transported from one location to another without properly disinfecting the hulls."

After that stern warning, emphasising all the environmental disadvantages, they tried again to sell the canoe and succeeded surprisingly quickly, which pleased Jan.

"Good. We need the money!"

She was right, cash was needed for many reasons. A goodly amount remained in the account but all earmarked for various purposes; eating, building materials, and equipment yet to come. Whether it would be sufficient verged between marginal and unlikely, so this small income instead of outgoing definitely felt good!

Immediately now the need was for a trailer. While working near the big waste heap, transporting stony waste over short distances a few hundredweight at a time in the digger's front bucket, had been reasonable. As the levelled area expanded, it became impractical and took too long to trundle such small amounts over the greater distances. With the vast quantity requiring removal, probably more than 50,000 tons, a strong new self-tipping trailer appeared the only sensible answer. This was not unexpected, they had always known one would be essential, that some of their remaining meagre resources would have to be utilised. The best model affordable cost £170, designed to hold five tons, a figure probably destined to be exceeded often enough. Cornish mine tailings, unlike coal or china clay, were broken rock, a hard and weighty material.

The trailer arrived drawn behind a large Landrover. Moderately light when empty, it looked three times the size of the towing vehicle. Unexpectedly it was driven by the salesman who, a week previously, had come to Relubbus with the illustrated catalogue from which the purchase was selected.

With the rear digging attachment already removed, the excavator looked much like a normal tractor, apart from the big loading shovel at the front end. A short demonstration quickly showed how the new trailer could be picked up, towed, tipped to empty then set down again, all without leaving the tractor seat.

"But," warned their visitor, "there *is* a disadvantage. Removing the heavy digging attachment is essential but now it's missing you'll find there's no weight on these." He slapped the excavator's big rear driving wheels with his hand. "They'll slip and spin when you attempt to thrust the front bucket into stone to load the trailer."

Seeing frowns of concern, the salesman hurried on quickly. "You can buy counterweights which hang from the same hitch that picks up the trailer," he laid a hand on the thick horizontal steel tube at the rear. "You can even construct one for yourself in concrete. I've a drawing."

He strode over to the vehicle, rummaged in a case, returning with a photocopy of a dimensioned sketch showing the counterweight. Passing it over he glanced at his watch, made the excuse of another appointment, and left smartly.

Gordon, arm around Jan, stood near the trailer watching the Landrover depart.

"Used the same ruse myself, to get away when buying the digger," he grinned ruefully.

* * *

A forge glowed redly in the ancient building. Dust coated everything, walls, the wooden joists above and piled-up items lying untended in odd corners of that dimly illuminated interior, light spreading weakly in from the open doorway. The smith, Eslea Lashbrook, shortish but muscular, leaned against a raised anvil studying a diagram of the steel bar needed for making the counterweight. On a bench along one side wall sat three elderly men, well into retirement, enjoying both the warmth and smell of the forge, and the company.

Placing the sketch on a bench and weighting it with a metal offcut, he reached for a round bar somewhat over an inch in thickness, unfolded a rule from his overall pocket and chalked a mark. Cutting it to size, he stuck one end in the forge and pumped the bellows. A roaring blast of air changed dormant embers by stages from dull red to a white hot living glare, tiny sparks flying continually upward in the draught. The blacksmith, one knee raised on some upturned item, chatted with the old-timers, waiting for the metal to heat.

The steel glowed as he swung it to the anvil, lifted a hammer and commenced to batter the end into submission in the shape of a crook. Satisfied, he reheated and treated the other end similarly, then formed the entire bar into a bent open-topped square, crooks uppermost both pointing in what would be the forward direction when the bar was cased in concrete.

The price asked was very reasonable. Gordon paid, then feeling unsure how long the steel could withstand the rough handling that would be its lot, asked the blacksmith to make another, to be collected next week. Reaching into his pocket, he held out another note but Eslea waved it away.

"You don't want to go paying people in advance, doesn't leave any incentive to do the work." He would only take for one. "Pay for the other when you collect it," he insisted.

Cornwall, a place of history, backward some might suggest compared to more modern communities, still retained in places the old values. Good chap, the St.Erth blacksmith!

The concrete counterweight, once hardened and in use, vastly improved the tyres' grip, though not quite matching the traction once available when the heavy trenching attachment had been mounted. In a search to find more weight, the rear wheels themselves were filled with water instead of air, a move that just about restored the original loading power. The drawbacks of this manoeuvre were not to be discovered until a puncture needed mending.

CHAPTER 7

The Perfect Loo

Good life it might be, provided one didn't weaken, but it could become so very much better if only planning consent would arrive. Progress in that direction had been achieved, at least in so far as the drawings now conformed to all known requirements and had long since been submitted. However, no permission was yet forthcoming for any building. Clearing and levelling had become a way of life.

The children, already broken up from school for summer recess, may not have regretted the delay unduly, at least in one respect. Until building commenced their usefulness remained limited, leaving them entirely free to play, barring those regular tasks that they had all learned to take in their stride. Few restrictions were placed on them except, like Stephen, both Christopher and Sharon had been warned never to approach too near the working excavator.

The three played together regularly, climbing, hiding, or accompanying Mum when she visited town for supplies. Having explored the nearer undergrowth, they ranged farther, to the outer limits of the site and along the valley beyond, but just as often Stephen chose to play on his own nearer to the caravan. The sight of Christopher sneaking off with the bow-saw led

Jan to conclude that some form of secret camp lay under construction but she decided not to interfere. New school friends turned up from time to time, joining either Christopher or Sharon in their play, staying mostly around the site but occasionally trotting off to a friend's house.

As August days ticked away and the children's tan grew deeper; Dad worked on, his own skin semi-tropical. Only Jan refused to discard her light blouse, but her face, arms and legs glowed smoothly brown. Though each day's progress under the hot sun seemed tiny, the jungle-like frontiers of untamed regions retreated slowly but inexorably away from the little caravan. Life, though enjoyable still, was hard and relentless as September approached.

Jan huddled under the blanket, knowing the alarm would sound any minute. Gordon lay asleep next to her. It was dark, half an hour at least until dawn would cast the first flickers of light through the caravan window. Days were drawing in, only a month ago it was light at this time; they rose later now but the routine hardly changed. She lay still, half listening for the bell, hoping it wouldn't ring yet but ready to reach out and stop it instantly to let the children sleep on. They wouldn't wake anyway, they never did! She and Gordon would rise, he rushing off to top Max up with diesel, grease the ram bearings and service the machine, knowing it so well that even in the pre-dawn gloom he scarcely ever took a torch.

She eased her weight over on one side, a hand reached for her in reflex action but he slept on.

"While he's getting the digger ready," Jan thought, "I shall have folded away the bedclothes and re-erected the table... that used to be his job! Ah well, gives him five minutes extra working time. Then I'll light the gas rings and cook breakfast. Shall I do egg this morning, or beans on toast? I think we'll have egg. Since we started doing the toast only on one side to save gas, I don't enjoy the beans so much. Perhaps..."

The alarm rang! Her hand shot out, pressing the button. Silence returned. Gordon's body moved, twisting closer. She clung to him momentarily, feeling the warm flesh, smelling his masculine scent and wishing there was time... Determinedly she sat up, fumbled for some matches and lit the little gas lamp overhead. Its soft light spread across the tiny room, hissing gently as she eased herself over the still recumbent form at her side. Halfway across two hands reached out, pulling her down, their lips meeting as she lay there straddling him. They both felt the pull, but in the little room, the light already on, with three children about to awake – it was hardly the time. She struggled up and went outside. Later they ate together when Gordon slipped quietly back to the caravan for breakfast.

As he trundled the digger off at first light to start the day's work, Jan roused the older children who took turns to wash in the bucket outside, fetching their own clean water from the river first.

"Mum," Sharon called, feeling the first crispness of approaching autumn in the air, "what will we do in winter when the water is really cold and it's dark out here?"

"Be very brave?" Jan laughed, calling back through the doorway with a question instead of replying directly.

"But what if the river freezes, and what about our baths?" Sharon's eyes had grown big with concern.

"Then we'll shatter the ice and bathe anyway," Jan

threatened, "but I don't think it ever freezes here."

Sharon, giving a little shudder, turned to dip her small pink face flannel back in the water.

With the washing and dressing underway, Jan turned her attention to Stephen, rousing him so they could all sit at breakfast together. Normally she would have made sure Christopher and Sharon were ready for school, but at least that was unnecessary for another two weeks while their holiday continued.

Later, the meal finished, she checked the water-carriers and seeing they were short, led Stephen on the half-mile walk to replenish the supply and collect milk, leaving Sharon to wash up and asking Christopher to retighten the steadies supporting the little caravan.

Gordon saw none of this, working on alone until Jan brought coffee. He seldom saw anyone else before lunch, the children tending to stay well clear, kept away by the twin deterrents, danger and work. Danger came from the big machine, and work from those extra little jobs Dad was apt to hand out to anyone within range.

Afternoons were no better. Hard, lonely days! Small wonder he talked ever more freely to Robin and Blackbird during any manual work when the engine stopped. Watching them at such times without pausing in his own toil, becoming so familiar with their habits and movements, he found himself seeing things ever more clearly from their point of view, beginning even to think like a bird. When moving to a new area, he could anticipate just which perch Robin would choose and predict Blackbird's selection of leafy debris, both with some accuracy. One afternoon shortly before Jan arrived with coffee, Gordon, quicker than either of the birds to spot a large worm under a recently extracted root, found his own mouth watering as it wriggled.

"I've moved over one hundred tons today," he mentioned it casually, slightly wearily, chatting with the children over tea.

"It doesn't seem to have made much difference!" Christopher had looked over progress when approaching cautiously to call Dad to the meal, and now voiced his disapproval.

Indeed he was right. Progress was slow, but not for want of hard work. Probably better than two thousand tons a month was being moved, but the area of land covered increased so slowly.

"Wish we could build the toilet blocks." Sharon's comment reflected everyone's thoughts. How could it take so long for a council to decide? Supposing they wanted yet more design changes?

Usually, within a few minutes of finishing the meal Gordon would leave, to work on again often until dark, or until stopped by fatigue as he used to be when they first arrived. In time the heavy clutch pressure began affecting certain leg muscles; he found difficulty in walking after climbing from the tractor each evening. Unable to talk to his bird friends while using the machine, and for want of something better to think about, he calculated that those injured leg muscles depressed the clutch pedal every seven seconds while actually loading, which formed perhaps one third of his working day. Some two thousand depressions each day, no wonder they protested.

Yet he couldn't stop; had to continue – somehow! In search of relief a long bar was welded to the clutch pedal enabling hand operation; awkward to use but at least transferring some pressure from leg to arm.

This period was difficult for Jan too. It was she who coped with and organised the Spartan living conditions, and managed the three children, though they were growing up to be more help than problem. All were becoming inured to minor hardships, former ideas of comfort fading in memory. The growing worry over money, however, did not lessen. It bore more heavily with the increasingly real possibility that their cash would run out, that they would fail before paying guests ever arrived at Relubbus.

"Will the valley see visitors at all?" Jan asked herself in odd unexpected moments of melancholy, struck by sudden doubts. Prodigious quantities of essential work remained to reach the minimum standards necessary to be acceptable to tourists.

For the children, of course, it remained one great adventure; they ran wild and unattended, unrestrained by any conventional force. They were happy, at least most of the time, in spite of a share of work forced on them and the unavoidable family economies. It was Christopher who discovered the grass covered banks on the site's northwest side were pure sand, probably the residue from washing for tin at some historic time, and Stephen who persuaded the trout to rise, snatching small pieces of bread from the surface. Sharon preferred work in and around the caravan. Since her seventh birthday, three weeks before at the start of August, Jan had felt sure that even so young, she was quite confident enough to run the home all by herself if she ever needed to, including most of the cooking.

"It's only a little job!"

Looking downstream from the bridge, numerous large stones lay haphazardly strewn across the riverbed.

Growing weed clung tenaciously to the surface of many, indicating clearly they had lain undisturbed for years. It was equally apparent they had once formed part of the broken-down stone wall that lined the west bank below the bridge, no doubt constructed at some past time to prevent scour. Having dragged Gordon out to look, she pointed down.

"There, you see. Just pick them up and plonk them back where they originally came from. Probably only take you twenty minutes. Come back for lunch an hour early – more than enough time for a little job like that."

Gordon, not regarding the task as essential, evaded the work for several days, in spite of Jan's regular hints that he should make time.

The following Thursday evening with the children soundly asleep, Jan yawned, announcing her decision to retire, and climbed into the bed without a nightdress.

"Because of the heat," she said.

Indeed it was warm, but now in late August not the sultry heat of the past midsummer.

"It can't really be the temperature," Gordon thought, and imagining a deeper significance, hurriedly climbed into bed alongside her. However, as he enthusiastically drew towards the warm unwrapped body, a restraining hand on his chest unexpectedly barred the way.

"No." she said softly, "You mustn't. I know you're short of energy, you don't even have the strength to lift a few little stones from the riverbed."

Friday dawned clear, and as the day progressed a combination of surprisingly strong sun and complete stillness of the air, hardly a breath of breeze, made clearing hot work. Dust from the arid ground stuck to his sweating body. By eleven o'clock he was pleased enough to seize the chance of working in cool flowing water, but events of the previous night were the deciding factor.

"I knew warmth was never responsible for that discarded nightdress," he thought, "I even guessed an ulterior motive, but never thought of one so devious. Typical woman!"

He climbed into the water and started, watched at a distance by Jan, a quiet smile of satisfaction on her face. As lunch time approached, the number of large boulders still dotting the bed revealed her estimation of '*a little job*' to be wildly inaccurate; he seemed hardly to have started. Levering the big stones free of the bottom, where silt and sand had accumulated, proved markedly less easy than it had looked from the bridge. Jan came to warn him dinner would shortly be ready, and stopping in surprise.

"You're not getting on very fast." she said accusingly.

"No. You didn't tell me they were iceberg stones."

"Iceberg stones?"

"Mostly hidden under the surface! They're bigger than they look. Come in and try if you like?"

"Hm. Lunch in five minutes." The invitation was ignored as she walked off in disgust.

Fitting stones back into the existing spaces was not straightforward either. Surrounding rocks had eased into the gaps, partly filling the holes. The ones from the bed could no longer be persuaded to take up their original positions. Hoisting the heavy boulders, turning them first one way then the other in an attempt to get the best fit proved no easier than pulling out gorse. When digging out roots, at least he could sit on the excavator whenever another load of fill was needed. The arrival of lunchtime provided relief, he was even decadent enough to pinch an extra ten minutes over the usual half hour allowed.

Starting again, hurrying to avoid losing more time, perspiration soon oozed freely. At least his legs were cool, the water coming in places as high as the thighs but usually just below the knee. He wore only a small pair of shorts and thick rubber shoes in case of sharp stones, just couldn't afford a cut foot. After a while something brushed his back. He straightened up, straining to peer over one shoulder, then reached round with a hand. Nothing. Whatever it was had gone. Imagination perhaps? The touch had felt spider-like, something hanging from above? He glanced upward, but no trees overhung that section of river. When it happened again he signalled Jan, working outside the caravan, and asked her to watch from the bridge. After a while she gave up, returning to her own jobs.

Time passed. A flash of light near the river surface just downstream caught him as he swung another large wet stone, dropping it with a thump on the wall. From the corner of one eye he saw a large dragonfly, black and yellow body, glossy transparent wings sparkling as the sun reflected from tiny panels between the intricate network of veins. Only this reflected sunlight warned of the approach, for it came in straight and fast.

He felt the tiny landing impact, this time making no attempt to turn but staying immobile, statue-like, hunched over the boulder just dropped into position. The feathery weight in the centre of his back worked gradually upwards.

"Its feet," he thought, "and maybe the end of that long body. Those occasional very light touches farther out are probably the wing tips."

It didn't stay long, ten seconds perhaps, climbing

129

about six inches up the spinal cord then flew off, a direct strong flight downstream again. He straightened to watch it go, reaching round to feel... nothing, just the wetness of sweat. Understanding dawned. Sweat was saline, it liked salt? Possibly, but no way to be sure.

It never came again, though he worked for another hour finishing the job, partly in the hope of being able to show his new friend to Jan.

Autumn arrived. Third September brought Stephen's fourth birthday. As with Sharon's over a month earlier, celebrations would be vocal rather than material, lots of considerate treatment and little favours, a special tea that few other people would think special, a handful of cards from the family, but no presents. It didn't matter. No one expected presents any more. Well aware of his birthday, Stephen rose early to swagger around, quite sure of his sudden increase in stature and importance. After all, he was four now, no longer a child of three!

Pampering him for once, Jan asked his choice for breakfast, and Christopher rushed to the river for fresh water before he washed, inviting him to be first instead of his usual third position at the wash bench. Sharon made a great show of folding up his pyjamas, a touch of deference surprising not only Stephen but the rest of the family too. He sat at breakfast, not squashed up with Mum and Sharon on the south side of the table, but alone with Dad on the north side, taking over Christopher's normal position.

No amount of presents could have been so flattering to his ego. His swagger moving around the caravan increased, almost a strut. When he moved, everyone stood aside, as if to royalty, winking at each other over his head, not in mockery, but in genuine pleasure at his delight!

Gordon chatted to Jan about it that evening as they watched the sleeping children.

"Do you realise that extra year represents twenty-five percent of his age? It's a big change for a youngster from being three to being four; as big in percentage terms as going from thirty to forty for an adult."

Jan nodded, silently continuing to gaze at the small sleeping head projecting from one end of the lower bunk, the only sound a gentle hiss from the single gas light. She turned back, feeling Gordon's hands enclose her own as they rested on the table.

"They do very well, you know," she smiled softly. "None of them have had any presents, not even clothes yet, and they don't mind, haven't grown to expect them, and they're all happy. They enjoy themselves now more than when we had money."

Autumn also brought blackberries, immediately to become a major part of the diet, appearing with custard, with apple, in pancakes, as jam, and mostly picked by the children, usually at weekends now they were back at school after the summer vacation.

To make jam, a large old preserving pan, similar to those suspended over fireplaces in bygone days, was hoisted onto both gas rings. Blackberries by the bucketful were tipped in and boiled with sufficient water to cover the fruit, not submerging it but leaving the top layer of berries just showing above the surface. Boiling for something under an hour softened and pulped-up the mixture, allowing the juice to be separated by straining through a muslin cloth into other utensils. Dregs in the muslin, tied to a broom handle suspended between table and sink, were left to drip, yielding perhaps another pint. So far it had cost almost nothing.

Midday passed with juice still dripping from those dregs. The small table lay entirely hidden by waiting jars, various utensils now full of juice, and the great preserving pan perched to one edge. Anticipating the problem, Jan and Sharon in a combined effort, served fried luncheon meat with mash and peas onto plates and carried them outside.

Afterwards Jan remained with Dad and the boys, seated strewn around on the sunny south side of the caravan while Sharon made coffee. Christopher took a sip, grimacing towards Stephen who following the cue pulled a long face. Sharon watching, immediately jumped up to face them, feet planted firmly apart, hands on hips.

"Don't you like it? You can give it back and go without, you know. You don't have to drink it!"

"Better, or Mum will tell us off," Christopher spoke ostensibly to Stephen but drained his cup quickly as Sharon walked towards them, then whispered loudly, "Worst I've ever tasted."

Sharon pulled up one sleeve, lifted her chin and searched for a response. "Expert, are you? Tasted lots of different coffee have you?"

"Yes, thousands."

"How many?" asked Jan, butting in.

Christopher turned, slightly abashed at the direct question from his mother. "Well, perhaps not thousands."

"Ha!" Sharon stamped her foot in triumph. "How many?"

"Well... Several, at least!"

Mum was laughing, such an infectious laugh, soon everyone, even Christopher, the brunt of the joke, was himself laughing.

With Gordon back working and the children off playing, she wasn't sure exactly where, Jan resumed her jam-making. Measuring juice into the now empty preserving pan already remounted on the gas rings, she added one pound of sugar for each pint of liquid. The resulting mixture, stirred steadily and brought again to boiling point, was simmered until ready, ladled into old jam-jars saved for the purpose, then left to cool and set.

Jan believed the jelly, rich in Vitamin C, would benefit everyone since their budget ran to very little fresh fruit. She was particularly pleased both to have enough stored for well into the winter and at such a very low cost, helping her minuscule budget. As an extra economy she had resorted to measuring water into the kettle in exact cupfuls, saving gas by not boiling more than necessary to make coffee.

Visitors were a rarity. Once in a handful of days some villager would wander along the valley surreptitiously observing their progress, or an unknown couple rambled by on the river path, but personal visitors were virtually non-existent. Apart from Jan's parents, no acquaintance from their previous life, not even relations, had visited since their arrival in Cornwall.

David Lincoln's sudden appearance was then, both pleasing and totally unexpected. An old friend of Jan's Dad, an accountant, he had offered help with the books when, or was it if, their business started. He drove across the bridge and stepped from his car just as Jan climbed aboard the digger after topping up with diesel. She raised the front bucket, backing the heavy machine round to see what lost stranger had arrived on her doorstep, only to be confronted by a face she knew.

David looked up with equal amazement. She had

been in an office, sedately dressed on their last encounter. His expression betrayed obvious surprise; he had never expected to find this previously pale neat girl as he saw her now – driving a heavy excavator, sporting a glowing suntan and more than slightly dishevelled!

She looked down from the high seat for perhaps half a minute, a smile spreading as she recognised him, then recovering from the unexpected appearance, killed the engine, swung herself through the cab doorway and jumped to the ground, landing lightly, skirt swaying nicely with the movement. David, about fifty, short, and certainly not thin, was Jewish by religion, immaculately dressed in a city suit. Both Jan and Gordon had always liked him in spite of, or perhaps because of, his different beliefs and background.

Gordon appeared round the bushes, drawn by the unusual sound of a car approaching. The old clothes he wore, tattered and stained, contrasted strongly with David's dapper rigout. A suit did lie hidden away, squashed tightly into the caravan wardrobe, but reserved for planning and other such meetings. After showing their visitor the reachable parts of their valley, they returned to the caravan for a coffee, David shaking his head at the primitive conditions. Afterwards, ignoring his natty togs, he insisted on having a go, thoroughly enjoying himself driving Max, the excavator. His whole short figure, right up to the black bowler hat that he still wore, became smothered in dust, hot dry weather having desiccated the soil, making it light and powdery. David would probably have made a great kibbutz leader; while surprised at first, he soon adapted, quickly at home in the new environment.

Christopher and Sharon had already arrived home from school, dashing madly down the road at the sight of the strange car, as they did with anything new. On Jan's insistence, they waited unwillingly at the caravan until David finally returned and climbed down from the big machine. Jan, introducing the children, offered him a small hand-brush for the dust. Christopher raced off to the river, returning with a bucket of fresh water, hoisting it onto the bench for him to wash. David, shaking his head again at the basic conditions of life, rinsed his hands and face, and took the towel Sharon offered.

Wash and brush-up finished, he joined the family inside the caravan for tea. With space short, Sharon ate on her bunk since she was making the coffee, while Christopher and Stephen squeezed in with Mum on one of the bench seats. Meagre fare graced the table. Apart from the occasional day when baked beans or some other hot snack was served, tea normally consisted of bread and butter, with jam or very occasionally a little cheese, and sometimes also a small piece of cake each when one of the grandparents sent a food parcel.

David didn't know about the economy slice. The first slice was special, the one everyone ate without jam. He reached for the home-made bramble jelly but hesitated when the children stopped eating to stare.

"First one without!" Stephen rebuked with a glance of reproach, showing no polite indulgence to their visitor.

"How would he know," Jan thought, mentally excusing Stephen's lack of tact, "we've never had a stranger to tea before." David looked taken aback as she quickly explained about the economy slice. Christopher and Sharon, who had held their tongues, hid smiles behind lowered faces.

When David finished eating, Stephen, unusually

talkative for a change, considering himself practically an adult since having turned four, asked, "Have you had enough?"

"Yes, thank you," David politely replied.

"Good," said Stephen, "'cos there isn't any more."

David went away fairly impressed with their determination if not with the food.

"You will," he said with conviction, "succeed!"

A sudden improvement to family circumstances occurred in early autumn – the first load of concrete blocks arrived on site. No building permission had yet materialised but the council promised it *imminently*. These first blocks were in anticipation, to avoid any delay when the good news came through.

The driver stopped before crossing the bridge and looked at it dubiously, unduly suspicious of bridges with no sides, with nothing to prevent his vehicle going straight over the edge.

Gordon, having done some rough calculations and believing the bridge good for well over fifty tons, took a leaf out of Christopher's book by exaggerating a little, suggesting the arch should take at least a hundred tons and as the lorry weighed only sixteen, what on earth was he fussing about at?

"The sides," the driver pointed, gesticulating. "It ought to have parapets."

"Why?" Gordon pretended surprise.

"To stop me going over the edge!"

"Tell me, on a normal bridge do you usually hit the parapets when you cross?"

"No never! Of course not!" The driver was indignant.

"Then they don't stop you going over the edge, do they? If you're new to driving, I can do it for you."

The man turned his back, climbed into the lorry, revved the engine fiercely, tiger-like, but crept across, gazing from side to side in concern.

Caught by the sight of something new, Christopher and Sharon again ran with excitement as they approached the bridge, waving and pointing across the river at the untidy pile still lying where the lorry had tipped its load. They were even unwise enough to volunteer help in shifting the blocks.

Up to this time the family could, without risk to modesty, only safely use the toilet after dark. Conditions had not changed, it was still the same chemical toilet bucket situated in the awning, an awning that still had no front. The side facing north lay entirely open to the air and even though walkers were rare, anyone strolling along the riverbank in daylight could hardly fail to notice a person employing the facility.

If things were desperate and the risk had to be taken, then a blanket left for that purpose always lay readily at hand. The person enthroned merely needed to toss this cover over their head to imitate some piece of inanimate clutter, keeping quite still until the walker had passed. This had actually occurred, way back two weeks after their first arrival in the valley.

The combination of hot weather, low budget and lack of a fridge, meant that eating something a little past its best was never totally avoidable. Gordon found on one particular day, a need to use this facility rather regularly, at times with considerable urgency. He had just rushed back again to sit down for the umpteenth time when suddenly Jan shouted through the caravan window.

"Two men coming, dressed in suits."

Sitting there, trousers around ankles, there was no

option. He grabbed the blanket, hoisted it up over his head and sat, statue-like in stillness, hidden by the side of the awning, the caravan, and the blanket, in a sort of tall triangular cubbyhole. One hand was hard against the aluminium caravan side, the other hooked over a bar supporting the awning, both well above head level so no skull-shaped outline would make it obvious that this was not just a pile of junk covered with a blanket. It shouldn't take a minute for them to pass by, unless they stopped on the bridge.

They did not stop! Instead the pair marched right up to knock on the caravan door, not five feet away. Jan opened it in surprise. They turned out to be Jehovah's Witnesses looking for a quick conversion. Jan insisted politely but firmly that she was not interested. The shorter one asked if her husband was around.

"I know he's somewhere nearby, but I can't see him at the moment," she said truthfully, adding as an afterthought, "would you like to wait?"

Gordon could hear the laughter in her voice, and his arms were about to fall off! He'd have to move in a minute, which would lead to inevitable discovery. He began to understand the words *captive audience*!

"Will he be long?" one asked.

"I'm not sure," replied Jan. "He can't be far away, but he might not surface for some time."

Gritting his teeth beneath the blanket, Gordon could tell she was really enjoying herself; they didn't get visitors often. He listened anxiously for the answer. Would they wait?

"No," said a voice, they must get on, there were other calls to make, but would she mind if they left a paper for her husband which would bring enlighten-ment and which they thought he might like.

"A paper," she replied, almost choking. "Yes, I think that's just what he needs at the moment, I'm sure you're right. It will be a great comfort to him!"

Knowing her voice so well, Gordon could tell she was practically biting her cheeks in an attempt to control the glee within, bursting to get out.

They left and before their footsteps faded away, Jan sank onto the caravan step so helpless with mirth that he had to peep cautiously out himself to make sure they were gone. Handicapped as he was sitting there, trousers still around ankles, he couldn't help smiling when she pretended to offer him the paper!

"We shouldn't laugh," he protested, struggling not to. "They were only doing as their conscience guided."

Had they only known, maybe they too would have laughed.

But now all that was changed. Now the family had a proper outside toilet; not perhaps entirely up to the standard of the traditional rural privy, but definitely a preserver of modesty. That first delivery of building blocks now stood stacked round in a hollow square, the toilet bucket hidden in the middle. A short blank wall of blocks concealed the entrance and some old plastic sheeting covered the top, weighted down at the edges with further blocks. What more could anyone want? Well-ventilated privacy.

True, first person out in the morning had to push upwards on the plastic, for a puddle of water sometimes accumulated overnight from rain or even a heavy dew. Left untouched, it dripped slowly through various tiny holes onto the user's head below, but one can't have everything. Luxury was relative, beauty in the eye of the beholder; they thought it beautiful.

Sharon was delighted!

Chapter 8

Little Accidents

"What is it?"

He glanced up, intrigued at the unexpected parcel, cylindrical, maybe two hands high, a little more across and covered in brown paper.

"I don't know, but it's heavy," Jan eased it carefully onto the table then slid back into the bench seat, picking up her cup, looking at the object, smiling back questioningly with eyebrows raised but not yet attempting to open it.

Gordon had brought the trailer back for a quick grease job at mid-morning break and sat drinking coffee when the postman, having made a special journey, handed it to her.

"Look at all those stamps!" Bending across she studied them closely. "London postmark, probably from Mum!"

Raising an arm in warning, Gordon leaned forward, putting one ear next to the mystery package.

"It isn't ticking, go ahead."

"Behave yourself, it's probably a cake. And my mother's not like that! I know she didn't want you to take me down here but that was before she visited. I told you, you've gone up in her estimation. Anyway she's more refined, more subtle; she'd never use a bomb. Poison perhaps – you can have the first slice." A glint of mischief accompanied the last suggestion, a teasing afterthought.

The diversion had been welcome, interrupting a disheartening discussion on the continued non-arrival of building permission for the toilets, and an absence of the long-awaited, much promised, delivery of three-inch water pipe. Jan reached forward, tearing off the wrapper to reveal a large, very old, round biscuit tin. Lifting the lid she extracted a big Christmas cake; dark, heavy, full of fruit and smelling terrific.

"I used to make these." Wistfully she cut two very small slices, passing one to Gordon, then sliced another as Stephen's head appeared round the door. He grabbed it, taking a bite. Jan rose, poured him a coffee and sank down again.

"Good?" she asked.

The little lad nodded, brushed straw-coloured hair from his eyes and continue eating but said nothing.

Looking at the texture inside the cut section, her desire to bake was rekindled. She sighed unhappily.

"I wouldn't mind discovering some way to cook just small ones but it's hopeless without an oven."

They had discussed ovens before. Her father Jim, reminiscing on his youth with the Guards in China, had often spoken about chickens cooked in a hole in the ground in some form of mud oven. That didn't seem practical in the sandy granular soils of the valley.

They sat quietly for a while. Stephen, comfortable in the silence, seldom demanding attention, finished his cake. Leaving the coffee he slid from the bench, dashing off to play again, probably remembering the stationary digger outside. Gordon, coffee still too hot, popped the last piece of cake in his mouth, slowly savouring the rich fruity texture.

"This one will never make it to Christmas."

Absentmindedly plucking a loose raisin from the plate and eating that too, his attention focused vaguely on the big cake tin, though he felt unsure why.

"An oven is just an enclosed space which is heated," he mused aloud, drumming fingers in an involuntary tattoo on the table and gazing into space.

Jan looked up at him in surprise. Her movement registered, breaking through his thoughts; he nodded slowly, reaching for the tin.

"If we place this on the gas ring it will heat inside, just like any other oven. It wouldn't cook anything big, but something small maybe?"

She listened, looked at the container thoughtfully, picked it up and took it across to the stove.

"Boil water in it first, to sterilise and test for leaks. You won't need much, just cover the bottom." Gordon picked up his coffee taking a sip, watching Jan empty a cupful of water into the tin, replace the lid and mount it over the gas. He was sitting at the table, not really paying much attention, his mind wandering silently over the whole idea. "That bottom is so thin, I could cut a flat disc of heavier metal to cover the gas. Sitting the tin on a disc instead of directly on the flame will spread the heat; that should protect the base *and* give a more even temperature inside."

After a while Jan moved back to sit on the opposite bench, watching him, waiting without speaking. Seeing the unfocused look in his eyes she could imagine a series of gleaming brass cogwheels churning within like the works of a watch, and fleetingly expected a report of the findings to eject, as tickets from a parking meter. He had temporarily forgotten her, she knew that; it would have been annoying once but now she continued to sit, waiting quietly.

Boom!

An explosion rent the caravan! Something flew with percussive force, smashing against the ceiling, falling back, bouncing from a cupboard to clang on the floor beneath. Simultaneously a cloud of steam burst hissing and writhing like something evil and alive above the stove, obscuring the far side of the caravan. The noise, blast of pressure, the threatening vapour cloud; all in that confined space – it stunned the senses!

Jan's eardrums popped, the colour draining from her cheeks. She couldn't understand, couldn't move, paralysed momentarily both in mind and body. Coffee slopped on the table, spilled from both cups in shocked reaction.

Fortunately the bench seats were just far enough from the stove to avoid the scalding steam. Jan rallied, drawing back in alarm, eyes wide, mouth slightly open.

"What happened?" her voice high-pitched and shaking, she swallowed, rubbing her ears.

Recovering himself, Gordon realised the cause even as she spoke – could have prevented it had he paid attention. "It's OK. My fault, I should have realised." He stretched a hand across and winked.

Still concerned she waited questioningly, but the tension had gone, reassurance like most other emotions, definitely contagious.

"That cake-tin lid fits too tight, steam can't escape," he shrugged. "Pressure build-up blew it off. Christopher would probably have told us; they do that experiment in schools. No harm done, except the chipped paint."

She followed his eyes towards the ceiling, then relaxed as they grinned at each other, holding hands across the wet table top. At any rate it had stirred up the blood a bit! Turning, she looked through the window at Stephen still playing happily on the far side of the field, then looked back, her expression serious.

"Thank goodness he wasn't in here! Not one of your brighter ideas!"

"It's only steam from the water, but most food contains water. I'll make some holes in the lid."

With the holes drilled they tried again, cutting the gas smartly when it boiled, dubiously sensitive the steam might not escape quickly enough. All was well. Heating without water revealed a further problem; a pungent smoke rose above the stove. Gordon cut the gas and using two cloths carried the heated tin outside.

The answer seemed to be, let it cool then sandpaper off the painted design that covered sides and lid. Having been caught out twice already, he cut two lengths of steel bar to lie in the bottom. On top of these was placed a shallow tart tin that had lain unused in the cupboard. The item for cooking would be placed on this smaller tin, the air gap beneath preventing burning on the underside. Explaining the arrangement, he suggested, "Now everything should work fine."

"Oh sure! Let me know when you intend to try it! I'll go to Penzance for supplies." She backed away, arms held up defensively in mock alarm, but smiling broadly.

Stephen had come and gone again several times, he seldom stayed long in the caravan. Jan sent him outside, then placed some bread in the tin and relit the gas. In five minutes it dried crisp without burning; a good sign. She dipped the bread in water before strolling to the bridge. Stephen, already playing upstream, raced back to cast small pieces on the current. Trout rose, viciously snatching crusts, no hesitation, speed and ferocity inbred from millennia taking flies at the surface.

Gordon, now behind schedule having expended over an hour attempting to solve the problem, hurried off to salvage such headway as possible from the morning's work. He had done his best, it was Jan's decision what and when to bake. However, she preferred to wait until Christopher and Sharon returned from school, involving the children wherever possible in family matters.

At teatime the choice was discussed. Agreement was never to be expected, at least not easily, and so it proved, but eventually they settled on Cornish pasties.

"Leave them 'til Saturday," Sharon suggested.

"No!" Both boys spoke in unison.

"Let Mum do it while Sharon's at school so it's properly cooked," Christopher urged. Stephen quickly nodded agreement.

Sharon drew herself up, hands on hips.

"*I* can cook properly!"

The boys grinned at each other in success. Jan, quietly observing, nodded knowingly. Some time her daughter would learn not to rise so easily. Watching the children's verbal battle develop, she waited patiently for an opening.

"We had an explosion in the caravan today."

Her comment, delivered casually, stopped dead all further argument. Young eyes grew wide and round with surprise and interest, particularly when her finger pointed to the ceiling abrasion. Intrigue, envy, doubt; mixed emotions shone on their faces, but most of all disappointment at not being present to witness the fun.

Gordon listened, Jan's lurid explanation differing from his own recollection in its more dangerous and dramatic description. But then, he had immediately, instinctively, sensed the cause. She had not; not known what exploded or the likely extent of damage, not even known if further blasts would tear them apart.

She paused, looking around at the intent faces, waiting, anticipating it would be Sharon who broke the silence but stepping in first with a warning.

"The first time I try it out, no one will come near!"

Gordon doubted the wisdom of relating the incident at all, visualising experiments at a camp fire or on a gas ring when Jan's back was turned, but watching the children's animated expressions and enjoyment he did nothing to interrupt her tale. Later, taking Christopher aside, he explained the expansion of steam that caused the lid to fly off, hoping to lessen the mystery and temptation. This same steam pressure once operated the old Cornish engines.

The actual oven trial proved both success and failure. Jan prepared short crust pastry, chopped potatoes, a small onion, some beef, and although not included in the traditional Cornish recipe, threw in a couple of smallish diced carrots for colour. Two pasties exactly filled the bottom of the inner tart tin. She cooked both at once for forty minutes as the book said, timed to finish for Christopher and Sharon's arrival home from school, the oven temperature complete guesswork.

In spite of all Gordon's efforts the bottom was somewhat burned, the top just a touch under-done and certain fumes still pervaded the caravan.

Jan cut thin centre sections from both pasties for herself, leaving four identical ends, cleverly avoiding arguments between the children. The general opinion was, "It's OK, makes a change; let's keep it for special, not have it too often!"

Not a resounding roar of approval, but no one left anything on the plate.

That night shortly after Jan and Gordon had retired and lay together comfortably on the point of sleep, a sudden snapping noise brought them both wide awake. Almost immediately a heavy thump sounded in the darkness, with a single loud grunt from Christopher. Sharon's high-pitched shriek and a howl of "Get orf" from Stephen quickly followed.

Pitch blackness, visibility zero, enveloped the room. Jan and Gordon both stumbled to their assistance, knocking over various items and colliding together, calling to the children and to each other for some light. Sharon's alarmed response mixed with Stephen's gruff comments cut across their parents' urgent calls, the verbal melee punctuated by bumps and bangs of over-turned objects. It was however, the total absence of Christopher's voice that drove both parents in their frantic, somewhat disorientated search to locate matches.

Noisy seconds passed... a pulse of light from a struck match flared, died down then grew again as the gas mantle flickered into life. In that yellow glow there emerged a scene of absolute, utter chaos.

The top bunk had collapsed, the circular timber rod supporting the outer edge having snapped. As it subsided to the bunk below and onto the other two children, Christopher's upper body had pitched to the floor, the left shoulder hitting with a thump. His legs, still entangled with the bunk's remains, rested on top of Stephen and Sharon who were struggling to free themselves.

Christopher, dragging himself clear, half rose to a sitting position to drop back against one of the cup-boards, a dazed expression covering his face. Sharon and Stephen peeped out from under the broken bunk, both holding part of it above their heads with one hand, their bodies still trapped by sleeping bags and the blanket wrapped right round them. Christopher's sleeping bag now lay crumpled near him on the floor with a pillow, his once folded clothes and several items off the dresser, knocked down for sure in the hunt for matches to ignite the gaslight.

Jan, matchbox in hand, knelt on the bed clad only in a short pyjama top, her pink bottom glowing smooth and satiny in the dim light. Gordon, a little slower off the mark, stood next to the cooker, hands outstretched, caught in the act of feeling for matches in what had been pitch darkness.

For an interval they stared, seeing the devastation but unable fully to grasp what had occurred. Who first recovered was uncertain. One minute they looked at each other in bewilderment, the next laughter engulfed everyone, even Christopher to Jan's great relief.

While the rest of the family tidied up, she brewed hot drinks to be sipped sitting on the convertible double bed, appropriately the bed that became a dining table in the daytime. Jan, propped in one corner had Stephen resting against her, while near the other wall Sharon sank back on Dad's shoulder. Christopher sat to one side, legs dangled over the edge, coffee on a low cupboard near his hand. They chatted about the accident, how each had felt in the darkness before the lamp came on and how to repair the bed – then drinks finally consumed Jan tucked the children in again, remaking Christopher's bed on the floor. He lay now on the hard boarding with only two spare blankets beneath him, for his bunk was made of canvas and had no mattress.

The breakage could have been dangerous, that splintered wooden spar might well have cut someone, or even worse! At the very least it should have been a nuisance, an event both tiresome and annoying. But was it? As Jan lay watching the children still chatting animatedly from their beds, she realised they were delighted with the incident, revelling as children will in danger faced and overcome. Rather than cause a problem, it had enhanced the family's closeness, that feeling of meeting and overcoming life's little challenges together.

It *had* been comical; remembering the scene when the lamp came on, there was no denying that. She had turned her head, still kneeling on the bed, the light shining out on the chaos behind her. The caravan, cramped at the best of times, needed little to endow it with the appearance of a shipwreck. She remembered another thing too. After the panic had passed, she had seen that look in Gordon's eyes as he watched her in the pyjama top under the soft gaslight. She felt warm inside; he would fix the broken bed for her in the morning. A hand slid up under her pyjama top and round her waist,

"Yes," she thought, "he's good at fixing things."

Later, happy but sleep not coming, she lay back contentedly reflective. Nothing like this could have happened in their former life, in the big safe house, where problems had been more imagined than real, like did next door have a better car? They had been part of the status race less than a year before. Their children could have grown up unable to grapple with real adversity, only concerned with the latest fashion or that one of their friends had a bigger TV. None of this worried them now, there was no TV anyway, nor any prospects of running one. Whether anyone else was better off no longer gave any concern.

"We *are* different." Jan thought, "It's the family

149

against our circumstances and they're not getting us down. In fact, the reverse; we're proud to live without what others think essential!"

Nevertheless, she fell asleep remembering the old saying, '*things happen in threes*'. Ridiculous superstition, she told herself, not quite able to sound convinced.

* * *

"Look!" Jan pointed at a column of small ads in *The Cornishman*. A local firm offered cheap second-hand two hundred gallon oil tanks.

Diesel oil storage continued to be in cans alongside the caravan. Two five-gallon drums were currently in use but needed constant replenishment. Purchasing such small quantities of fuel had proved both inconvenient and unnecessarily expensive.

"How much will we use before next season? Could we save money by buying in bulk, enough money to cover the cost of this tank? Remember to add the cost of petrol each time I go for more."

Gordon thought for a while, absent-mindedly stroking his chin, before answering her question.

"Won't use so much once we start building, if they ever pass the plans, but still quite a bit – digging the foundations, carting things about. Then there's towing the mower, digging and backfilling drains, and don't forget there's water to bring in all the way from the village." He paused again, mentally calculating. "Well over a hundred gallons, maybe nearer two hundred. Should be quite a lot cheaper, taking everything into account."

The tank was ordered, and having checked its dimensions, Gordon stopped work early that evening, enlisting Christopher's help in carrying concrete blocks to form a solid base that the tank would stand on. Of necessity the blocks were borrowed from those stacked around the toilet bucket, lowering the roof level slightly. This platform needed to be sufficiently high to ensure the small old milk churn used for topping up the digger with diesel would pass easily under the outlet tap. Christopher was intrigued that such care went into constructing the base's top, not level, but with a one-inch slope.

"Why?" he asked.

"So any sediment will settle on the side away from the tap. We also need two strips of timber on top. A tank resting directly on blocks will rub; metal tanks expand and contract in hot sunshine at a different rate from concrete blocks. Wood does too, but it's less abrasive."

Three days later an oil tanker approached, bouncing over potholes, an empty cylinder, very obviously second-hand strapped on behind. It turned across the bridge and stopped. The children were at school, Stephen asleep on one of the benches in the caravan.

Two men jumped out, manhandling the old tank into position on the newly formed platform, thumping it down without much care. Quickly unrolling a long flexible hose from the lorry they lugged it into position, obviously in a hurry to finish and depart. The engine note deepened as pumping commenced.

Jan saw Gordon emerge from some bushes drawn by the noise, and expected Stephen to wake but he never appeared. How pleasant to watch someone else doing something for a change, even though the workers were unsmiling, intent solely on speed. So different to be, for a short while at least, only a spectator. Oil entering the tall cylinder was rather like filling a bottle, the tone changing nearer the top. It could only be heard from quite close because of the engine noise.

Jan stood idly to one side when a great spout of foaming diesel oil gushed in the air drenching her to the skin, her hair, clothes, everything! Something to do with the machine blowing air when the lorry tank became empty, so the driver claimed. His tone hovered between apology and annoyance, not admitting that his own overriding dash to finish had prevented him lowering the engine speed as pumping neared completion.

One local farmer had said diesel oil was a sure cure for ringworm. "Not many people know that, but I don't suppose it's meant to be administered ten gallons at a time," Gordon thought, dashing across to grab Jan's hand. Funny how trivial unimportant things flash across the mind in an emergency.

She felt herself dragged bodily at speed towards the far side of the caravan, Gordon shouting back over one shoulder for the men to stay where they were.

No time to heat water!

"Take off anything that's soaked," he urged, snatching a bucket.

"Everything is! I can feel it penetrating right through, even my underwear is saturated and it's still running down inside." She looked round uncomfortably, "Out here?"

"Unless you want the caravan covered in diesel. And hurry, that stuff can affect your skin!"

Without waiting he dashed off, returning at a run, the bucket now full with cold river water into which a good portion of washing-up liquid from a squeezy bottle by the sink was speedily emptied. Jan had stripped entirely but held the diesel-soaked skirt to shield her lower body. The blanket kept in the awning beside the loo had also been moved closer in case it was needed.

Holding the sponge used for river baths, Gordon began dousing her with the cold sudsy water, starting with her hair then working downward, splashing on small quantities directly from the bucket for speed. With the worst of the oil washed off, he squirted more undiluted liquid soap directly onto her bare body and head, massaging it quickly into hair, shoulders, back, and was reaching further round when she protested,

"I can do the front, thank you! Go for more water to rinse me off."

He raced away, returning with another bucketful, tipping it straight over the now soapy hair, rinsing suds from the rest of her shivering body on its way to the grass below. Dashing back for one more, he doused her again before wrapping a large towel round the wet body and bundling her into the caravan. Less than four minutes had elapsed since the diesel spout; the men were still rolling up their hose – she would do a more thorough job in the river after they left.

A few days later no skin rashes had appeared, prompt action may have saved the day, but the tank had begun to leak. The ground below was stained for some distance, so back came the same two men with a new square tank, unfortunately at extra cost. Jan remained firmly in the caravan while they transferred the diesel.

Two further days elapsed before a drip, drip, drip, betrayed escaping oil from a drain-hole plug near the new tank bottom. Another mushrooming dark stain spread relentlessly outwards over the dusty soil below. Reluctantly the men returned, a large Stillson wrench hanging pendulously down from one man's hand. They tightened the offending nut, all muscle and very little technique, leaving without a goodbye.

Gordon looked on dubiously, returning again to the caravan shaking his head. "I'll be surprised if that does much good. I'd remake the joint myself but it's not possible without draining the oil first. The way they treated it, the thing will probably leak worse than ever. Good job we haven't paid for it yet."

Sure enough, a day later it dripped even faster.

"Nothing more we can do," said the man on the telephone.

"Oh yes there is," Gordon replied. "Take the useless thing away." At least that's what he told Jan when she returned from Penzance later. She cocked her head on one side, frowning dubiously, "Your actual words?"

"OK. So what I really said might be just a fraction more colourful, they wouldn't have understood anything less!"

A new supplier achieved success first time, no leaks. That was essential, and not just for economy. The tank's eventual resting place lay inside the service passage of the first toilet building, at some future time, hopefully not too distant if building permission would only arrive.

* * *

"Pfpfpf!" Stephen, kneeling on the bench, blew a raspberry against the windowpane.

"What is it?" Jan, washing up after lunch, turned at the noise.

Gordon, still at table, lying back in the cushions for an extra minute before rushing off again, also looked up.

"Moo!" Stephen's eyes were fixed on something outside as he uttered the word, chin dropping down on his chest in an effort to copy the low note, oblivious of his parents' attention.

"What is it?" Jan called louder, having received no answer.

"Cows." He didn't look round and said no more.

She bent to look through the window in the top section of the stable door, then quickly swung it wide open and gazed out. Cows indeed, dozens of them, all gathered close outside, one actually licking the caravan wall.

"Where have they sprung from?" She had hardly uttered the words before Gordon's hands were round her waist, squeezing gently as he smiled down while moving her bodily clear of the doorway and slipping through.

The animals turned, trotting off sharply when he approached, but followed him back again at an almost constant distance, much as the hurricane lamp's light pushed away the darkness when someone headed for the toilet at night, only to follow the carrier back again at a fixed distance during the return journey. No doubt associating humans with food, they regrouped around the caravan to gaze at its occupants with mournful eyes, giving the occasional "Moo," both louder and deeper than Stephen's otherwise good imitation. Hoof-prints along the riverbank indicated the cows had come from downstream, and they were soon herded back in that direction. A hundred yards down they took off at a run.

Several such calls occurred after that, but only once did they find the owner. Fortunately the visits suddenly stopped. Somewhere a fence had been repaired. Just as well, for as they were to discover after one incident, in wet weather tremendous damage could be done to the turf. Not that any of the turf was special, but some of the holes were nearly six inches deep, easily enough for someone to turn an ankle. These imprints took hours of patient work to fill.

* * *

"They've arrived!" Jan rushed round, waving her arms at Gordon who was loading yet another trailer although teatime fast approached. He switched off the engine and looked at her blankly.

"The pipes. They're here!" She shouted frantically, her voice sounding loud as the engine died, one arm stretched out waving, pointing towards the entrance. "The lorry! It's parked near the bridge. Come on, hurry up. Help unload. It's late, the driver's looking at his watch. Don't let him drive off with them!"

There was good reason for her excitement.

Telephone cable had arrived weeks ago but the water main had taken an inordinate amount of time to organise. First the company had pushed for a six-inch pipe but had not been prepared to pay for the extra expense, then there were supply difficulties. Now at last the finally agreed three-inch pipe had come. It only remained to dig the half-mile-long trench and put them in the ground.

The telephone company were good, supplying the multicore cable within the connection cost; it would carry fifteen separate lines. However, Gordon had to order and pay for the water pipe himself, as well as paying the water company a high connection charge based on the total number of units allowed on site.

"It's to cover work by the company to increase our own capacity accordingly," one of the water reps explained gravely.

This included enough for all the static caravans permitted even though these were not expected to be sited for years, if ever. However, arrival of the pipe, encouraging as it was, did not mean that work could commence. A legal document sanctioning pipe-laying and connection was still awaited.

Returning from a special trip to the Water Board offices in Cross Street, Penzance one afternoon with the completed paper, Gordon waved the Agreement in triumph through the van window as he crossed the bridge. Braking hard, the vehicle skidded to a halt, sliding on the loose surface, stirring up a minor dust cloud. Leaping out as Jan rushed from the caravan, he passed the document with a flourish.

"There you are, the Section 25 Agreement, or is it 52? I forget. Anyway, that's our permission to lay the water main."

"Is this all that's been holding us up?" She demanded scornfully, turning it over to glance at the signatures.

He nodded.

"We can go ahead now?" she wanted to be sure, eyes alight with eagerness to hear his confirmation. They had waited so long for their own water supply.

He knew she would ask, had planned his response on the journey home, guessing her reaction. "Certainly, yes. I'll do a few more day's filling, then maybe stop for a while and dig your water trench."

"A few more days? You start that water tomorrow morning first thing – *or else!*"

Concealing a smile, he nodded back at her with an almost straight face, about to voice agreement but was cut short.

"You...!" Dropping the document on the ground she threw herself bodily at him, pushing hard in the direction of the river, "I'll drown you! You intended to start tomorrow all along. *I* can tell when you're smiling!"

Stephen appeared in the caravan doorway, tumbled down the steps, picked himself up and rushed over, unsure whether to be concerned at the tussle or worried about missing something. Seeing him coming, Jan hesitated for a moment, just long enough for Gordon to say "Hello, Stephen," drop on one knee and quickly put an arm round the lad, frustrating her effort to push him farther towards the water.

She looked down at them both, not angry, laughing at his ploy of using Stephen for defence but annoyed with herself for having fallen so easily into his trap; hating to let him win and escape totally unscathed.

Gordon looked back from his kneeling position, smiling equally broadly and wondering what was coming

Reaching out to rest a hand easily on his shoulder, she looked down, speaking slowly but without sound.

"Just wait till I get you to bed tonight!"

He read the message on her lips and relaxed. This he could deal with, look forward to in fact. In that disarmed moment she heaved forcefully against the shoulder on which her arm rested, sending him sprawling in the dust.

"Oh, Daddy's fallen over," she said to Stephen in mock surprise, dusting hands together as if cleaning something unpleasant off them, an even broader smile now flickering on her lips. Looking down at the slowly recovering man for a moment, she straightened, body swivelling towards the caravan, head thrown back and sideways, eyes still watching the fallen figure, the stance typical of a triumphant matador. With a flick of the neck that sent her hair bouncing, she minced off, retrieving the precious legal agreement on the way.

Although water had become a family joke, the amusement was partly a facade, at least for Jan whose frustration had escalated with passing weeks, growing as she lugged each carrier full of water. She more than anyone regretted the hold-up, and Gordon knew he should not have baited her about further delay. The telephone was secondary in her eyes, obviously necessary to receive bookings but in no way comparable to the arrival of their own water supply!

The children who had always carried the non-drinking water, drawing buckets from the river, were uncertain whether to believe Jan when during tea, she made the disclosure.

"Laying water pipe starts tomorrow!"

All through the summer they had asked "When?" finally giving up. Arrival of the pipes had refired their enthusiasm and questions, but when work still failed to start they began to wonder. Now, unsure if Jan teased, they held back, looking from one parent to another, bursting into smiles of delight on receiving nods of confirmation from both. However, having watched the clearing and filling work, they expected slow progress.

Sharon, anxious concerning anything connected with washing, asked doubtfully, "Will it take long?"

"Probably Christmas." Christopher muttered under his breath, but loud enough for all to catch.

Stephen sat for a while, listening to their scepticism but not commenting. In a silent period as they ate, he murmured, "Dad fell over."

Two heads came up, keenly curious, no longer eating. They glanced from Stephen to Dad, but neither gave anything away.

Jan, smiling faintly at the memory, responded

evasively, "Oh yes, I believe he did." She raised her eyebrows, glancing in Gordon's direction, leaning back as the silence lengthened and wondering who would speak first. Sharon probably.

"Mum pushed him." Stephen uttered the words quietly but with relish.

Jan breathed in sharply with surprise. She didn't think he knew. Was he more astute, or had she been less subtle than she thought? The two older children were staring at Gordon who adopted a martyred expression. They turned to her, amazement and accusation on their faces.

Stephen sat quietly in his chair taking no further part, his little four-year old face covered with a demon grin, illustrating well the inner pleasure of stirring up this minor sensation.

Jan looked back at them, realising an explanation was expected. "He deserved it! She spoke with feeling. "What I really wanted to do was push him in the river!"

* * *

A final *Bang* sent the last pin home, refixing the rear digging attachment to the excavator. Shortly afterwards it trundled off towards the village, a dozen long plastic pipes sticking out each side of the front bucket. Jan waved from the caravan doorway.

Later, as eleven o'clock approached, she walked down the road accompanied by Stephen and carrying a coffee flask. The digger was already a hundred yards from the entrance, the road beyond obscured by untidy heaps of excavated soil. When the engine stopped, she stepped closer, placed one hand on the digger's yellow jib and leaned over to look along an almost straight trench stretching back to the village.

This excavation, alongside and in places under the road, explained why no attempt had yet been made to fill any but the major potholes.

Following an early lunch they worked together with the surveyor's level, Stephen playing on the riverbank nearby. Gordon set the instrument on a tripod before climbing into the trench holding a twelve-foot long wooden batten. This staff was marked in inches by the simple (and more importantly, cheap) expedient of sticking on two cloth tape measures; tapes permanently borrowed from Jan's needlework basket.

Stepping behind the instrument, Jan looked through the eyepiece, delicately turning focus and line knobs. Fifty yards away Gordon cleaned and adjusted the bottom levels according to her shouted instructions.

Water and telephone company requirements specified pipe and cable runs be supervised throughout. True to their promises, the inspectors arrived promptly by two o'clock and checked not only that the services were properly laid, but stayed during re-filling and compaction of the first nine inches of soft sandy soil.

After their departure, Jan helped shovel material into the trench and compact it in layers, then drove off in the digger to fetch fresh stone for the top six inches while Gordon spread surplus soil at the road edges. Stephen had played nearby throughout the day, happy by himself, even being allowed to run along the bottom of the partially filled trench; it helped to tread down the soil. They were still working on the last few yards when Christopher and Sharon ran down the road, arriving home from school.

"How did you get so far!" Sharon's eyes shone at the unexpected progress.

Gordon basked in her surprise, chest expanding, saying proudly with a little wave of the hand towards the now covered trench, "I'm just a fast worker."

"Tell me about it later!" Jan whispered.

"Must have had help." Christopher looked at the long length of disturbed surface, frowning suspiciously.

All proceeded well until the third day when some emergency elsewhere delayed the water inspector. A successful morning's work left a long length ready for approval. Due to the river's proximity, the road here was narrow and now completely blocked by the open trench and continuous uneven piles of spoil alongside. Moreover, this lay in front of the old miner's cottage where Minnie and Emma Jenkins lived. Fortunately they had never owned a car, so that problem did not arise. As luck would have it the two old ladies arrived home in mid-afternoon while Gordon waited in hopes of an inspector turning up. He saw them standing by the far end of the trench, debating the best way to gain access to their home.

Minnie, the more sprightly, thought she could walk over the line of excavated material but Emma, her elder sister, drew back aghast at the prospect.

"I could carry you," Gordon offered, having walked along the trench bottom to meet them.

They looked at each other, doubtful but amused.

"I'll try walking. Emma, you watch, see how I get on." With that Minnie put one foot on the loose soil and started out. They watched her go, Emma's head shaking.

"I could never manage that. Go on, carry me if you can." She moved close to the trench edge.

Gordon, standing in the bottom, reached out; one arm below her shoulder, the other just above the knee, the elderly lady uttering a slight "Oh!" as she was swung off her feet. He carried her the fifty or so yards, still walking along the trench bottom while she smiled, looking pleased, her light weight balanced easily in his arms. As they caught and passed Minnie, struggling over the soil heaps, Emma urged her sister on.

"What's keeping you, Minnie, this is easy, I could do this reg'lar!" She was obviously enjoying herself.

As they approached the cottage, Gordon regretted his tattered and somewhat muddy trenching clothes, thinking, "Hardly suitable for carrying ladies around, I should have a cape like that fellow Raleigh, to rip off and spread across the muddy entrance." But he said nothing, depositing her carefully in front of the gate-posts without leaving the trench.

In little over a week, pipe and cable covered the complete half-mile length to the site, including working elsewhere at the weekend when inspectors were not available, and two days waiting for a large diameter steel tube. This tube, which was fixed to the bridge, carried the three-inch plastic pipe across the river. Just before the crossing a meter was placed, and before that a fire hydrant. The water main terminated in an inspection chamber from where a smaller pipe lead off a short distance to a tap on a wooden post driven in the ground near the bridge.

The telephone cable ended coiled up in the same inspection chamber, a phone promised for installation the following week. The caravan, being sited back near the bushes, originally because of the exposed chemical toilet, lay too far from the cable for easy connection. Before the following spring their home must be moved nearer the entrance into a position suitable to welcome visitors. Then the phone could be indoors. Meanwhile they would have a true outside phone, fixed to a stake driven in the ground and covered with a big plastic sheet.

The two older children arrived home from school at a gallop, knowing that pipe-laying was almost complete. Stephen rushed to meet them. He had watched Dad test the water pressure earlier that day by sticking a finger over one end of a short hose connected to the tap, and sending water flying in an arch of spray. Attempting to duplicate this process the lad turned it back on, pointing the nozzle in Christopher's direction to stop him crossing the bridge, a tiny finger applied to the end controlling the flow. He succeeded, ignoring jets of spray that were drenching his own clothes.

"Stop wasting it, we're on a meter!" Jan yelled, suddenly aware of the standoff.

They all trooped into the caravan, Christopher and Sharon with their satchels, young Stephen trailing wetly behind.

While discussing their day at school, Jan carried on with the meal; fried sausages, mashed potatoes and baked beans. She seldom cooked in the evenings but final work on the water main had allowed time for no more than a snack at midday. With only two gas rings, she juggled saucepans as usual, removing the potatoes but leaving them in their boiling water to retain the heat, slipping baked beans over the flame to cook. On the other ring, sausages already spat and sizzled in the frying pan.

Carrying leftover lengths of pipe and cable to a less exposed place, Gordon observed this premature arrival from school, ten minutes earlier than expected, and joined them early for tea. Knowing the water might be on, they had probably run most of the mile and a half home. Unfortunately Jan, unaware of their haste, had planned tea for the normal time. With nothing yet ready, there would be a delay.

Stephen, never very conscious of time since it had little meaning in the valley, failed to understand that they were early. He spoke gruffly and with a typical bluntness.

"Mum's slow, you'll have to wait."

Sharon jumped to Jan's defence, "You ought to try cooking on only two gas rings."

Gordon, winking at Christopher, said conversationally, "You'd think with water laid on almost to the door, Mum would at least get tea on time. Too much easy living makes women lazy, don't you think?"

Everyone started to talk at once, Christopher agreeing, Sharon indignant.

"You couldn't do it if you had all day!" she asserted.

"'Course he could." Stephen muttered.

And Jan? She just rested one elbow on the sink, smiling at Gordon, mouthing quietly, "You stirrer, I'll deal with you later."

Some minutes of argument passed before Christopher noticed his parents leaning back, grinning at each other. He broke off in mid-sentence and stared. Sharon and Stephen puzzled at his sudden silence, turned, uncertain. Both parents broke into quiet laughter at the bewildered expressions.

Realising their legs had been pulled, first Stephen, then Christopher joined in, but Sharon, always easiest to rouse, put her chin in the air and spoke with all the dignity she could muster.

"I think you're horrible!"

Chapter 9

Caravans and Luxury

The bridge needed attention. Built many years before, it had according to official documents replaced an older timber bridge sited somewhat upstream and previously swept away. Indeed some parts of what appeared to be the old structure were still clearly visible.

The concrete arch, flat of course across the top, lacked parapets, an omission the children had become carelessly familiar with. Stephen, in spite of Jan's warnings, often stood close to the abrupt drop, or sat feet dangling over the edge. He liked the bridge that way, never realising it was unusual. Visitors however, might view the matter differently, particularly those with young ones of their own.

When the first load of building blocks had been delivered to the site, the lorry driver, not a profession known for its great sensitivity, had indicated just how unpopular the bridge might be. On a foggy night a stranger could easily drive over the edge and land on the riverbed eight feet or more below. It was simple to imagine that anyone finding themselves in such a position, providing they were still conscious after the drop, would not be in the best of humour. Sitting there, unable or unwilling to open the door against the force of water, twelve to eighteen inches up the bodywork and probably already seeping in, one could scarcely expect a good-natured reply to the question, "Are you all right?"

Fortunately, local gossip estimated the incidence of foggy nights in the valley as one per year or less, almost a fog-free zone.

"I don't care. It's just not good enough! It doesn't need to be foggy to put people off. Standing looking down into the water they'll think they're walking the plank. *Do something!"* Jan spoke forcefully with an exasperated smile, digging a finger at her husband's chest as he backed away in pretended alarm. Only that morning she had seen Stephen lying full length on the bridge, head and shoulders over the edge, craning to look at the water beneath where the trout liked to wait, shaded from the sun. Quiet suggestions had been made before. Now she was pressing, a thing she hardly ever found necessary. Gordon would sort it eventually, she knew that, but fully expected him to play with her for a while, shaking his head, drawing in breath, tutting a bit and generally trying to rouse her further. It was part of life's fun, this understanding. She would go along, pretending to get angry. Usually they would end up in each other's arms.

The acreage purchased included land half a mile upstream in the village, a plot alongside the entrance track, the place where Jan's parents wanted to live. Official searches attached to the deeds referred to five miner's cottages that had at one time stood on the land. An old photo showed two of them, their image reflected from a lake of standing water completely covering the track that now led to the site.

These cottages had since fallen into disuse, then fallen apart, probably assisted by scavenging of the more reusable materials. Still strewn across the plot however, lay many granite slabs whose sheer weight formed a deterrent to such opportunistic removal. Some of these Gordon struggled to load in the digger's large front bucket, then trundled them away down the track. He chose shaped, elongated stones, of necessity varying in height, and used these to form a natural-looking random bridge edging, between twelve and eighteen inches high.

After the cement had set, these low, uneven parapets became a favourite place. Here one evening the two parents sat, as so often lately, the children off playing elsewhere. Idly they watched four swallows dive and skim backwards and forwards along the water surface, passing below them underneath the arch, now and then picking up water with a little splash and a slight reduction in speed. What control to lower a beak under the surface, skimming off a mouthful without being pulled down.

"What are they finding?" Jan asked. "I've never noticed gnats in the air. I thought midges might be a problem by the river when we first came, but I haven't seen any. So what are they chasing?"

A week or so earlier, swifts too had skimmed and wheeled, all black against the sky. Rather than flying beneath the arch, these bigger birds powered their way above, sometimes swooping very close, almost in attack. They were gone now, borne on scimitar wings for a journey half across the globe. No bird spends more time in the air. The swallows too would leave in a day or so.

Below, a trout kept station, mastering the easy current with leisurely tail flicks, to dart off and be lost where sunlight reflected golden off the smooth water. On other days when wind ruffled the river, that same surface had glistened and sparkled so nothing in the crystal water beneath could be seen.

Seconds later the fish had returned exactly to its previous place. Gordon pointed it out to Jan, mentioning he had often seen hover-flies do a similar thing. They watched for a while, the trout darted off and returned again.

"Almost as if it owns that bit of river." Jan pulled her gaze from the water, turning to ask lightly, "Freehold or leasehold, which d'you think?"

Tired from the day's work but contented in the cool evening sunlight, idly he pondered before answering.

"Neither. Just until a bigger one comes along."

Sitting there holding hands, Jan's eyes returned to the fish just before it rose suddenly, leaping more than a body-length above the water to take an unseen fly. She squeezed his fingers and leaned closer.

"How lucky we are. You never warned me marriage would feel this romantic."

* * *

Meetings with council officers over toilet buildings had now ceased and all drawings had long since been submitted but still the waiting continued. What did they do in those council offices, hibernate?

Jim's bungalow design had recently caused a spate of renewed conferences. Such meetings were easier to arrange now, using their own phone, no longer dashing to the village with a handful of coins, although with the instrument outside, certain drawbacks remained. Holding a telephone conversation while squatting on the ground making notes on a pad, proved cumbersome and difficult; doing so during those infrequent days when it rained, verged on the impossible. Trying to keep telephone and notepad dry under a plastic sheet that tended to move in the wind, with rain somehow dripping down inside, certainly kept calls economical. Even worse was answering in the dark, clad in pyjamas; that inevitably added a touch of abruptness with late callers!

Sleep had scarcely come one night when the bell sounded. Several rings echoed across the sleeping valley before Gordon, coming fully awake, made to rise from the bed but Jan reached out a restraining arm.

"Leave it. No one will hear. The ringing will only stop just as you reach it."

He rolled back, pleased enough to give way. They waited but the phone rang on, waking all the children.

"Shouldn't we answer it?" Christopher asked.

"No, it must stop eventually."

Of course she was right, it did.

Sleep however, would not return. She lay awake well after the even tenor of their breathing indicated Gordon and the children had dropped off, her mind wandering over the isolated phone. Should anyone hear it, the sound of that bell miles from anywhere, ringing away in the darkness; it would have seemed very odd – even stranger had they investigated, finding the phone fixed to a stake driven in the ground. It was unlikely the little caravan some distance away near the bushes would be visible in the darkness.

Discussing it at breakfast, eaten together now the mornings were darker, she asked the children how they thought someone might react, walking beside the lonely stream when a bell suddenly rang in the middle of nowhere.

"Probably fall in the river," Christopher offered.

"But what would he think, finding it fixed to a

piece of wood, all on its own, remote and isolated?"

She looked round the children's faces, waiting. No one had an answer. What could anyone think? They resumed eating.

"Should have fixed it to a tree instead," Gordon suggested quietly.

"Why?" Sharon asked, pausing, a part-eaten slice of bread in her hand.

"Our midnight stranger would have known then, what it was for."

The others looked up, no light of understanding in their faces. Suddenly, Jan lunged at him, digging his ribs before turning to the children.

"Dad's being clever. At least he thinks so. Why is a telephone fixed to a tree? – for *trunk calls*!"

Leaning over, she dug him again with a finger but blank faces round the table made her realise; of course, the children had never heard such an expression. She explained, "They're long distance calls, we avoid them, cost too much, a letter is cheaper."

So far as they knew, no one did hear the bell, though a few nocturnal rodents and maybe a fox or the odd badger might have made off in a hurry.

* * *

A warm and largely dry spring and summer had favoured the family, offering no inkling of trouble ahead. The children played for long hot months in the sheltered valley, scouring hidden corners, building pebble weirs in the stream, catching butterflies and trying to catch trout. This splendid weather continued through early autumn. Only when some crisp October days heralded the first approach of winter did a new problem make its appearance, and as the weeks passed it became worse. Increasingly, Jan worried!

With five souls living in such a confined space and no proper form of heating, condensation began covering most inside surfaces by morning, even with windows left partially open all night for ventilation. Particularly worrying were bedclothes, especially the children's bedclothes. The material never felt truly dry. On fine days matters improved, for she could hang the sleeping bags and blankets on a line outside in the air. When it was warm, leaving doors and windows open during the day evaporated most of the condensation before it started to form again the following evening.

In wet weather neither of these tactics worked and windows on at least one side of the caravan had to be closed at night. If, in addition, it was cold, then the situation deteriorated further. Under such conditions more windows must be closed to retain such warmth as possible, which was precious little for heat continued to escape quickly through the thin aluminium walls.

One night when the temperature dropped sharply lower, Jan lit both gas rings in an attempt to raise inside comfort levels. After a time the flames glowed less fiercely but she left them burning all evening in spite of the cost, extinguishing the gas only when retiring to bed. The following morning condensation hung in globules from every surface, having trickled down the walls in such quantities as to saturate one side of virtually all the bedclothes. The caravan felt not only damp, but cold, the air outside noticeably warmer.

"What are we to do?" Jan asked at breakfast. Even the bench seat they sat on felt damp. "Should I leave the gas rings running all night?"

"You can't." Gordon shook his head and seeing

Jan prepare to argue, held up a hand, stopping her. He glanced at the children before continuing, "Gas is part of the trouble, when it burns it produces water, more than its own weight in water vapour. The more you try to heat the caravan that way, the wetter everything will get."

He paused again, marshalling his thoughts. "Another thing, it wouldn't be safe. I know there are vent holes in the floor and the rooflight doesn't close right down, but with both those rings alight, the gas bottle may eventually freeze. Did you notice the flame burning lower last night?"

Looks of disbelief appeared on the young faces but Jan nodded thoughtfully. "Maybe, but will that matter?"

"Yes. When the gas freezes the burners go out but are still turned on full. If the cylinder thaws later, the gas will flow again, filling the caravan. These gas rings have no safety devices to cut them off."

The weather warmed over the next few days but the problem only reduced, never disappeared, and it returned later in the week. Just the act of breathing itself created condensation. The parents even discussed whether they should start sleeping outside, under the stars as it were, regardless of the awning having no front – taking a chance that any sudden rain could soak them. Two fewer people breathing inside would reduce the condensation a little for the children.

* * *

Jan stood alone in a stony car park looking back towards their little green mini-van, Stephen had fallen asleep on her lap during the journey; she had eased him back gently onto the seat, closing the door quietly.

A long line of large caravans, well spaced, some of them occupied, stretched across the adjoining, partly wooded area.

They were near the Lizard, a site advertising a forty-foot caravan, the size Jim wanted. Gordon had already walked over to someone standing nearby, the two men stood absorbed in conversation then turned and walked off without a backward glance. Making no attempt to catch up, Jan tagged slowly along behind glancing from a distance at various caravans, intermittently moving closer to examine the empty ones – those with For Sale notices. An old, very cheap, twenty-two foot model caught her eye. Much too small for Jim, but...?

Sixty pounds read a label stuck inside the front window. The men had passed by, not even noticing; she moved to follow until they stopped some distance farther on. As Gordon slid underneath to inspect a larger caravan's floor and chassis, Jan quietly retraced her steps to the smaller unit, checking round the outside then opening the door. Ah! She had guessed so from that pipe projecting through the roof – a stove! Glancing round the interior, she hurried back as Gordon emerged, wriggling out from his under-floor survey with a shake of the head. The other man had gone. Offering a hand ostensibly to help him up, she hung on, dragging him back to the smaller caravan.

For a moment he stood waiting. Seeing his uncertain expression change to understanding, then resistance, she spoke quickly.

"I know we're desperately short of money and this will make the position even more precarious, but I don't think we can survive the winter in our present caravan. Condensation is already bad. As the weather gets colder, even if it doesn't freeze down here it will still mean the children sleeping in constantly damp or wet bedclothes. We *must* buy it!"

He listened, heard urgency in her voice, felt her little hand more tightly gripping his, whether from anxiety or to prevent him turning away was not clear but there were lines of concern on her face. She was never normally this pressing. And she was right of course. He had known all along that something had to be done but pretended to himself they could manage. Well then, better look more closely. This caravan was very old but not too dilapidated. Crawling underneath he inspected chassis and flooring, expecting the worst. Plenty of rust, all superficial, no wood rot either, amazing really for its age. Certainly not overpriced and as Jan pointed out, it had a boiler. He crawled out and opened the single door. True enough there it stood, luxury of luxuries, a small solid fuel boiler centrally placed on the long wall opposite. This really appeared a bargain, the price exceptional. They would just have to spend less on something else. What that something would be he couldn't for the life of him see at the moment!

The site owner returned as they closed the door.

"Twenty-two feet this one, too small these days. Not so popular now with just the one room. Replacing it with something larger – more profitable." He rubbed his hands unconsciously together at the thought before adding, "That's why it's ridiculously cheap!"

Gordon, keeping enthusiasm off his face and hoping madly that Jan would do the same, made one attempt to lower the price but the owner absolutely refused to consider it. At that price, why should he? So a caravan was purchased, though not the forty-foot model intended for Jim; that one had a dangerously soft floor which needed replacing.

The seller declined at first to make delivery but Gordon dug his toes in; delivery included or no sale. No way could it be safely towed by a Mini van! They would perhaps reach five miles an hour on the flat, but with no hope of control downhill. Twenty-two feet might be considered small, but it was more than twice as long and certainly four times the weight of their tiny Eccles tourer. Eventually delivery was promised for the following day using a Land Rover.

"But," the man said clearly, "it's transport only. I'm not setting it up for you!"

Gordon nodded agreement.

They climbed aboard the Mini van, waking Stephen who remained ignorant of the whole transaction and fell asleep again early in the journey. Dashing home full of enthusiasm and bursting with happiness, they pushed completely to the back of their minds any monetary problems the purchase would be likely to cause. Jan started cooking a late lunch, keeping Stephen with her while Gordon prepared a flat site in a new position nearer the entrance, then dug a trench and quickly laid a duct to take the water and telephone cable straight to the caravan. They were really going for comfort this time! By mid-afternoon, the site lay level, the trench refilled and everything ready to receive their new home. While Stephen played in the field, they debated what to tell the children.

"Tell them nothing," Jan urged. "Just hope it comes early tomorrow. We can set it level for their arrival home from school as a surprise."

It had seemed a good idea, but Christopher, more observant than expected, noticed the flattened ground straight away and asked its purpose.

"It's ready for our new home one day." Jan told the

youngsters. True, if a little deceptive! They played on the new levelled area for a while after tea, then forgot it.

Before ten o'clock next morning a Land Rover bounced down the road, caravan bumping along behind. It crossed the bridge and stopped in the wide level area made for tourists arriving the following season. The driver uncoupled his load, quickly said goodbye, waved and was gone. He made little conversation and though cheerful enough, had offered no advice on the task of levelling.

In spite of Jan's impatience, Gordon, who had stopped work to watch the delivery, insisted on returning to finish loading the half-full trailer, tow it away and tip it at the area being filled. It took less than twenty minutes but in that short spell he had seen Jan and Stephen visit three times at a safe distance, the look on Jan's face clearly saying, "Haven't you finished that yet?"

His own impatience was hard to contain but he never left a partly loaded trailer; empty was kinder on the tyres – and tyres were expensive! Eventually he finished, drove back and walked towards the waiting caravan. Seeing Dad approach, Stephen dashed to the little tourer, climbed the steps and looked up at Jan with an expression of urgency. Turning without a word, he jumped down again, rushing to the new caravan. His mother followed behind almost as quickly.

Manoeuvring over such a short distance with the Mini van proved easy, it didn't matter about moving slowly, accuracy not speed the essential ingredient. The caravan reversed cautiously, ending up approximately central over the prepared ground, not at the first attempt, but fairly smartly. Jacking the axle and supporting it on building blocks with timber packings, then winding down adjustable corner steadies, completed the caravan levelling.

Asking occasional questions, Stephen climbed into the doorway some eighteen inches off the ground, not really in the way, his irrepressible enthusiasm adding to Jan's own quiet delight at seeing her new home made ready. There was nothing Stephen could damage, she allowed him complete freedom to go in, around or even under the caravan as he pleased. With hot water boiled in the tourer, she washed and cleaned while Gordon prepared a pile of logs for the boiler. After the first hour, interest lessening, Stephen ran off to play in the field, dashing hurriedly back now and then, anxious to miss nothing.

Jan insisted on lighting the boiler to air the caravan, and on the gas bottle's immediate connection for testing the rings.

"Still only two, but we can't have everything." she leaned back to assess the other advantages as they sat for a first coffee in their new abode. The table was bigger, it would easily take five people, and the boiler was great – it roared pleasingly, every window open slightly to assist with the airing. Broader and more comfortable seats too, the very atmosphere felt better. Moving forward, elbows on the table, chin resting on the back of clasped hands, she looked at Gordon and in a sudden burst of euphoria made an impulsive decision.

"We can sleep in this tonight! It's already drier than the tourer. I can carry most of the things we need over. Can you take the afternoon off, make the steps, connect up the water, then give me a hand?"

"Take the afternoon off?" Gordon echoed, pretending to be scandalised. He prepared to say more but she rose, coffee cup in hand, moved round the table and stood over him looking down, expression half threatening, half laughing, cup raised towards her lips but with just that suggestion that it might land elsewhere!

"You wouldn't like to reconsider, would you?" she asked sweetly.

"Well, I might."

A few spots of coffee splashed on the table.

"I think it's a brilliant idea," he agreed hurriedly.

"Right! Drink up and let's get started." She had fire and spirit in her voice. It was hardly surprising. Twenty-four hours ago they were not even aware this caravan existed, now they owned it and might yet move in that very afternoon!

He smiled up at her, knowing how she felt, and somehow they floated together. Her kiss was not one of passion, just excitement and eagerness. He would have liked more, knew from the intensity of her embrace and the warmth of those soft lips that it easily could be. But she was too unsettled, the urge to create a new home too great. He loved her far too much to interrupt the transparent thrill she displayed in preparing it. Like a bird building a new nest in spring he thought, releasing her with a sigh, and left to pinch more blocks from around the toilet to make steps for the caravan.

Water and telephone were quickly connected while Jan carted bedclothes, pots, pans and a panoply of other articles, including coats from the wardrobe. She called down to him as he lay, flat on his back under the van, connecting the last nuts.

"These winter clothes from the wardrobe, the ones we haven't started to use yet, they're beginning to go mouldy. Shows how bad the condensation was!"

Completing everything by the time Christopher and

179

Sharon were due home proved impossible. Stephen, interested again as Jan swept to and fro with various armfuls, had been quickly pressed into carrying smaller articles. Some things remained to be transferred but the essentials were in and working. They stood outside waiting for the older children as their usual time of arrival approached.

Christopher saw the caravan from a fair distance up the lane, Jan could see him pointing and speaking to Sharon, then both started to run, arriving out of breath, bursting with questions.

"Whose is it? How did it get here?"

"It's ours!" Stephen, sitting on the top step, muttered the reply into his chest, then lifted his head with a grin of delight, daring anyone to contradict him. As the older two stared doubtfully, he jumped up and disappeared through the doorway.

They looked at Jan. She nodded, standing aside and signalling them in, watching the wonder on their faces as they entered, feeling the warmth of the stove, the smell of cooking and all that space everywhere!

"It's enormous!" Christopher turned from one end to the other in amazement.

"Space is relative," Gordon murmured, his thoughts running off at a tangent again. "The salesman sold it cheap because to normal people it's much too small. To us, after the tourer, it's as Christopher says – enormous!"

Life in the new home proved fantastic! At least, it was so long as memories of life in the little tourer remained fresh. Later no doubt, it would become first normal then substandard as comparisons altered. For now 'fantastic', Christopher's word of course, found no one arguing. For one thing, the stove had a small water tank at the back which, when filled with a jug, heated enough water for washing. Bigger cupboards and two tiny wardrobes offered more storage space; the sink was larger too, and boasted a single tap connected directly to the water supply – no more carrying buckets from the river – this was opulence! Most important, however, warmth now spread throughout the caravan totally curing any condensation problems and making possible thoroughly dry bedclothes. How much nicer after a strenuous day, to climb into a bed feeling warm and crisp, rather than cold and limply damp!

Jan purchased a tin bath, not the long one a person could sit or even lie down in, she could never heat sufficient water to use it; this bath resembled a small clothes basket, both in size and shape. Any member of the family could strip out, stand in hot water and bath inside the caravan, right next to heat radiating from the stove. The children could even sit down in it, knees crunched up to their chests, although rather a squash for Christopher.

The improvement went beyond baths, beyond the extra space and dry bedclothes. They were seated in the caravan, weak winter sunlight had turned to a cold clear night. All five basked in warmth radiating from the stove, still a new enough sensation to feel incredibly good!

Gordon sat back idly, his book resting on the table, watching the children sprawled upon the floor playing cards. At the moment everything was OK. He and Jan could draw the little curtains and bath in the daytime when the children were at school, but he recalled his old worry: there was still only the one room. Before they were many years older, Christopher and Sharon at least would want some privacy for themselves.

Sleeping arrangements while more comfortable, were in one respect very similar to those experienced before. Although Christopher no longer slept in a bunk above their heads, the two youngest still had to share sleeping quarters, head to toe on a bench seat. This too, could not continue for long. For the moment however, these were minor drawbacks, everyone delighting with the bigger caravan. Drying clothes, a real difficulty as the weather began to change, now presented hardly any problem at all.

The outside privy remained, the caravan had no space for a loo. It lay farther away now they were close to the bridge, but no one seemed to mind. Gordon lifted his gaze to find Jan in the other bench seat looking at him, leaning forward, elbows on the table between them as she often liked to do. He moved to a similar position, bringing their heads close so they could talk without drawing attention from the children, absorbed in a game of their own on the floor.

"No person living under normal conditions would think of this as comfort, but look at them."

They sat for a while, watching and listening. She continued quietly, "Think of all those people still in the rat-race, making themselves miserable yearning for things they think they can't live without. They should live with us for a while, give them a whole new outlook on what constitutes a necessity!"

* * *

A motorcycle lay against a bush on the far bank of the river, Gordon spotted it as he returned, slightly earlier than expected, for coffee. "Whose is that?"

Seeing him glance towards the machine, Jan waved

an arm roughly in the direction of the river path. "A young couple, teenagers probably. Went off downstream hand in hand."

The subject was forgotten as they drank, resting comfortably at the table.

"I was about to bring the coffee round; what made you come back?"

"Missed you madly!" Seeing the disbelieving smile, he admitted, "Need another pair of rubber gloves, these are getting smelly inside."

"They shouldn't be, I gave you a fresh pair only this morning."

Reaching over to pull open a drawer and passing him another pair, she took the ones he pulled from a pocket, holding them between two fingers like something distasteful, and sniffed delicately. Smelling nothing she turned them over idly then stopped in surprise, looking up at him accusingly.

"Smelly nothing. You've torn one almost in half!"

Draining his cup, he rose.

"Have I really? Nothing lasts these days, does it?"

She threw the gloves as he jumped through the doorway.

Later in the afternoon, a movement of something white, high up on the waste heaps caught his eye. Strange. Occasionally someone passed along the foot-path, perhaps once in three or four days, at times not for a week or more, but he had never seen anyone in that part of the valley. Walking to the bottom of the rise and looking up – whoever it was had disappeared. Gordon called, "Hello!"

A quick exclamation floated down on the wind but no one emerged. He started to climb, shortly reaching the top, hunted briefly round but could find nothing and soon returned to work.

Ten minutes later an attractive young woman in a white blouse appeared, standing hesitantly, watching him from a distance but making no move to approach. When he started towards her, she turned as if hunting an escape route, then seeming to change her mind, stood waiting in confusion.

"Hello, are you in trouble?"

As soon as the words were out, he wished they had been said differently. It was not the sort of question one asked any woman, particularly a pretty young lady, but her obvious agitation had suggested something was very wrong. She looked about to reply, opened her mouth then glanced again over one shoulder as if ready to flee. Was he such an ogre? The torn and somewhat tattered clothes perhaps, he thought hopefully.

After some moments she forced herself to speak.

"I've lost my boyfriend." Nervous eyes looked down, her hands rubbing anxiously together, weight shifting uneasily to the other foot as the silence lengthened. The girl's expression suggested those few words were reason enough, but mislaying a companion hardly seemed to explain her present distress.

"Lost him? Where?"

There was that expression of fear again, something she wanted to avoid telling. He stood still, waiting, making no attempt to move closer.

She drew a deep breath. "He knew of an apple tree, in the wood above the waste heaps. We walked along the riverbank, cut back out of sight and climbed to the top. He went in to see if any apples remained, telling me to keep out of sight. I waited just at the edge of the trees." She paused, looking like a little roe deer about to prance off into the forest. After a minute, seeing the explanation was not enough, she continued.

"You must have seen me, you came closer. When you shouted I heard a big crash in the wood, something falling and a yell, then silence. You came up, I hid behind some ivy. When you left I called softly but there was no reply and I can't find him. I looked but the brambles stop you going right in. He may have fallen from the tree and be hurt!"

At last he understood. The wood above the waste heaps was indeed fairly impenetrable, mainly elm with masses of ivy and brambles. Although forming part of the park they had never explored this area. Lying as it did above the waste heaps, hidden mine shafts were a distinct possibility.

"Do you want me to help search?"

"Would you?" Her expression held relief, almost gratitude. They climbed the steep path yet again to reach the fringe of the wood. Gordon signalled to stop, and hunted around on the ground, eventually finding an old bough some six feet in length. Stripping off the small side branches by brute force, he made a knobbly bent staff.

"You want to come?"

She nodded. He had guessed she would.

"I've never been inside there before, it may be dangerous, there could even be shafts. Hold the end of this stick and follow me. If I go down a hole, back off and get help. Understand?"

She nodded. They set off, Gordon forcing a way through, stamping down the brambles and other low vegetation so she could follow. There was no sign of a body near the apple tree; he pressed on, leading the girl, using one foot to feel ahead, testing the ground. It was slow! Overhead the foliage was thick, little sign now of the sky that had disappeared behind them, but ahead the trees were thinning. Fifty or so yards in that direction, southward, must lie open ground.

Suddenly the sound of a distant motorcycle kicked into life, wafted from far below into the wood. It revved up, fading away along the stony track at speed. The boyfriend had escaped. Escaped from what? Neither of the two would-be rescuers were sure.

"Perhaps," Gordon suggested lamely, "he's been looking for you and thinks you might have left?"

The girl looked half furious, half like she might burst into tears. At a loss to know how to handle young females possibly on the point of breakdown, he smiled at her and shrugged.

"Come on, let's find a way out. Straight ahead looks easiest. Step where I step, we may have problems yet!"

Threading their way forward, they came at last to a Cornish hedge, two layers of stone with soil between. It stood some two feet high. Jumping on top he held out a hand, pulling her up, discarding the no longer required staff. The field beyond lay some five feet below, the wall on that side taller by more than twice the expected height. Gordon slid and jumped down, pushing a break in the tangled foliage, then leaning back in the gap, took the girl in his arms, lifting her down. Strangely, he recalled Emma, carried along the trench in a similar manner some weeks before, and realised he had felt more at ease with the old lady.

Setting the girl's feet quickly on the ground, he stepped back smartly, pretending to stagger slightly, alarmed at the close contact but not wanting to admit it. They walked together down the sloping field, back towards the bridge. As the caravan came into view, he stopped.

"My wife, Jan, will run you home if you're stuck."

"No. *He* may be waiting along the track. What I want to say will best be said alone." The girl paused, but as he made to leave, she laid a restraining hand hesitantly on his arm, "And thank you."

For a moment she looked directly at him, then her eyes returned to the ground, uncertain. With a little nod she walked off. Gordon strode towards the caravan.

Jan, having observed their approach and the little scene before separation, stepped quickly outside, glancing suspiciously at him as they stood together watching the young lady walk somewhat listlessly up the track, to disappear from view.

"Who was she?" There was an edge of something, surprise, mistrust, amusement perhaps, in Jan's voice.

"I don't know. We only just met."

"What's her name?"

"I never ask their names."

"You never...!" Jan spluttered, rounding on him, "What do you mean you never ask their names? Anyone would think glamorous young girls are two a penny out here in the wilds. What I want to know is, what were *you* doing with this one?" She dug a finger in his ribs on the word '*you*'.

"Can't help it – like moths to a flame!" He drew himself up, running a hand through bedraggled hair, straightening an imaginary tie on his torn open neck shirt, then ducked low as she aimed a haymaker at his head. "Make me a coffee and I'll tell you the whole curious story."

"OK!" She made for the door, laughing and mumbling loudly, "Now where did I put the arsenic?"

CHAPTER 10

Man Engines

With the water main installation completed and no other disturbance of the road surface planned, rough filling of the major potholes had become worthwhile and was speedily carried out. Final stone surfacing, a much longer and more meticulous job, would be left until all heavy lorry traffic carrying building materials had finished. At least the postman now delivered to the caravan, though letters were still rare.

The arrival of planning permission had been so long expected, that even when Jan read the postmark '*Penzance*' she remained doubtful. Was this it? More important, would it be approval or rejection?

Lunch already simmered on the gas, tended by Sharon as was usual on Saturdays. Jan looked at the letter, handling it nervously, wondering? Perhaps she'd leave it for Gordon, he'd be back for the midday meal soon.

"Open it, Mum!" Sharon urged, when she learned what the letter might contain, and took a knife from the drawer, placing it on the table nearby.

Hiding a sense of foreboding, Jan picked it up, slit the envelope quickly, extracted the contents and scanned several typewritten sheets.

Sharon watched, seeing the intensity of expression on her mother's face and the nervous twitch of fingers as she studied the sheet. Gradually, the frown faded, replaced as the corners of her mouth turned slowly upwards in a broad smile.

"We've got it!" She looked up, eyes shining, voice triumphant. "Watch the lunch, I must tell Dad!"

Sharon, on the point of protesting, not wanting to be left behind, glanced at the stove then back towards her mother but it was too late. Jan had whipped through the doorway at a run!

Ten minutes later she returned at a canter, bustling up the steps and into the caravan.

"Change of plan. Lunch needs impact, something with flair! How can we pep it up quickly?" It wasn't really a question, more a thought said aloud. She looked at the clock. "Ten minutes, just over, before Dad comes back. Christopher and Stephen are down by the stream, I think they're trying to catch a fish. Are the potatoes done?" She spoke rapidly with a certain tense energy, restless, eyes bright like a bird, hand reaching to open a cupboard door, not waiting for the reply. A more experienced observer might have suspected champagne but it was stronger than that. The excitement of success coursed through her body!

"Should be another five minutes," Sharon picked up a fork and prodded. "Yes, needs a bit longer. Water's boiling for peas, shall I put them in?"

"Go ahead." Jan ferreted in the cupboard for another saucepan, pulling out her biggest complete with lid. Reaching for the kettle, always kept heating on the stove to save gas, she poured its contents into the wide saucepan before pushing it onto the gas ring having temporarily removed the now boiling peas. Being already very hot it boiled quickly. Sharon watched with interest as she swapped saucepans again, then placed the bigger one on top.

"Pass me a teaspoon then get three eggs from the cupboard, prick them and lower into this top saucepan. We can boil them there, steam from the peas will keep the top one roughly at boiling point. At least I hope it will, I've never done it before."

Jan took the teaspoon, poking the handle between the two pans to form a tiny gap, and seeing Sharon's slightly raised eyebrows, explained, "To make sure the steam can escape; we don't want another explosion! I'll have to hold the top saucepan – seems a bit wobbly. What else can we use?"

Sharon lowered three eggs into the water with a tablespoon, watching as her mother juggled the pans round again to bring the water back up to boiling point. Looking in the cupboard, she returned with a bunch of carrots.

"I could throw these in with the peas, or cut them in rings, raw like with salad."

"Raw – the colour's nice, only two, they're really for tomorrow's lunch. There's an apple I think. Cut it in segments with the skin left on; looks good that way."

"With the main course?"

"Americans do it all the time, usually pineapple."

Sharon made a grimace but fetched it from the cupboard, then pushed the potatoes aside, replacing them with the frying pan and added slices of luncheon meat. Jan reached with her left hand, taking over the frying, flipping the thin slices around while retaining a hold on the top saucepan, simultaneously casting glances at her daughter slicing the carrots.

"I'll leave the apple until we dish up, it might go brown." Sharon suggested. "How will you divide three eggs between five people?"

"If this works, and I'm not totally convinced it will, we want them hard boiled and cut in half. Half each, the extra one for Dad."

"Why two for Dad, he always gets extra!" Sharon's lips formed a little pout, a token objection with no hope of changing anything.

"Don't you think he deserves it?"

"No! We work just as hard."

The statement lacked conviction. Jan looked at her daughter questioningly, not disagreeing, but Sharon looked away, both women tacitly knowing it to be untrue.

"Extra energy might help him finish the toilets faster."

Sharon's expression turned thoughtful.

"Yes, Dad *should* have the extras!" she nodded.

They laughed at each other as Jan pulled off the peas, which were done, putting the eggs directly over the gas for a few more minutes before fishing them out and running under cold water. Sharon drained the peas, laid out plates then took over peeling eggs while Jan mashed and served potatoes, chivvying luncheon meat one final time around the pan before serving that too. They could hear the boys and Dad approaching as she added peas, then carrots. While Sharon segmented the apple, Jan dived back into the cupboard for a small chunk of cheese from which she cut five fairly miserly slices. Plates were whisked to table as male members of the family entered, clustering round the sink to wash hands.

Quality in food lay not only in the taste, appearance and aroma made an impact, but most important of all – how did it compare with expectations? Even before they sat down, the uncommonly colourful display promised a more than usually tasty meal. It alerted the boys that something was afoot, though they had no idea what. Sharon was bursting, containing herself with the utmost difficulty until all were seated.

Her delight flowed from two sources. First, the boys had been absent when the letter arrived and therefore she knew something they didn't: a secret to tell. Savouring the prospect she waited impatiently, sitting erect, shoulders back, living in advance the little scene with them hanging on her every word. Secondly, the likelihood loomed closer now, not only of real toilets but the dreamy, almost magical prospect of hot showers.

Between mouthfuls of an unexpectedly appetising meal, Sharon, centre stage and basking in the limelight, revealed the tidings. Her parents watched with interest but avoided interfering, other than to give a nod when Christopher turned to them for confirmation, pleased with the news but not entirely happy that his sister had known first.

Content with her revelation but confidence faltering, still unsure the prospects were really true, Sharon turned, eagerly anxious to Dad. "Now we can have a proper toilet with a door and a chain to pull?"

Gordon nodded but she continued, a touch of suspicion in her voice.

"When? How long will it take?"

"Don't hold your breath." He smiled and seeing her blank expression, explained. "That means it will take some time, maybe months, but the best is worth waiting for and these will definitely be the best toilets you ever saw!" Gordon spoke with a certain amount of pride and conviction.

"What can be different?" Christopher looked doubtful. "Like Sharon said, a toilet has a door, a loo and a chain to pull. What else?"

His father didn't reply immediately. The family watched, all curious to hear the response.

"What do you notice most about bad toilets?" he asked rather than answering directly.

"Smelly." Christopher promptly replied.

"Dirty." Sharon answered almost simultaneously.

Stephen looked confused. Never using any toilet other than their own, his memory of the previous house's toilet had already faded. To Stephen an outside bucket was perfectly normal and satisfactory.

"Let's take smelly first." Gordon selected the easiest answer. "Smells come mostly from loos. In our design all the loos will be against outside walls, with a window high above to carry smells away."

Christopher nodded.

"And dirty?" prompted Sharon, having established a certain standing during the meal and not prepared now to be overlooked.

"Well no matter how excellent they are, only regular cleaning will keep them sparkling, but certain things can help." Gordon stopped, marshalling his thoughts. So many features had gone into the design; where should he start?

"First, pipework is ugly – the less that shows, the less to get dirty. We'll fix all the basins on the wall that divides ladies from gents but it's a double wall with a passageway between. That's where all the pipes go, into this service passage; the heaters will be in there too, close to the basins so hot water reaches the taps quickly. Using an inside wall makes it easy to mount mirrors and hooks above the basins," Gordon paused looking round; they nodded. This talk of proper loos and basins with taps, it had their full attention!

"Don't forget the floor," he continued. "If we try

to make it flat, any spilled water will stand around in puddles, so we'll make it all slope to a drainage point."

"Sloping floors?" Sharon screwed up her face.

"Not a slope you can see, a tiny slope, just enough to run any water away. Like the pavements in Penzance, they all slope you know, to shed water into gutters."

The older two nodded, they understood pavements.

"Where the floor meets the walls it will be slightly rounded instead of square, easier to clean, and we'll have lots of hooks. Oh, and a special gadget on the outside doors to stop them banging. There, I told you we could build the best toilet facilities anywhere."

Stephen had lost interest, these technicalities beyond his real understanding; he had no memory of flush loos, or why anyone would want two taps on one basin, and certainly saw no point in door closers. In his opinion, doors were made for banging! He slid from the bench to wander off, Christopher glancing after him as he climbed down from the doorway. Sharon however, remained deeply interested.

"What about showers, hot showers with tiles?"

"Showers yes, with hot water..."

"Hot water!" Sharon interrupted, wrapping both arms round her chest, hugging herself at the thought, turning to Jan in delight. "Hot water," the young girl repeated, closing her eyes as in a dream, breathing in deeply with an ecstatic little shiver.

Her father waited until she turned back before continuing. "No tiles. Can't afford them; perhaps later. The walls will be cement rendered and painted white, floors just smooth cement. For the rest, wait and see!"

As a young engineer, Gordon's admission into the Institution of Civil Engineers had been achieved on the strength of a toilet building design, admittedly a two-storey affair for a large industrial complex, so not exactly similar to the present problem. Nevertheless he had poured every drop of expertise into designing facilities that would please the customer and not only stand the test of time, but be low on maintenance and easy to keep clean. Moreover, it had to be done within the budget set aside for building. It formed the severest test of skill to achieve this by eliminating every inch of wasted space rather than sacrifice quality anywhere. He felt sure the aim had been achieved.

The council's final planning approval meant that no redrawing would be required. The drawing board at which so many hours had been spent could now stay where it was, in the Mini van, rather than yo-yo back and forth as it had earlier in the year.

Jan displayed her delight with a large hug.

"You clever lad," she clung round his neck, lifting both feet off the floor while she kissed him again, a kiss of pleasure and exuberance, bubbly like lemonade, certainly no prelude to anything serious. "Thank goodness that's done. Now when you get the first building finished you can store that drawing board in the roof, then it won't need to stay in the back of the van either."

* * *

Brrmm! Four heads turned, the sound breaking that pre-sunrise quietness, cutting across sporadic early bird-song as the engine roared into life. They were gathered under the first streaks of dawn, sky still coldly grey, cheered only by a hint of pink on the eastern horizon, but nothing could depress the jubilant spirits of the watchers. The excavator's main boom moved, a well-worn bucket swinging from the end. It hesitated, swept upwards and forwards, teeth projecting like giant talons extending to grasp some hapless prey, then arched down to earth again at the full extent of its reach. The engine note deepened as the claw dug itself deeply into soil, grasping its pound of flesh, ripping away that first massive bite from the virgin ground. A little cheer rang out, the boom lifted, swung to one side and dropped its load.

Climbing from the high back seat down into the driving position, Gordon turned the key. The engine died. Placing hands on the cab sides, he swung down, leaping to kneel on the ground. Three children rushed towards him, Sharon with arms outstretched, Christopher more reticent but excited still, Stephen following behind, unsure about the celebration but caught as so often before by the enthusiasm of the older pair. Jan walked slowly after them, smiling. She stopped, gazing down on the young heads, listening to the animated questions and comment before finally interrupting.

"OK. That's it. I declare our toilet building officially started. Now back for breakfast!"

The little party in high good humour, returned to the caravan where Jan served boiled eggs. They were quick, a breakfast she could cook in one saucepan all at the same time.

The last day and a half had been spent tidying and making safe the area that had been half levelled when news of the council's approval had arrived on the Saturday morning. Now on Monday, the toilet building was under way at last.

After so many months of clearing, an essential task but tediously slow, steady and unspectacular, the commencement of work on the first building's foundations gave a boost to everyone's morale. Conversation over breakfast had a lightness of spirit quite natural after the crushingly long wait. Jan suppressed her own exuberance, trying to damp down the children's expectations of how soon these facilities would be available, but with little effect. She gave up and concentrated on eating. Though not now in the mood for discouragement, they would remember her warning as weeks passed. She listened to their continuing over-optimistic chatter, only Sharon waiting to empty her mouth before speaking.

"Must talk to them about that," Jan thought, not for the first time, but couldn't bring herself to interrupt the feeling of euphoria pervading the caravan that morning.

Watching the small smiling faces and answering questions between mouthfuls, Gordon hoped they would be as happy in a few months time. His own standing had perked up considerably with the improving outlook and the rise in comfort levels in their new home.

* * *

"Mum, what's a Man Engine?"

Christopher and Sharon had arrived home from school to find tea almost ready, but dashed across to inspect progress on the foundations before returning to the caravan. They sat down as Jan pushed beans on toast in front of them, setting a double portion before Gordon.

"Cheat!" Sharon noticed first, objecting loudly and pointing. Stephen and Christopher both looked up adding exclamations, turning to Mum, then back to Dad with expressions of protest.

Gordon smiled broadly.

"Some people are just more special than others," he suggested, with a royal wave of the hand.

His final word disappeared, drowned in a combined

verbal protest, the words 'greedy', and 'unfair' detectable above the general hubbub. Jan, having failing to get their attention, reached for her paperback, swishing it down with a heavy thump. Plates jumped on the table, cutting arguments dead. A small "Oh!" as Sharon jerked upright in surprise, hung on the sudden silence.

"Eat! You can argue later! Actually I just bought a bigger tin of beans. Anyway, Dad is special, he does more work than anyone." She paused, watching Gordon put on a superior expression, making a little '*I told you so*' nod towards the three children on the other side of the table, before she continued.

"*And*," she paused again for effect; "he's bigger and uglier than any of you!" She finished with a broad smile and a triumphant flourish, bringing complementary grins to three young faces and a fake frown to Gordon's.

It was shortly after, as the last beans disappeared that Christopher asked his question.

"Mum, what's a Man Engine?"

The teacher, he explained, had given them the task of finding the answer as homework. They had a week to prepare and could seek information from any source. Unfortunately, no one round the table could help.

Jan visited Penzance the following day to purchase cement from the builders' merchants. Five bags were collected, all she felt the springs would continuously support, for of necessity this cement must stand in the Mini van. No point having a load delivered; nowhere dry to store it. While there, she borrowed a book from the library. However, it was Gordon who, having an interest in the subject, picked up the book that evening. Earlier darkness had made work outside impossible, offering plenty of browsing time. He read not only of man engines but scanned the absorbing mining history of eighteenth century Cornwall, occasionally reading snippets aloud to the family.

A common problem of Cornish mines was the vast amount of pumping required, for in the fissured rock water drained through various strata to the mine bottom. Some were said to be over a thousand feet deep. Only the invention of steam engines made possible continuous clearance of great quantities from such depths. Steam power operated huge pistons, some large enough to contain a whole modern car.

"It says here, that there are two Mine Engines in Camborne, both are preserved and open to the public." At Gordon's words, heads lifted. "They're actually working but only for demonstration, using compressed air instead of steam. Apparently, according to this, in that early era vessels holding the steam often exploded, killing those around not by flying metal but by scalding them to death. Definitely gives a new meaning to the expression, getting into hot water!"

"Human lobsters!" Christopher gruesomely commented, as Sharon gave a little shudder.

Jan looked at him in surprise. How had Christopher known about lobsters? Meeting lads at school with fathers in the local fishing industry she realised, perhaps working from Mousehole or Newlyn.

Old tin and copper mines had an enormous wheel mounted over the pumping shaft. Steam-driven pistons turned this wheel, and attached to its rim in one place was the first rod, a great balk of timber that hung down into the shaft, moving up and down as the wheel above rotated. At the end of each rod, a further rod was attached, like links in a wooden chain going down into the depths of the earth. Counterbalances usually took some of this weight at intermediate points lower down.

At the shaft bottom a pump was installed. One might think of it as a bicycle pump magnified many times, forcing water out on each downstroke, and on the upstroke as well, sometimes. Fixed to these timber rods, from ground level to pit bottom, were little platforms just large enough for a man to stand on, spaced exactly the diameter of the wheel apart. These were the moving platforms. Fixed to or carved out from the shaft sides, were other somewhat larger stationary platforms at a similar spacing.

At the end of any downstroke, a miner wishing to leave the pit would jump onto a moving platform on the rods, the upstroke taking him level with a stationary platform above, which he stepped onto, waiting there for the next moving platform to descend. When it arrived he jumped aboard, riding again to the top of its movement before stepping off onto the next stationary platform fixed to the shaft wall. Repeating the procedure he eventually reached the top without climbing a single ladder. He could go to work the next morning the same way, jumping on at the beginning of the downstroke instead of the upstroke. This is where the name Man Engine originated.

It was, of course, not without risk. There were several hundred to a thousand feet of nothing below. In a tragic mine accident at Levant, about a dozen miles from Relubbus, the rods broke near the top with many miners clinging to the platforms. Everything below the break level went away and all were killed. The fiftieth anniversary of this mining tragedy had recently been commemorated in the local paper, *The Cornishman*. There was no Safety at Work Act then. Probably if there had been the costs would have pushed Cornish tin out of production in favour of that mined in more primitive conditions overseas, priced out of the market as it was later anyway, largely due to the depth of the mines and the cost of pumping.

One might expect that the old miners who dug by hand and with blasting powder, would start their mine in the valley bottom, reducing the amount to be dug, but they were smarter than that. The shafts were always started well up any hillside, and for a good reason. It was easier to have the steam engine bring mined material to the top, then tip the unwanted waste downhill. Massive quantities of waste was dumped by hand-barrows or by baskets suspended from a sloping wire, always tipping them downwards from the higher ground.

For this reason Gordon did not expect to find shafts in the valley, he knew they should be above the waste material higher up the hill. There was one visible not far up on the neighbouring farm.

Sometimes, to avoided pumping water so high, the old miners cut horizontal shafts, called adits, to come out lower down the hill but well above any flood level. In moving the waste, might he not find such an adit, and might it be possible to crawl along, reaching the main shaft. Would those little platforms still be fixed to the walls or rotted away? With water at less than twenty feet down, what about diving gear? Could such old mysteries be explored further?

"Best not to suggest it to Jan or the children," he thought. "Would I really do it if an opportunity ever occurs? Who knows?"

* * *

Small cuts and bruises were commonplace, totally unavoidable in the wild and unkempt surroundings with three healthy youngsters braving imaginary perils in their private jungle playground. Frequently the boys returned with scratched skin or their old play clothes torn where bramble thorns or worse, wild rose thorns, had caught as they squeezed and pushed through small openings. Sharon, reasonably tomboyish but just that bit more careful with her appearance as girls often are, mostly avoided such damage.

"Listen carefully," Gordon said to the three children when more concrete blocks and other building materials began to arrive. He made them sit on the ground, waiting for their full attention to emphasise the warning.

"Building work is dangerous! More people get injured doing building jobs than almost any other work! Always be extra careful when doing anything connected with building!" At this stern caution, all appeared suitably impressed.

"But how long will they remember?" Jan thought, looking on. "I'm glad he warned them though, it will make more impression than I could have done. He's a little hard on them sometimes, especially if he's extra tired. I don't think when they're given so many little jobs they realise just how hard he works himself, struggling to get things ready."

Gordon looked up and caught her watching. She smiled, nodded approval and disappeared back into the caravan.

The older children were most affected. It was they who spent time each evening carrying materials around, moving concrete building blocks and pipes to positions convenient for the next day's building work. They, at least, appeared to heed the warning and work carefully.

At still only four, Stephen, while not entirely free of little tasks, lacked the strength to carry blocks and for the most part, played at whatever pleased him. Stephen took chances. He was the first to be told off for walking on the bridge parapets.

"Get down!" Jan shouted urgently.

He stepped off unhurriedly, oblivious to the peril.

"Isn't he brave?" Sharon whispered, standing near her mother.

"No. Just too stupid to know that it's dangerous!" Christopher murmured, more sagely.

Jan nodded, "That's not far wrong, but he's young, still needs to develop a proper sense of risk."

Crouched over a line of pipes, kneeling awkwardly in the narrow trench, Gordon forced in another twist of tarred rope before filling the joint with cement. Christopher, the next length of pipe ready in his hands, squatted at the trench edge watching intently. Not far away Sharon helped Jan carry concrete blocks for laying next day, leaving Stephen to his own devices.

Aaaagh! A sudden scream rent the air!

Actions froze in mid-movement as breaths were drawn in and heads turned... a split second later, blocks, Christopher's length of pipe, the trowel, all were sharply dropped as feet raced towards the source of the shriek.

Stephen, wearing only shorts, lay face down and very still beside a tall pile of building blocks that he had obviously been climbing. Several fallen blocks lay around the unmoving body, blood streaming from a wound on his back.

Jan reached him first, dropping to her knees beside his still form. Her heart that had skipped a beat at the scream, now pounded strongly, more from fear than from the short dash to his side. The long gash, blood spreading and trickling down, but most of all the absolute stillness of the small body, all this drew the sudden horrible thought that his spine was damaged. She slid her hands under his head and he moaned. Her concern heightened.

As he struggled to rise, a great sigh of relief escaped her lips but blood welled up in increasing volume from the wound. She glanced up at the family gathered close, her eyes bright with unshed tears.

Apart from his first loud cry, Stephen didn't yell and wail as many children do, but remained quiet and suppressed, saying nothing. He had behaved like this before when hurt. Animals react to injury in the same way; hiding, lying still, stoically enduring the pain and waiting for recovery, trying not to draw attention to themselves in their weakened state.

Knowing him as they did, his quietness was far from reassuring. The wound looked bad, needing medical attention, and quickly! After one glance Gordon rushed to the caravan for something to wrap him in, returning speedily. Pressing a large clean towel tightly over the laceration, together they wrapped him in a blanket. Carefully Gordon lifted the injured but still quiet boy, following Jan to the Mini van and as she slid in, placed him gently on her lap.

"Use up the cement if you can," he yelled to Christopher, then jumped into the driver's seat and set off to Penzance hospital. Torn between the opposing desires of speed and smoothness, he forced aside the former, driving slowly enough not to jolt the injured boy unnecessarily, particularly along that still rough track leading to the main road. Their route led past the surgery at Marazion where the windows blazed with light. They stopped and dashed in, asking whether to drive straight on to hospital or bring Stephen into the surgery.

"Bring him in, a doctor will see him straight away."

As Gordon carried the small figure into the building, blood soaking through had spread across the blanket. Jan's blouse was stained with red and they still wore grubby working clothes and boots but neither noticed, concern for their son dominating all thoughts.

A doctor appeared quickly to clean the wound, probing the jagged torn flesh but the bleeding had eased. He thought butterfly plasters preferable to stitches on one so young and applied fifteen down Stephen's back, covering the torn skin with a large dressing.

Darkness met them on leaving the surgery. In spite of prompt attention, the repair job and accompanying medical check had taken time. Jan, usually good in a crisis but already feeling slightly sick with concern over Stephen, now worried about the other children. They had never been left on their own after darkness fell. Her anxiety proved groundless. After a careful and slow drive, they arrived home to find Sharon had prepared the children's beds, lit the gas light and boiled the kettle for coffee. Christopher had finished the cement on a near perfect drain run, washed all the tools and generally cleaned up. He was not yet nine and Sharon still only seven! Both were concerned about Stephen, but obviously pleased with themselves. Jan hugged them in delight, deeply thankful to have the family still together. She lifted Stephen, easing herself back onto the bench seat and arranged him on her lap. He lay back, slightly skewed, shoulder against her chest, head nodding sideways resting above one bosom, her hand lightly supporting the back of his neck well clear of the damaged area. It was a measure of his shaken confidence that he stayed clinging to her rather than struggling to get down as he normally would.

Sharon placed coffee on the table as Christopher, having put the tools away, came through the doorway. Gordon, standing to one side, indicated with nods of approval how proud he felt of them.

Stephen's back healed as the young usually heal – very quickly. Even so, he had slept on his side and been stiff for many days. A long scar that might well be permanent, still remained vividly clear on his back. The experience certainly taught him more caution around the site, though Jan had doubts as to its lasting effect.

* * *

Gordon's mother and father, Frank and Ivy, were coming for the first time; just a short visit. They planned to stay at the same bed and breakfast used by Jim and Audrey.

Jan viewed this pending event with less concern than that felt for the arrival of her own parents many weeks ago. Sitting discussing the matter one lunchtime, she showed none of the apprehension that had hung like a shadow before Jim and Audrey's visit. Her manner was easy and relaxed.

"Things have changed quite a lot. You don't think about it now we've had this caravan for a while, but there's lots more room. I know the children still won't be able to sit at the table with your Mum and Dad, but they can sit on the other benches rather than on the floor. There's running water too, to wash their hands; the old bucket on the bench outside has gone. I know we still have the chemical toilet, but at least it's hidden and under cover, not close to the door like it was at first. I feel quite a bit better about everything."

Ivy and Frank arrived mid-morning, wanting to see

the children of course. Ivy complained that if they waited until someone brought the youngsters to Buckinghamshire, they might wait forever, which was untrue or at any rate slightly exaggerated. Stephen dashed from one to the other during coffee, then dragged Frank off to watch fish from the bridge, pulling him back again almost immediately to look at the digger. Having persuaded Gordon to lift him high in the bucket, he waved from above and when lowered again, tried to drag Ivy in for a repeat performance but she absolutely refused.

Jan and Gordon, knowing that curiosity had been partly responsible for the visit, conducted them with a certain pride on a site tour. Explaining intentions as well as showing work already done, the little group made their way eventually back to the caravan for lunch.

Asked his opinion on the site, Frank shook his head doubtfully. "I can see a hell of a lot of work."

However, both agreed they liked it; if only it wasn't so far away.

Arriving home from school, Christopher and Sharon led them off again, guiding none-too-willing grandparents into other less accessible places. Gordon, as he had on and off throughout the day, returned again to laying more concrete blocks.

Neither chicken nor any other meat had appeared on special that week, so Jan prepared potatoes, thin slices of luncheon meat and vegetables, a cheap meal that figured only too frequently on the family menu.

"In any case," Gordon said, "it won't hurt Mum to know how we normally live."

That had been a misjudgement. Being an exceptional cook herself, Ivy was not impressed! Never having been short of good food in her life, or at any rate, not in the past twenty years to Gordon's certain knowledge, she expected a big spread as a welcome, and looked with obvious disapproval at the meal.

"Think yourself lucky, we usually eat midday. Do you remember," Gordon asked, "telling me how not long after you were married, the pair of you sat by a canal near Aylesbury, eating sandwiches rather than pay for a meal? Well, luncheon meat and mash by the river can't be that much worse! Wait until next year. If we have a good season, Jan will show you the best meal anyone could ever expect from two gas rings!" The promise was given with more confidence than he actually felt.

The grandparents stayed late. With work continuing during daylight, evenings were the best times, with all the children home from school. Only after dark did the family relax together and enjoy each other's company. What a difference that roaring stove had made to the caravan atmosphere. As they left on the first evening, Ivy paused before reaching the car, looking up towards the dark, now invisible, valley sides. Pivoting slowly round, not another light could she see anywhere. The children, chattering away, became suddenly quiet and unsure. What had she heard? Only water sounds from the river, magnified in the silence, reached them. A solitary owl hooted.

"How can you live in such a lonely forsaken place?" Ivy asked in a whisper, pulling the coat closer around her shoulders.

The pleasant two-day visit passed quickly, no sooner started than ended it seemed, as they were off again driving away up the still rough track and waving.

"Well, that's all the parents been to inspect." Jan commented as they turned to the caravan, "Your Mum's fun, so full of energy, but at least they're not planning to live here too. I don't think they liked it quite as much as Jim and Audrey."

"Maybe. But you're Audrey's only child, naturally she wants to be near you. I've a sister. She's not bright or good-looking like me of course, so Mum probably needs to stay close to where she lives to keep an eye on her."

Jan looked at him, eyebrows raised, grinning.

"Must get my ears tested; could have sworn I heard *bright and good-looking*! Is that bright like the gas lamp when the mantle's broken, and good-looking like a fresh cow pat to a horsefly?"

While Jan looked after the home, simultaneously managing almost a full day's manual work, Gordon continued laying blocks from first light until darkness fell, seething with frustration at the contracting length of daylight. Wall heights increased daily, the corners always a few courses ahead. Little galvanised wall ties regularly spanned the two-inch cavity connecting both leaves of the wall together, all at the correct spacing, with extra ones next to each solidly built-in window or door frame, right alongside the vertical damp course. The complex web of under-floor drainage was also now complete. Every loving care had been lavished on the building. Nowhere was quality sacrificed for speed, in spite of the urgent need for progress.

In some respects but not all, family enthusiasm grew with the building. Jan mixed cement in batches throughout the day, and each evening, with Christopher and Sharon's help, great numbers of building blocks were moved from untidy heaps where the latest lorry load had been tipped. All were piled in neat stacks outside and inside the building, within easy reach for

Gordon to grab as he built extra courses next day. This work on the children's part was seldom entirely voluntary, but the family motto, "Everyone eats, everyone works," which had applied since arrival, led them to expect no less. Though they would not have wished to be left out, fewer blocks might have been welcome.

"Look!" Jan called one evening as they appeared walking down the track after school. "They've seen the new pile that arrived today. Weeks ago it would have had them running, now they've actually slowed down."

Stephen helped less, unable yet to carry anything but smaller broken pieces, but his turn would no doubt come.

Although these facilities were primarily for visitors, the family themselves keenly anticipated use of both flush toilets and hot showers. Each layer of blocks, each window, each doorway, was seen by the children as a step towards this end; their partiality for concrete blocks might be at a low ebb, but anticipation of proper facilities burgeoned with the building.

There remained the lintels to fix – those concrete beams over doors and windows. After that, only two courses of blockwork above and gable ends to build before starting the roof. These lintels were home-made, Gordon insisted they were not only cheaper, but stronger and better than bought ones; the only disadvantage, they would be heavier. Over the previous weekend he had shown Christopher how to make wooden moulds to pour the concrete in, and where to place steel bars for proper strength. They had cast these beams early since each one took a minimum of seven days to harden properly. However, the final blockwork courses went so well that lintel level was reached two days before they had sufficiently hardened, causing a delay. He had intended to drop back onto clearing work while waiting, but another caravan advertised in the local paper caught Jan's attention.

"This could be just the one for Jim. I know you don't want to stop working but you'll have to some time, it might as well be now. You're held up anyway."

She was right, of course, now was the ideal time to look. Reluctantly he agreed. Jim's bad leg and more particularly the blank cheque he left, meant that only a bigger caravan in fairly good condition would fit the purpose. The one advertised measured forty feet and was sited near Helston. Arriving, Jan looked it over, holding Stephen by the hand, ignoring his struggles to escape, knowing too well his tendency to dash off, impervious to any sense of danger.

She recalled when over a year earlier at their old home he had suddenly disappeared, putting everyone in a flap. Eventually the boy, not yet three at that time, was sighted. A hundred yards away across the main road, lived a gander. This belligerent old bird, having chased off women, children and even some men, had been caged for its troubles and for everyone's peace of mind. Stephen had somehow entered the pen and was sitting unconcerned with the gander who tolerated him as if he belonged. The lad had been totally unafraid, the secret of his success maybe, but only one person had been prepared to enter and bring him out. Jan looked down, gripping the small hand more tightly.

The caravan, in decent condition but far from new, looked suitable. Its central heating promised help for Jim's joints, though a radiator in the double bedroom at the end of a narrow corridor offered virtually no chance of working effectively. A small empty room that could have taken a narrow bed also opened off this corridor. In the other direction a central kitchen led to a lounge with French windows opening onto a balcony. Gordon crawled underneath, scratching around for a bit, then emerged to confirm that though it showed signs of age, there was no rot and the inevitable rusting had not weakened the chassis. It was claimed to be only seven or eight years old and after some bargaining, cost two hundred and sixty pounds, delivery included.

Because of those not quite hardened lintels, the afternoon and following morning Gordon spent clearing and filling. Happily he renewed acquaintance with Robin and Blackbird who had visited only occasionally during building work in spite of his habit of carrying bread-crumbs in one pocket.

Shortly after lunch the following day Jim's caravan arrived right on time, exactly as agreed with the seller. Levelling up, connecting mains water and Calor gas, took less than two hours, making it habitable before the children came home. About four o'clock they stormed breathlessly down the road, a normal occurrence when anything new had appeared. Both stood for a moment, recovering, looking at the side with the door before running round in a tight circle, jumping up to peer in various windows, then rushing again to where their parents and Stephen stood waiting.

"It's huge!" Christopher sounded pleased, a touch of wistfulness in his voice.

"Why does Gramp have a caravan so much bigger than ours for only two people?" Sharon's jealousy showed more clearly.

"He's got more money."

Dad's explanation was simple, and readily accepted without resentment – they understood money but a touch of that envy remained.

"Can we go inside?" Christopher asked.

Receiving a nod they dashed back to enter the caravan, followed by Stephen, short legs pumping to keep up.

"Here we go again!" Gordon held out a hand, palm upwards. "I told you space is relative. Last week our caravan was luxury – now Jim has a bigger one, ours is only second best. They've already half forgotten the little tourer we managed in a few weeks ago."

Blockwork to the new toilets neared completion, the lintels having somehow been erected using a method of working likely to give any good safety inspector apoplexy. It was always known that lifting them would be difficult with only three planks and two trestles as scaffolding. These were used for the entire building and required moving each time a new section of wall was worked on.

The largest lintels, those over the high windows in the gable walls weighed nearly three hundredweight each. They were lifted in stages, first onto two planks, then up again onto the final one, and from there to over the windows almost twelve feet off the ground. The owner of Jim's bed and breakfast house who had called in, stayed for the morning to help hoist them up.

There now remained the gable tops and one course all round to reach roof-level, but the inside walls to shower and toilet compartments lagged well behind, needing considerable work to raise them to the proper height. This final blockwork would be slower, entailing much checking to ensure these internal partitions were exactly upright, ready to receive the door frames later.

With the last pile of blocks now exhausted, it became

necessary to take some of those surrounding the outside loo. At first it was still possible to use this facility, just the roof and the top layers having disappeared. As the next few days progressed the stack gradually lowered and a person could gaze around at the landscape while sitting on the throne, a 360-degree view, clear vision for at least a hundred yards to the closest cover. It was quite a novel experience. Fortunately no one using the footpath could see more than a head projecting above the surrounding blocks and even that could be hidden by bending over horizontally. However as each layer was removed the situation became increasingly embarrassing.

When the bucket had been in the awning, at least it was only visible from the northeast. Now the user could be seen from both directions along the river, from all the rising valley sides and even from the farther hills. One could imagine the comments of some distant bird watcher with powerful binoculars.

"Hello, hello, what have we here? Never seen one of those before!"

As the stack diminished, now below waist level, something had to be done! Gordon carried the bucket over to the new toilet building, placing it inside one of the cubicles that would later take proper toilets. Even though there were no doors and no roof, this worked fine except for a very wet seat one morning after a shower of rain.

Sharon tried to avoid leaving the caravan after dark. Christopher increased her apprehension by saying how spooky the building became at night. It was not all bluff, he had looked less than normally confident when returning from his own first evening visit. Little Stephen had never actually made the journey on his own at night, Mum or Dad always accompanying him, though he did once venture alone a dozen paces in the dark. After a particularly tiring day when neither parent felt inclined to move, he had asked to go. Jan looked across at Gordon, who declined with a small shake of the head. Turning back to Stephen she offered a suggestion.

"Go water the nearest bush."

He had stood for a moment, puzzled. Slowly a smile spread across the small face. Jaw set, chin tilted up, he left slamming the door as usual, to reappear some minutes later, his expression decidedly less self-assured.

Nevertheless, he now followed Christopher's lead with remarks on the blackness and noises in the night.

The first time Sharon needed to use the loo after dark, she carried the hurricane lamp to light her path, returning after a while at a canter. Bursting hurriedly back into the caravan, she tried to speak, gasping and struggling to recover her breath.

"It *is* real creepy! I don't like the way you can't see what's in the other compartments... especially just as you reach the main doorway and have to walk into the blackness. All those spooky shadows! Anything could be hiding there!"

Jan noticed she said 'anything' rather than 'anyone'. It did feel a bit like that. The whole area lay so quiet and isolated at night. Entering the unlit, half-complete structure with rows of doorless dark cubicles and no roof, it must have been frightening for a seven year-old girl. The building lay just under a hundred yards from where the family and caravan waited, the route passing several dense clumps of trees and bushes.

Seeing a small shiver pass through her daughter's body, Jan thought back a few days to her own first trip. The unfinished building had stood, a derelict hulk dimly visible against the night sky as she approached. At the doorway the swinging lamp threw moving shadows on bare block walls, highlighting nearer surfaces, casting farther recesses into deep gloom. She had to force herself to step inside, cold fingers of fear running down her spine, almost like some hidden hand reaching out to touch her. Sitting there, she heard the faint sound of wind in the silence, then a sudden night noise of unknown origin. She had kept her eyes rigidly on the opening ahead, frighteningly aware that anything *could* be hidden just beyond the blockwork, waiting... An opening she must pass through to regain – she had almost thought freedom – but just to regain the outside air.

She left, hurriedly glancing at the other dark compartments, bursting through the invisible barrier of that open doorway into the night air beyond, then quickly on towards the caravan. Passing some low bushy trees, something scuttled away in the fallen autumn leaves. "A rabbit? Yes it must be a rabbit, or..." She moved even faster, almost in a run, and rounding a taller tree felt the hairs on her neck rise at a brief unexpected glimpse of shadowy branches overhead just visible in the lamp's glow, then rocketed across open ground towards sanctuary in the gas-lit caravan beyond.

Jan shook her head, clearing the memories from her mind, turning again to watch Sharon, now sitting very close to the stove, the young girl trying to remove a chill that might not be just coldness.

"Even I felt the urge to keep glancing over my shoulder," she thought. "Thank goodness we can't watch television; none of us except Gordon would walk across there after a film about little green men."

CHAPTER 11

First Christmas

Part of man's nature is never to be satisfied. Like cows in a field, the grass beyond the hedge is always greener. In earlier months when only clearing work was possible, a keen desire for planning permission to arrive had been at least partly to give some variety. Now building had started in earnest they longed for a simpler life again, with not quite so many jobs demanding attention. Blocklaying, foundations for the next building, casting lintels, building a septic tank, spreading topsoil ready for seeding next spring, the road surface, site signs, underground pipework, the list lengthened. Fortunately, the choice remained simple, at least it appeared to. The first toilet building took total precedence on two counts; one from sound logic, the other pandering to their own desires.

The logical reason, no visitors would come unless at least some facilities were working, and not just working but looking attractive. For that, the roof must be weatherproof and the rendering applied, and soon! No one knew how wet the winter might be or how long the unheated building would require for drying out before decoration could be applied.

The second factor, sheer self-indulgence, hinged on a collective family desire, and particularly from Sharon, to have a proper loo. Even more she wanted a hot shower instead of the weekly wash-down in the tiny bath, or worse, in the river! Jan found the little tin bath restricting. It had proved far more difficult than expected to wash the children thoroughly as they stood in it, and even more so for herself. No matter how carefully she tried, the caravan carpet and wooden floor beneath became saturated after every use, which must eventually soften and rot the floor.

Because of these problems, Jan often preferred the old method in the river, in spite of approaching winter. Cornwall, and particularly Relubbus, might be warmer than the rest of the country most of the time, but that didn't prevent a person feeling a drop in temperature. Certainly it could not stop the children shivering when plunging naked into the cool clear waters of a spring-fed stream on an unusually chilly October day, with the wind whistling round those parts normally hidden snugly inside warm clothing! In the mind of everyone except Stephen, that first building symbolised a promise of comfort to come; a dream! Nothing should be allowed to delay it. Gordon could hardly be surprised then, when his popularity took a nose-dive.

"Tell them," Jan suggested with an unfriendly stare, "about the phone call."

The three children seated round the table stopped eating, looking from one parent to the other. Gordon breathed deeply, speaking with a shrug of resignation.

"There's a hold-up. Our roof timbers won't be coming this week after all."

"Why?" Sharon's annoyance showed clearly.

Christopher's disappointment was less obvious and Stephen showed no concern. Gordon spread his hands in a gesture that in any language said "who knows?"

Not content to let the matter rest, Jan insisted, "Tell her why – the real reason!"

"OK." Gordon's response held a defensive '*if I must*' quality to which she nodded decisively as he continued.

"They say there's a technical fault at the tanalizing works. That's where they put the timber in a vacuum chamber, suck out the moisture, then pump in fungicidal liquid under pressure. It stops timber going rotten."

Sharon's frown of annoyance only increased, but Christopher nodded understanding. Jan however, was not yet satisfied.

"If we had ordinary timber like everyone else, it would be here now. Who was it made the decision to have the stuff treated in the first place?"

The accusation was clear. Three small heads turned back to regard Dad with suspicion. He faced their looks of censure with seriousness.

"Timber treatment is important. If all timber was treated, less trees would need to be felled. In our case it will mean that these roofs will last for as long as we live; none of it will ever decay or need replacing. That often happens you know, with untreated roofs."

Doubt showed in the children's faces. With the possible exception of Stephen, they understood these arguments but also sensed that their parents disagreed, a rare event. Seldom did any of the youngsters become involved in such differences of opinion. It forced them to think, to try to decide; showed them perhaps that right and wrong was not always so clear cut.

Jan watched for a while before leaning forward, a slightly Machiavellian smile on her lips.

"Treated timber costs more!" she whispered.

Sharon strangled a gasp as she looked at Dad in incredulous accusation. Christopher and Stephen's eyes both widened at the dreadful revelation! Few crimes in the family rated worse than wasting money! Doing so and simultaneously causing a delay in the long-awaited new facilities put Dad inescapably in the wrong.

Jan slapped one hand lightly on the table, turning to Gordon with a grin of triumph, then swinging back towards the children, her smile broadening.

"Never mind, I expect he meant well. Just not very bright at times." She spoke with a touch of condescension. "Don't worry, plenty of other jobs to do. Keep an eye on him though; make sure he's not slacking!"

What for a few minutes looked like a serious rift, had turned quickly into a huge joke at Dad's expense. He didn't really mind, rarely had to defend himself, and as the children continued to eat and discuss other matters, he answered automatically, paying little attention, already arranging those alternative jobs in his mind. For a start, two days of that week could be well spent on the half finished area that looked so untidy. By quietly approaching lorry drivers at certain local building developments, they had already accumulated a dozen piles of good topsoil; not nearly enough, but at least a start.

"Work's a funny thing," he thought, while shovelling the following morning. "When I had no other option, clearing seemed tedious. Now, when work should really start on the second building's foundations, the two days I intend to spend finishing this area feels like a holiday, stolen almost. How many thousand blocks have I laid over the past weeks?"

He looked down at cracked fingertips, effects from both cement and blocks, a combination of chemical attack and abrasion. The soreness became so bad he had started wearing rubber gloves regularly for building.

"I could go off concrete blocks for life!"

Now spreading soil, he worked bare-handed again, thankful for the chance. As always when the ground was being disturbed, Robin came flying up, soon joined by Blackbird. He talked to them a lot, and particularly that afternoon, having returning from lunch totally in the doghouse with Jan. Working with the land again felt so good he even sang as he toiled, thinking how tolerant birds were, wondering if they had any sense of music, admitting ruefully they were unlikely to gain it here. He had forgotten the time and rushed back thirty minutes late for the meal. Stephen had disappeared, having eaten already and gone off to play. The food was largely spoiled.

"It's not easy to keep things hot with only two gas rings, you should come on time!" she said, lips tightly compressed, face unsmiling.

The excuse of reaching a tricky stage in the work received an icy look. He knew it would be unwise, but Jan was so difficult to annoy normally that he couldn't resist. Perhaps it was the way her angry eyes sparkled, or the hollows of those indrawn cheeks? Whatever, something drove him to pass little comments during the otherwise frosty silence of the meal, half to himself but intended for Jan.

"Prefer my sausages less crispy round the edge," and later, "Are these really peas or airgun pellets in disguise?"

She said nothing, but steam issued from her nostrils. There is a point, he told himself, when even the brave call a halt. It seemed sensible to shut up, finish anything at all edible and quickly return to work.

Saying as he slipped through the door, "I hope coffee will be on time," was another mistake!

The remains of the meal whistled past his ear less

221

than five paces from the caravan. They were still on the plate! He felt the wind as it passed, to smash in tiny shards on the stony ground and would have done the same on his head if Jan's aim had been better.

He turned, speaking softly, as to a naughty child. "Temper, temper," and would have patted her head if he dared go back within reach. Seeing the explosive intake of breath, the knuckles of her small hand whiten where she gripped the caravan doorway, he beat a hasty retreat while still in one piece. Plates, after all, were expensive!

Mid-afternoon, shortly after Robin had located and tugged free a small worm returning with it to his perch, Jan appeared in the distance carrying coffee. Gordon, working on happily for the past two and a half hours, reliving his success in arousing a normally unflappable wife, was half surprised to get coffee at all and a little apprehensive.

As she approached dressed in a bright red anorak he quickly warned Robin to watch out, explaining her lunchtime eruption and unreasonable behaviour.

Robin replied *"Well, what do you expect? They're bound to get ideas above their station if you let them wear red that bright!"*

At least Gordon thought the bird said it. It was so clear. Perhaps he *had* been working alone too long.

During autumn the old ten-foot tourer that had been advertised for the second time, finally went. Jan sold it on her own one morning with the children at school and their father away at some meeting on the design of Jim's intended new bungalow at the site entrance.

Having washed and waxed it with Christopher's help the weekend before, she was rewarded with a bundle of crisp notes, £65, five pounds more than the twenty-two foot caravan had cost – a salutary lesson in economics. It's not what a thing is worth; what matters is who wants it! Nobody had wanted the twenty-two foot, it couldn't be towed behind a normal car. The small tourer was different, almost any car could tow that!

Later, when Gordon arrived back she said nothing, waiting, but he failed to notice. Changing into working clothes, he pecked her on one cheek in a perfunctory manner on his way out, rushing off to catch up with work. She watched him go, seeing the determined look on his face.

"If I ducked my head at that vital moment, would he have kissed the door-post instead?" she wondered. "Bet he wouldn't even notice!"

Stephen had seen the little tourer go, but failed to see any significance in its disappearance. Jan continued to say nothing, smiling to herself with pleasure; someone would notice sooner or later. She could wait, in fact she relished it!

Christopher was first to twig, at tea with everyone seated and waiting for Jan to put food on the table. Looking idly out into the dusk he missed the familiar dark outline. "Where's the little tourer?"

Dad and Sharon swung to stare in the same direction. Stephen, knowing what had happened, looked towards Jan, but she put a finger to her lips warning him not to speak.

Having scanned the yard and finding nothing, three faces turned again as Jan, carrying coffee, stepped back to the table.

"I sold it," she said, setting the two cups down.

No emphasis, so casual, the most normal thing in the world. She reached round to pour more coffee, leaving them looking at her back, unable to see her grin of satisfaction. Struggling for control she pivoted slowly round with two more coffees, face now impassive, to find three pairs of eyes staring at her.

Depositing these cups on the table, she made to swing back again but a strong hand grasped one wrist, detaining her.

"Well?"

"Well what, dear?" She was having a terrible job to retain a neutral expression.

"Mum!" Sharon cut in, but the eyes of her parents were locked, a ghost of a smile on both faces. Seconds passed, Jan strained not to give way, waiting.

"Well, how much?"

She relaxed, smiling broadly, the exact words she knew he would say. He was smiling too; how well they understood each other. Another man might have said "How clever," but it didn't matter, she had won – he had spoken first!

Reaching over with her free arm, she flicked off the lid of a tin on the side cupboard, lifted the small bundle from within, then swung back scattering a handful of five-pound notes across the table with a flourish.

The tourer sale represented a minor triumph, an ego-boosting increase in funds, something talked about over coffee for days, basking in the glow of success. However, they were not out of the wood yet. This extra money might aid survival until spring but it would never last another year. The site still *must* be open for business in only a few months.

Everything hung finely balanced; the time until opening, money to finish the job, and even perhaps the physical stamina to continue. But they had paid their bills, bought all the machinery – plus many building materials, and owed nobody anything. Enough remained in the account not only for final materials, but to pay plasterers who would apply cement finishes to walls and floors, inside and out. At least, calculations indicated it would be enough if all went to plan, provided the plasterers didn't take too many hours and nobody ate too much!

Life in the valley remained good, the family were happy, ever optimistic, laughing a lot at their brief meal-time meetings. Only Gordon, working almost non-stop, would occasionally sit quietly reticent of an evening, haunted by a lingering apprehension. The idea of failure, of letting the family down, kept entering his mind, recurring unbidden at odd unguarded moments, much as he tried to dismiss these thoughts completely.

November approached, the working day still dimin-ishing. Darkness offered timely relief to tired muscles, yet simultaneously it caused renewed frustration. So much needed doing but no way to do it, no way to continue once night fell. He could not see to build and even though the tractor had lights, danger prohibited working by them alone to load stone when those little telltale signs indicating an imminent rock-fall would be hidden. He did use the tractor lights for short spells on one or two evenings as illumination to saw wood for the boiler. These logs lay where they fell; later the boys would stack them under the caravan to dry.

Generally, evenings were for reading, for fun with the children, for chatting and planning the work ahead. Sometimes they played simple card games together, but often both parents read while the children played on the floor. Jan noticed as days continually shortened, that

225

Gordon, although he needed the respite, increasingly exhibited periods of restlessness, looking into space or drumming fingers on the table, completely unable to concentrate on the book before him. Did he feel guilty sitting in the caravan unable to do anything useful, she wondered? He must realise the short days were not his fault? At such times his mood could turn sombre and withdrawn, even on rare occasions becoming intolerant of small transgressions by the children.

There was no television to watch and they missed the daily newspapers, but did take the local weekly, *The Cornishman*, to keep abreast of neighbouring events and for the small ads. It was here that Jan spotted an article concerning a forthcoming series of evening talks on the history of Cornish mining at the Technical College in Camborne.

"That's what he needs, to mix with people, have his mind diverted to something else, if only for a while! But how can I persuade him to go?"

She considered the problem. Visitors would expect them to know the area's history, would ask about it from time to time. Was that enough? She must be careful, emphasise the advantages, a little honest exaggeration.

"Admit it," she corrected herself, "when you say honest exaggeration, what you really mean is dishonest deception, a little lie. Can you deceive your husband like that?" She paused, considering for a while... "Of course you can; you're a woman, aren't you?"

That little battle of conscience over, putting qualms aside and warning herself to be subtle, Jan determined to try. Having mentioned the lectures one evening and detecting a flicker of interest she started.

"If we're to live here the rest of our lives, we ought to learn more local history." She hesitated, turning to the children for approval, confident of gaining support. When they nodded, she continued, "Our holiday visitors are bound to ask about those old derelict engine-houses with their tall chimneys. We ought to know. It would add interest to their holidays, persuade them to stay longer, perhaps to come back the following year."

He was nodding thoughtfully; she changed tack.

"You might meet interesting people, even find out more about the mine that produced our own waste heaps." She paused again, giving the ideas a chance to take hold, before adding casually, "What else can you usefully do on these dark evenings?"

In that final sentence, *'what else can you do?'*, there lay the crux of the matter. She knew it to be the clinching argument. No more need be said; he would go.

In truth, they knew little of Wheal Virgin, whose stony waste was absorbing so much of their time. It was said to be neither a prosperous nor an extensive system. Had it been created, as many were at that time, merely to draw money from financial backers before going bust, a South West, rather than a South Sea, Bubble? Probably not, if the size of the waste heaps was any guide.

The lectures discussed great men of that era, the structure of command in the mines, with the Mine Captain at the head, his powers sweeping and final, with no appeal; powers like a sea captain's, almost of life or death. Many miners worked on a freelance basis, paid solely by the amount of ore raised. Few lived above fifty, dust affecting their lungs. Speakers talked of transport systems from mines to docks, of washing wastes on great flat tables to separate tin residues, and about the stamps, a series of enormous hammers for pounding and crushing ore, often driven by waterwheels. Muscular women known as Bal-maidens, shovelled the ore to and from these stamps.

"I wonder," his mind wandered off while listening, "how many real maidens lived in those mining camps, even at Wheal Virgin."

The copper ore was transported by ship to Wales (Cornwall had no fuel for smelting) and on the return journey these ships were laden with Welsh coal for making steam to drive the mine engines. Stories were still heard today, handed down through the generations, of how those Welsh robbers never gave fair money for the ore and charged ridiculous prices for their mucky coal.

"Did they say the same about the Cornish, or were they proud of being sharper businessmen?" Gordon wondered. "Never mind, we got our own back. We grow better daffodils!"

He passed the information to Jan and the children, it gave an extra topic for talk in the evenings after Christopher and Sharon finished telling of their day at school and completed any homework.

Later, the older two read while Stephen liked to look at the pictures or draw, all suddenly abandoning their books to play together again. Naturally, in time an argument burst forth on who had won, who had cheated, or some other terribly important matter of absolutely no true consequence whatsoever, but having very real, if short-lived, concern to the youngsters.

Children's arguments, like politicians', tend to have a momentum of their own, each striving to win, with no regard to truth or merits of the case, and certainly no one listening to the other's point of view!

***

The roof timbers were late again. Gordon had cast the concrete lintels for the second building, determined this time they should not create a delay, then started the foundations, dropping back onto clearing while waiting for the council's surveyor to make his inspection. At Jan's request, vegetation cleared over the last month had not been burned, but saved for the coming Bonfire Night.

The inspector passed the foundations midmorning on the fourth. Gordon watched him drive away and headed back to the caravan to make an urgent phone call. Before he could lift the receiver, Jan spoke.

"You do realise the special significance tomorrow has?"

"Yes. It's Bonfire Night."

"It's more than that. Tomorrow is November the fifth – five months exactly since we arrived here! Well five months and three days. It calls for a celebration!"

He shook his head, immediately on the defensive.

"I've come in to order Readymix. I must concrete those foundations before any of the sides fall in. It's no good you asking me to take tomorrow off."

"You don't need to. The children will want the bonfire after dark anyway. But you know what would be nice... if we could go out Sunday afternoon. Since the earlier evenings started to set in, you've worked every single Sunday. How about it?"

"We had half a day off early in September. Some women are never satisfied."

The good weather held, with a morning fine and dry. Before nine the concrete lorry arrived and two hours later they walked back to the caravan together, both drenched in sweat in spite of the lower temperature but pleased with the result of their efforts. They sat long over coffee; that was the great thing about really hard work – so good to relax afterwards! Jan again broached the question of Sunday, to which last time she had received no definite answer. She knew after the help just given with concreting, he could scarcely refuse her wish. This was the time to pounce! As she guessed, he reluctantly nodded agreement. Yes okay, they would go out Sunday.

Talk turned to the coming evening. There would be no fireworks, too expensive, but they had flares, plastic bags containing screwed up newspaper soaked in old oil saved after servicing the digger. Christopher and Dad prepared them in secret without Stephen's knowledge.

The weather held and just after dark on a fine, wind free evening, the bonfire ignited with no problem. This was a night for gathering and celebration. Here however, they watched alone, just the five still isolated in the valley, observed no doubt by other pairs of eyes, but none of them human.

The flames caught hold, rising vertically with more moderate intensity, the materials less dry and crisp than that bonfire made earlier in the year. A ring of warm flickering brightness edged its way outwards as the fire's ferocity grew. Half faces glowed in the warmly red light, sides away from the flames cut off, disappearing then reappearing as they turned in excitement this way and that, laughing, shouting to each other, ignoring the dense blackness lurking beyond.

Thrown into the fire from a distance, the flares were only moderately successful, a quick whoosh of flame, hardly worth the effort but better than nothing; sufficient to illuminate for a second the dark coppery foliage of more distant trees. Stephen found throwing difficult until adding small stones gave weight to each plastic bag. The dry vegetation soon burned down and Sharon, with minimal help from Jan, roasted potatoes in the hot ashes, some foil wrapped others just in their skins, all pushed between fading embers. In a predictable effort to belittle her ability, the boys loudly suggested at intervals that the potatoes were ready, would burn, would be charred to a cinder. To their disappointment, for once Sharon refused to rise, brushing the comments aside and ignoring their advice.

"I'll know when they're done. You keep out of it."

After a time she fished charred-looking remains from the embers into a pan, then back to the caravan. Some were partially burnt, a few slightly underdone, bound to happen in a bonfire, but most were close to perfect.

Jan cut them open one at a time, keeping others warm on the stove top, mashing the insides with a knob of butter, some salt and pepper. They were excellent. Both boys had second helpings in spite of continuing critical remarks. While eating Jan laid a map of the area before the children, ignoring Dad and discussing where to go for that coming Sunday afternoon, craftily forestalling any chance of him changing his mind.

Over the following two days Gordon pushed on laying blockwork above the second building foundations up to floor level, leaving gaps where drainage pipes would pass. The network of under-floor pipes, laid out on a fine stone bed, needed exact positioning. An outlet must rise through the floor for each of the ten toilets, with absolutely no possibility of altering the position later, short of cutting up the floor. Though not available all the time, Jan continued to help, intermittently mixing cement, carrying blocks and pipes, and later driving the excavator to fetch bucket-loads of stone. Working together in this way, apart from the companionship, produced better progress.

Sunday dawned overcast. By mid-morning light drizzle fell. Gordon pushed on regardless, but Jan, not really able to help at that particular stage, remained inside with the children. After a while the rain's intensity increased and he returned to the caravan.

"Don't I have waterproofs hanging somewhere?"

Opening the wardrobe, Jan rummaged about inside, eventually passing the bottoms. Three young heads that had looked up from the table when he came in, returned to their game. Searching again she extricated the waterproof top holding onto it while he struggled to tug on the trousers. Taking the jacket he pulled on one side, reaching round and sliding into the other sleeve.

Jan had half turned away when from the corner of one eye she saw him stiffen, jerk upright then struggle frantically, striving the pull the garment clear. Jumping back, she stood not understanding as he tugged at a sleeve that clung to the already damp jumper below, resisting removal. The children, their game forgotten, looked on in confusion. Sharon sat unmoving, her mouth slightly open; Christopher rose, backing away until hard against the window, only Stephen's face held a grin of expectation.

One arm came out, Gordon swung it round violently, scrabbling feverishly with the cuff of the other sleeve. He jerked suddenly again, eyes narrowing, wincing in pain and tore harder at the adhering garment, snatching the arm free.

Jan had no idea, no explanation for the erratic behaviour; the word 'What' formed on her lips but no sound issued forth as she saw a wave of relief cross his face.

Dropping the jacket he looked intently along his own right arm, particularly around the wrist, and finding nothing, turned to the family with a wry grimace of relief. Gingerly he took up the waterproof top and commenced carefully turning the sleeve inside out.

"Ah!" A look of triumph crossed his face as the large queen wasp, slow moving and sleepy, came into view. Crossing to the door, he flicked it through the opening with a spoon off the worktop, and continued to reverse the sleeve, carefully examining every inch for other assailants. The family watched... it was Sharon's turn to cringe back as two more emerged from the same sleeve, both of which were flicked carefully, still alive, through the doorway.

"No wonder he tried to rip off the top!" Jan thought, "Wasps aren't like bees, don't lose their sting. They can strike several times!"

The other sleeve came up empty, as did the rest of the interior. She crossed, reaching for his hand, pulling it to her, turning the arm towards the children. Two swellings showed red and angry near the right wrist.

"What made you set them free?" she looked in puzzlement at his face where a light-hearted smile now replaced his frantic expression of moments before.

"Not their fault. What would you do if someone squashed you?" He leaned forward to kiss her, winking at the children before donning the jacket again and leaving to continue work, pressing on, hoping to avoid the arm stiffening, as was prone to happen with stings, ignoring the rain now pelting down with some force.

Satisfied with the layout, he spread more stone placing it carefully around pipework on the Ladies side, before levelling off and compacting over the remaining area to form a solid base for the Ladies floor. This base would first be covered in plastic, both to prevent damp penetration and to avoid loss of cement grout from the wet concrete. Pipes that projected upwards would be temporarily stuffed with old newspaper and the plastic cut to fit round them.

He worked on through the afternoon, finishing as darkness approached. Jan had stayed with the children in the caravan, periodically looking at the sky, waiting, still hoping the rain would clear. No one mentioned that intended half-day break.

The following day saw completion of the stone base on the Gents side too, the entire floor now ready. When the concrete arrived, it was spread with Jan's help as before, working carefully to avoid knocking the projecting pipes. As always when handling a full lorry load, they returned for coffee drenched with sweat but happy.

Happiness however, did not extend to those roof timbers, which still had not arrived over two weeks after the already revised date. Calls to the builders' merchants produced only vague replies and promises with little confidence in the voice to suggest they would be kept.

Jan, with firm backing from the children, reminded Gordon on frequent occasions that it was he who had chosen to have the timber treated.

"But for that," she said, "the roof would be on by now and we'd have a dry toilet!"

Dad's popularity reached a new low each time the promised lorry failed to appear.

With drainage in both buildings finished and ready, all remaining pipework and inspection chambers, right up to the future septic tank could at last be finalised...

or should the remaining blockwork take priority? Decisions! The water main must be extended too, to serve both buildings. Everything needed doing and time was flying. Well... the drains and water pipe first, to get the trenches covered before Jan's parents arrived, the date of which remained uncertain.

As if there wasn't work enough already, a lorry carrying topsoil drove up looking for a place to tip. Another distraction! But such chances were too good to miss. "Sure, bring it all in." Load after load was dumped on a stony area. When the driver left for the final time, Gordon slipped a meagre tip into his hand, a little *beer money* in the hope of getting more another time. Common sense dictated that the soil be spread immediately, before rain came making it soggy and unworkable. Ah well, so be it. Three days later, work on the trenches resumed and still the roof timbers had not arrived.

Time rushed on, the final sewage chambers not quite complete when Jan's parents arrived on Saturday 20th December, giving themselves comfortable time to settle in before Christmas. They rolled up in their little car, a Hillman Imp, stacked to roof level with essentials, all the furniture and other possessions left in store until completion of their bungalow next year.

As the car covered those last few yards, the children cheered, hanging on and proudly pointing to the long caravan. While Jim struggled from the driving seat, they waited impatiently; eager to show the new abode and expecting both grandparents to be impressed since it was almost double the length of their own home.

Audrey and Jim, leaning on the little car, stretching and eyeing up the caravan for the first time, certainly regarded it in a less rosy light after living in a house. Smiling and nodding agreement to the children's plethora of favourable comments, their faces did not totally reflect a similar enthusiasm. Audrey was impressed however, with the balcony in front of the lounge, facing south with views along the valley and river.

Jim, more concerned at the steep steps, struggled to mount, managing with an effort, taking one at a time. Christopher's offer to make them longer but shallower with additional blocks and to start right away, was forestalled by a cry from Sharon.

"Presents!"

Naturally inquisitive, she had peered at the vehicle's contents, spotting parcels inside wrapped in Christmas paper and shouted her discovery aloud. Steps promptly forgotten, everyone carried inside some part of the car's copious load. A welcoming warmth radiated from the coal central heating boiler in the lounge. Audrey and Jim seated themselves, trying the small, rather Spartan armchairs with a sigh of relief after the long journey, Jim stretching aching legs out before him with a passing wince of pain. They sat talking to Jan as the children unloaded the remaining boxes and parcels.

Curiosity combined with prompting from Sharon leaving them little rest, they rose again to inspect the rest of their new domain. Audrey looked with approval at the kitchen adjoining the lounge. It sported a gas oven as well as rings and the sink had two taps, one giving hot water direct from the lounge boiler. Sharon reaching the sink first, demonstrated by leaving the tap running with her hands beneath in the just bearably hot water, a wistful look covering her face.

"I should turn it off or you'll lower the radiator temperature." Jan prompted mildly.

Part way along the corridor lay the small, box-like room. Audrey poked her head round the door to gaze at a brand new chemical toilet, bought a few days before.

"My Lord," she murmured. "Whoever thought we'd come down to a bucket."

Jim, a large rugged man, a one time army boxing champion, found the corridor narrow – partly due to his stiff leg. The end bedroom when they reached it, showed no hint of the lounge's warmth. Gordon had warned that being all on one level and without a pump, circulation would always be sluggish, so nothing could be done about the coldness, except perhaps hot water bottles.

Having seen all, Audrey sighed resignedly. "Never mind, it's not forever; just until our bungalow is built." She glanced across at her daughter's smaller more primitive caravan, "It could be worse."

Catching her mother's expression, Jan wondered momentarily about her own home; would she ever have another house? – but dismissed the thought. There were more immediate concerns. A little family difficulty had arisen about Christmas Day. She had already spoken to Gordon, insisting he take the whole day off.

"The whole day off!" he repeated. "That's decadent. Couldn't possibly."

They had crossed swords on this subject several times since, but all his reasonable arguments had been brushed aside by feminine illogic, or so he felt.

"We'll see later," he said in answer to her latest attempt, not admitting defeat but certainly not scoring a victory.

At last! In spite of renewed promises, they had almost given up hope of seeing anything before the Christmas break, but around mid-afternoon the lorry appeared. It bounced down the road, crossed the bridge with inches to spare and halted as the extended family gathered round to look.

The roof timbers had arrived!

Jim, reckoning himself good with a saw, volunteered to cut them up. "After all," he pointed out, "it's only my leg that's stiff, nothing wrong with my arms!" To prove it he would stretch out for any shoulder within reach and grip it powerfully enough to leave a bruise on anyone who failed to agree smartly.

A saw-bench was prepared using branches of a fire-damaged tree with a hollow rotting trunk. These branches were stripped, cut to length and fixed with the same four-inch nails intended for the roof. They went to work. Gordon marked while Jim cut. A two-foot steel square was the usual tool for marking angles and bevels on roof timbers. Some old carpenters were brilliant with them. Rumours in the trade suggested the best could use one to calculate next year's Grand National winner. Not having such a tool, they made do with a wooden ruler, using a child's protractor to measure the angles. As an extra precaution, the first two rafters were tried on the roof before the rest were cut, an insult to any top-class carpenter. However, considering the price of timber, humiliation was preferable to expense!

Having waited so long, and taken so many jibes from the family as a direct result of having the timber treated, Gordon brushed every newly sawn end liberally with timber preservative. At Jan's instigation, Christopher and Sharon regularly inspected these ends, hoping to find one missed. No doubt if they succeeded he would never live it down, and claims that the treatment could not have been necessary in the first place would have followed, but they never did find one!

Fixing the horizontal timber wall-plates on a bed of

cement along the top of the now complete external walls provided a solid level base to which the main roof timbers would later be fixed. This and other odd jobs took until Christmas Eve. That evening, with everything ready to pitch the roof, Jan again raised the question of not working the following day. Gordon had begun to realise that this was one argument that could not, or perhaps should not, be won – but a certain stubbornness prevented his giving way. Late that evening with the children asleep, the lights out and only the moon dimly lighting the caravan interior where it shone through and between the skimpy curtains, Jan asked the question yet again, but she did it in such a way that he just could not refuse.

Someone once said that promises extracted under duress were not binding, but then a man's word is his bond. He fell asleep wondering if he'd have any energy for work tomorrow anyway.

"Wheee!" Sharon pirouetted round, simultaneously trying to peek over one shoulder, attempting to see how the new skirt swirled out. Stopping, she swayed sideways a few times feeling the hem of thick winter material slap softly against her thigh, then looked up at Jan with a gleam of approval, stepping over quickly to hug her mother in appreciation.

"It's great!"

The boys, sitting on the floor, cards spread out face down all around them, looked up at Sharon's excited comments, wrinkled their noses and turned back to the former pursuit. Ostensibly less interested in their own presents which were also clothes, they sat playing *pairs* at which Stephen's young memory excelled. In spite of pretended indifference, he still wore his new black calf-length Wellingtons.

Christmas at River Valley proved a happy affair; unusual, different from any previous Christmas but happy all the same. Even the turkey dinner thought to be lost, had been reprieved, courtesy of the oven in Audrey's kitchen. The smaller caravan was now hung with mainly home-made Christmas decorations, while chocolate and sweets were plentiful, provided by both sets of grandparents – and of course, no work!

The children dashed to Jim's caravan as soon as his curtains were drawn, and later followed a trail of clues their father had laid around the site, each one leading to another, Stephen only catching up when the older pair stopped to work out the next location.

Lunch, including chestnuts from their own tree, gave rise to profuse praise.

"The best since May!" Christopher declared.

He spoke for once without the slightest exaggeration. Sharon, equally impressed, asked more technical questions on preparation but Stephen said little, sensibly concentrating on the eating.

Resting in the smaller caravan late that evening, Jan suggested and everyone agreed, a body could get to like idleness. She had put the children to bed some time before but they lay talking to each other just as long as they could force their eyes to stay open. Finally sheer exhaustion quietened them and they dropped off to sleep.

Jan continued to sit, staring thoughtfully into space, thinking about the future. Her eyes flicked back to the sleeping children; they were so young and vulnerable. Where would they be next Christmas?

The timbers lay cut and waiting. Horizontal ceiling

joists, those timbers forming the loft floor, were already firmly fixed. Only the rafters, the sloping members that support the tiles, remained to be erected, a job for two people. Working solo was possible, but the first pair of rafters at each end would be tricky and take much longer. Jim's bad leg prohibited him from helping, so Jan would have the job of holding the rafter tops together and upright at the very summit of the roof. These timbers needed support while Gordon first nailed their bottom ends, then fixed in the ridge piece that joined the tops permanently.

Altitude and stability would be the problems. The joists moved somewhat underfoot, and once standing on them Jan would not be tall enough to reach. Two wooden boxes balanced above these open joists and spanned by a single plank were arranged for her to stand on, to gain the necessary height. She climbed the ladder, eased herself carefully onto the roof, walked shakily across the wobbly timber joists, and knelt on the single plank. From this precarious perch, looking down she could see straight through the widely spaced timbers to the concrete floor nine feet below. These joists, the boxes on them and the plank above on which she knelt, all rocked slightly at any movement.

Gordon watched her rise unsteadily into a standing position before passing up rafters, first from one side then the other until she stood, both arms above her head holding one timber in each, waiting for the bottom fixings to be driven in.

Climbing back down the ladder to retrieve hammer and nails, he looked up at her and on a sudden whim, waved.

"Won't be long, just going for a coffee!"

She could do nothing. No way could she let go

without the timbers falling on her head, or herself falling from the plank she stood on – but no one could stop her speaking!

He listened waiting, struggling to suppress a smile, adopting a shocked expression. When she paused, forced to stop long enough and draw a deep breath, he stepped in quickly.

"Such language, and I thought you were a lady!"

The second tirade flowed vehement and unrepeatable. She never said anything really crude, but he marvelled at how, without actually swearing she could cast such inferences on his character and origin!

He climbed the ladder again, carrying the necessary tools, placed them near the roof edge, then carefully balanced his way across the joists. Standing very close he leaned to kiss a cheek. Her head recoiled sharply, like a cat trapped by a dog. When he ran his hands slowly over her body, she was so furious at being unable to move her arms in defence, it was touch and go if she didn't just let the timbers drop and have them both fall off the roof.

He stepped back smiling,

"There, there. It's wrong to lose your temper," and seeing the livid intensity of her eyes, quickly retired to start driving in the nails.

With the first four rafters fixed and braced, the rest became an easy single-handed job, no longer requiring assistance. He helped Jan down and safely across to the ladder. She accepted the assistance frostily. It was definitely going to be difficult persuading her to help with the next building's roof.

CHAPTER 12

Apple Custard

Things were coming together. By New Year, grey-green tiles, including those rounded cappings along the very summit, covered the first building's roof. On the Ladies side which now housed the toilet bucket, an outside door complete with lock swung smoothly on rust-proof nylon hinges. Again, Sharon displayed most delight. She, and of course the rest of the family, could now visit the loo with much more confidence and comfort.

Using the toilet during the past few weeks had, on one or two bad days, been distinctly unpleasant; sitting there looking up past uncovered roof timbers, captive to rain falling steadily through. Returning to the caravan on one such occasion, water dripping off her hood and mac, Jan spoke with feeling.

"Gene Kelly may enjoy 'Singing in the Rain' but there are certain things a girl prefers to do in the dry!"

Gordon had looked up in surprise.

"Gene Kelly? Showing your age a bit, aren't you?"

Happily that phase had past; one could now sit with a roof overhead and privacy assured. However, some draw-backs remained. Temporarily, the old chemical bucket continued in use, flush loos would come later with the plumbing – and the wind blew in draughty as ever, for the windows still had no glass. Never mind, it was dry!

At least so far it was. Rain *could* still enter by the high windows, but these were on the north face, sheltered from the normal south-westerly direction.

The second building progressed steadily; concrete floors had well and truly hardened and walls were already sprouting. Piles of blocks, window and door-frames, roof timbers, tiles, rolls of felt; all lay stacked and strewn around ready for use, and all paid for! This second building could be important in mid-summer when visitor numbers increased – essential if the site's reputation was not to be lost in their very first season with queues for a shower!

The appearance of the valley with these materials laid haphazardly around, was chaotic. Even the building with the roof already finished looked stark; with bare walls like some second rate warehouse. That rough blockwork must be covered in a smooth cement coating known as rendering, to give a finish that visitors would find attractive. Two local men agreed to do this work. Percy and Charles were father and son, and like most builders in country areas, could turn their hand to nearly anything. If they finished before the second building's blockwork was complete, they would help with that too, then apply the cement finish there as well.

Rendering walls had always been an anticipated expense, but money reserved for wages had dwindled somewhat as other unforeseen costs arose. For instance Jan, who normally mixed cement for the building work, could never be expected to keep up with three men! Percy and Charles could of course mix their own but the extra cost in hours would be greater than hiring a mixer. In the event, buying proved cheaper as Gordon found one that attached to the excavator. Having no motor of its own, this mixer hung from the rear and worked directly from the digger engine. With it Jan could mix, reverse the heavy excavator to the exact position required for each batch of cement, tip it out usually into wheelbarrows, then drive back to the sand heap and mix again.

She felt relieved, relieved and profoundly grateful as progress flowed more swiftly. Gordon had worked every day for months, still refusing to take Sunday afternoons off. She had watched his tiredness increase day by day, seen him taking five minutes less than his half-hour lunch break and work on until almost too dark to see in a vain attempt to beat the constantly ticking clock.

"Nearly there," she thought, "just a few more weeks!"

Life's pace increased, not from harder work, that was scarcely possible, but the constantly changing tasks created an impression of rapid development. River Valley had become a hive of increasing activity.

Stephen, always present somewhere but seldom seeking attention, played on his own, investigating here and there, and spent much time with Audrey in the bigger caravan. His freedom to roam was complete, without restraint, he could go anywhere, visit anyone; everyone was pleased to see him. Even so, he did not entirely escape little jobs, like carrying empty cement bags to the bonfire pile. Jan, without pausing in her own work, glanced in his direction from time to time, checking; only occasionally dashing off to search when his presence had been missed for too long.

Stephen watched his older brother and sister leave for school each morning; Jan could see envy in his expression though no comment passed his lips other than to ask once, months before, "When will I be old enough to go?"

"Next autumn, September, you'll be five by then!" Jan had told him, wondering where they would all be by that time. He had never asked since. The little lad would be amazed to know how much his older brother and sister envied his own freedom *not* to attend school. That greener grass again!

Stephen often waited near the bridge for Christopher and Sharon's return, knowing they would rush to the buildings to inspect progress before going to the caravan. One evening, instead of waiting, he raced off as they approached, and having a head start managed to reach a doorway first, leading them in. Some time later they returned to the caravan together, conspiratorial smiles passing between the three.

Tea was not ready, it would be eaten when darkness fell. Jan offered coffee for a stopgap, something more often done by Sharon when her mother was working. While drinking, the children continued to glance at each other, small sniggers bursting out which they tried hard to conceal. Stephen in particular could not restrain the satanic little grin that spread across his features each time Mum looked at him.

"What's happened?" she asked.

"Nothing." Sharon shook her head, the attempted air of innocence marred by a badly disguised smirk.

"Happened?" echoed Christopher, looking at the ceiling.

She had not expected a reply from Stephen, his grin just broadened as he looked her defiantly straight in the eye. Later when dusk fell and Gordon returned for tea, the little charade continued, still without any indication of the cause. It recurred in little outbursts all evening, even in bed, until they finally fell asleep.

The following morning, breakfast over, Christopher and Sharon hurriedly finished dressing for school, even though they were not yet due to leave. Jan wondered why, having detected knowing looks and concealed sniggers during breakfast. Minutes afterwards the three children dashed off again to the first building, returning with straight faces but a certain undercurrent of wicked merriment that raised their parents' curiosity.

Jan, grasping Gordon's hand, pulled him towards the building.

"Goodbye!" called Sharon, as she and Christopher started up the road at a run, ten minutes early. Stephen had disappeared.

Jan stopped, watching them go. "Why?"

The parents looked at each other smiling, mystified and perhaps a little concerned. What was it? Where was Stephen? They hurried off towards the building as a small figure crouching behind the caravan emerged unseen to follow.

An inspection of the Ladies, still showing bare blockwork, revealed nothing. Quickly they entered the Gents. A cement render finish now covered many inside walls, its smooth monolithic surface hiding joints and imperfections; nothing seemed out of place. Jan looked quickly round, then checked again more carefully, but even so almost missed it. When her eyes did rest momentarily on the cause of the children's mirth, at first she passed by, returning suddenly to stare.

Drawn by the exclamation of surprise, Gordon joined her; they gazed together at a perfect tiny hand print; four fingers, a thumb and the edge of a palm etched deeply in the now set cement. Broad smiles of amusement and intrigue spread across both faces. How had it happened – a stumble and fall, or had he reached out, carefully placed one hand, then deliberately pressed an imprint into the wet, still soft finish? At a slight sound Jan turned; a little head peering round the doorway disappeared instantly. She walked to the opening and looked out but the landscape was empty. Stephen had disappeared again!

While cooking meals and brewing extra coffee, Jan bent at intervals to peer through the small windows. These little snapshots of activity reminded her of nothing so much as the rapid erratic movements of the Keystone Cops in those early non-speaking films.

On the first day Charles and Percy arrived she had seen them at work in the first building, applying a finish to the internal walls. Gordon went with them removing the outer door from the Ladies, placing it and the old loo bucket in the service passage before returning to more block laying on the second building. As Jan operated the excavator, mixing cement for all three, she saw that blockwork grow. A day and a half later Percy and Charles, having finished rendering the Gents, moved to tackle the Ladies, only to return again to the Gents in a further two days to start on the floor.

Immediately following completion of both floors, jobs swapped again. Abandoning blockwork, Gordon returned to start plumbing, working in the service passage, connecting pipework to tanks in the roof, unable to enter the building itself until the floor hardened. Meanwhile Percy and Charles, ignoring the outside walls, switched quickly to continue block laying on the second building for the short remaining distance to roof level.

In another two days, with these walls at full height, it was all change once more, as the two builders returned to surface the external walls of building number one, while Gordon stopped plumbing temporarily to mark out the second roof timbers which Jim would then cut.

Jan, dashing to mix cement immediately the children left for school, declared herself dizzy trying to find who was working where.

Jim, industriously sawing away, had the timbers ready and the cut ends treated with preservative by the time the latest blockwork had set. Now however, Jan refused to climb on the roof.

"No! After the way you treated me last time, you can do it yourself."

"I can't." Gordon replied, both palms turned upward in a gesture of despair, appealing to her better nature, "It's difficult on your own. I could fall."

"Good!" She tossed her head and stamped off, laughing, well aware of the plentiful alternative help now available. Had they still worked alone she would probably have made *him* hold the timbers while she drove in the nails!

Despite Jan's refusal the work went well. Even with three days back on plumbing while the wall-plate cement hardened, the entire roof was on in a week, complete with tiles.

Standing inside the building one could now look up through the joists and see right into the loft space, for as yet there was no ceiling. Against one wall rested a stack of plasterboards which must somehow be nailed to the joists above. But these boards were eight feet long and as wide as a double bed. It would not be easy! Fortunately, having made her point, Jan was helping again – and she had assistance from George. George was a square wooden pole just long enough to wedge between floor and ceiling, with a two-feet wide piece of timber screwed to the upper end, making a tall 'Tee' shape.

George had acquired a mop of hair, two eyes, a nose and a mouth drawn on with a thick carpenters pencil – Charles had sneaked in during one lunch break, returning quickly to his own work. This pole supported one end of the plasterboard sheet during erection.

The system of work was rather awkward. Together they lifted a big sheet roughly into position above their heads but still well below ceiling height. Then, while Gordon balanced the full weight on outstretched hands, Jan quickly pushed George underneath at an angle, supporting one end. Working his way to the other end, Gordon slowly climbed the already conveniently placed stepladder, still holding the unwieldy ceiling board which was tugged and pushed exactly into position.

"Now!" he called, and Jan promptly moved George upright, wedging the board tightly against the joists. Continuing to support the weight, this time with his head, Gordon reached out, nail in one hand, hammer in the other. Once the first half dozen nails were driven in, things became easier.

A small argument arose when one of the big sheets slipped and fell, breaking in half.

"I can probably use these two pieces at the ends," Gordon sighed as they prepared to lift a new sheet. "Do try to hang on this time, stand closer to George, hold him firmly!" Tiredness had imparted a sharply critical note to his voice, a tone he hadn't even noticed. But Jan had!

"Don't make out it's my fault, you should bang some nails in quick... I've seen snails move faster! What were you doing, having a snooze or waiting for next Christmas?" Her eyes blazed defiance, daring him to take issue on the matter, but fatigue prevented it. He shrugged and reached for the next board.

Still smarting, Jan picked up George, lifting the

pole close, arms flexing as if to throw it, "Certainly I'll hold on tight to George, he's the best-looking guy around here by a long way!"

Later, argument forgotten, they finished and stood back, leaning together, arms round each other's waist, heads close, appraising the effect. While gazing up, half resting, half admiring their own work, footsteps approached. Percy, no longer hearing the hammer, poked his head round the doorway that as yet had no door. Tools in hand, he came prepared to start the internal cement finishes.

"Progress!" Jan thought, "I begin to believe we'll be ready."

Sharon and Christopher that night after school, hurried down the road as usual. Stephen joined them as they rushed from one building to the other before returning to the caravan, jubilant at the apparent increase in pace created by rapidly changing appearances. A ceiling actually took surprisingly little time to erect, but visually the impression of growth was splendid. As usual in the still short evenings, the family ate together when darkness fell. Sitting at the table, discussing with enthusiasm the building work, Christopher passed a comment.

"Good thing Charles and Percy came. They certainly know how to get jobs done!"

Jan, smiling, nodded encouragement. "They do, don't they. Isn't it nice to have really competent men around?"

Stephen dipped his head momentarily in a short expression of accord, but continued eating.

In an attempt to be ladylike, Sharon swallowed her mouthful in a gulp before asking innocently, "What does Dad do?"

"I don't really know." Jan's puzzled expression as she looked towards Gordon could have been real, so well did she hide her feelings, only those slightly indrawn cheeks betraying her effort not to laugh.

Later with the children lying asleep she leaned forward, elbows on the table, gazing at her husband's face. He seemed relaxed enough now but she knew the pace of work was telling.

He looked up and catching her close scrutiny asked, "Well? Will you keep me, or throw me back?"

She detected the faint smile, more in the eyes and pursed lips, quizzical, questioning.

"I'd have thrown you back this afternoon! You realise how close we came to a blazing row. How long is it since that happened?" She waited but he said nothing, a slight shrug of the shoulders, perhaps a small change of expression, but she could see the tiredness there; he'd be no use tonight. Small wonder, it was months since his last break, working all day and every day. At least she went to town regularly for supplies and cement; he never left the site. She leaned closer.

"Why don't you let up for half a day. How many times have I asked you now? When was the last break? September, four months ago! Don't tell me it's winter; I know already. But it isn't cold, many days are sunny." She waited again, looking at the slight frown.

"We had Christmas Day off," he argued quietly.

"I'm not counting that. Everyone has Christmas Day." She thought momentarily of farmers around them with milking cattle and realised it wasn't true, but pushed the thought aside to carry on. "And we didn't leave the site! I could do with a break too, so could the children."

It was blackmail she realised, doubting it would

252

have any effect. Her hand reached out, touching him, sliding her fingers round under his palms, softly feeling the work-roughened skin.

"Percy and Charles don't work Sundays," she added without stress. It could have been a mild complaint or just an observation.

Was that a nod? Her fingers involuntarily squeezed. His expression changed, not greatly, slowly warming as she watched, looking back to meet her own gaze; something in his eyes sent a tingle of feeling up her spine. Perhaps the evening was not lost after all?

Plumbing work continued, but with some reluctance Gordon stopped at lunchtime on Sunday, which Jan had deliberately brought forward by nearly an hour. It was she and the children who chose the route, chatting spiritedly over the meal. An extremely mild temperature for late January, around fifteen degrees and sun shining from a clear sky, removed any excuse Dad might have used for evasion.

Briefly they visited the old mine engine-houses at Camborne, formerly looked after by the Cornish Engine Society but now under the care of the National Trust. At the larger house, contrasting with the enormous old engine, a beautifully made scale model demonstrated to the children in a more easily understandable way, how this system worked.

Leaving Camborne they followed the road to Portreath, took a walk on the sands and a bite to eat from Jan's sandwich packet, before turning west. The B3301 between Portreath and Gwithian lived up to its spectacular reputation, the route coming close to cliff edges, some breathtakingly steep. They stopped in one place, parking temporarily beside the road to look down over an almost sheer drop of nearly two hundred feet. Gordon hung back; he had a suspicion of heights that years of working on tall buildings and climbing up tower-cranes had never entirely overcome. A local chap with binoculars hanging round his neck chatted to Jan and the children telling of gulls nesting in springtime, way below, clearly visible in niches in the rocks. They could well believe it, their gaze descending dizzily to the white frothy breakers at the very foot of the cliffs. Jan held Stephen tightly in her grasp, which for once he made no attempt to escape. As her eyes followed a seagull floating gracefully downward, she felt the pull of the abyss and sharply ordered Christopher and Sharon back to a safer distance.

Farther along the same road it was possible to park clear of the carriageway and walk across the dunes at Godrevy Towans, the only place cowslips grew locally according to the orchid man. Cowslips need chalky soils, the sand on these dunes was very alkaline, some used by farmers near their own valley as a substitute for lime. Over ages, shells of crustacea were ground by the action of tides to a fine sand and lifted on the wind.

Walking over these dunes Gordon held Jan's hand as the children raced in front, outlined against a deep blue sky, glowing with health, Sharon's hair like her mother's but darker, blowing in a light breeze off the Atlantic coast ahead. Watching them he wondered why anyone would want to live anywhere else in the world.

It took perhaps half an hour strolling on towards Godrevy Point, looking out to Godrevy Island and the lighthouse, wandering along the sands to the mouth of the Red River then south towards Gillick Rock, there to relax while the children played.

Sitting close to Jan on the fine, light-coloured sand

of that wide beach overlooking the sea with not another soul in sight, neither felt any inclination to move in their contentment. Stephen ran backwards and forwards with handfuls of shells, amazingly numerous on that stretch, a complete contrast to the southern Channel coast near St Michael's Mount. Christopher and Sharon approached the water's edge, near as they dare, racing each incoming wave up the beach. Where *did* they find that surplus energy? At last Jan rose, reluctantly leading the way back towards the van, Hayle, and home to Relubbus.

Like most people, the children believed completion of the roof indicated an almost finished building. They somehow expected that in a matter of days, flush loos and hot showers would suddenly become operational. Assurance that such a state of affairs remained weeks away, met with considerable suspicion. Sharon grew even more sceptical the following week after the glaziers had been, leaving the buildings completely weatherproof. Darting a resentful glance from the corner of her eye in her father's direction, she protested.

"It must be nearly finished now, Mum?"

It was part statement, part question, implying Dad was somehow deliberately delaying, or at the very least not trying sufficiently hard. She became even more convinced when Percy and Charles left. Gordon wanted to keep them both, but money, a continuing problem, prevented it. The belief, pay promptly or go without, applied to wages as well!

No member of the family escaped work. Absolutely the most monotonous, and unfortunately extensive job, was knocking holes. This became Jan's Dad's speciality. Jim hammered holes for water-pipes, holes for drains and holes for waste-pipes; struggling to sit on the floor, unable to kneel with his bad leg, and struggling even harder to rise afterwards. Each position was marked on the wall in pencil by Gordon, who would himself later knock the smaller holes that needed precision placing. Every screw required its own hole filled with a plastic plug, but these must await completion of the decoration. There would be screws for hooks, basin brackets, pipe brackets, toilet-roll holders, soap-dishes, cistern brackets, gas-pipes, shower sets, and even to fix the toilets to the floor – hundreds and hundreds of holes everywhere. How easy it would have been with Jim's electric drill, but for that they needed electricity!

While Jim knocked, Gordon pressed ahead with plumbing, forming a maze of copper pipework spreading web-like in the service passage.

"Plumbing," he claimed, "is a gentle art, requiring inspiration rather than perspiration. I like it."

Soldered joints were utilised virtually everywhere, being cheaper than nut type fittings and less prone to developing leaks, but difficult to undo once soldered. Precise measurements and meticulous cleanliness of all joints before applying the blowlamp should, with luck, avoid any need to take joints apart later! Ordinary brass fittings were banned in the southwest – they de-zincify; that is, zinc dissolves from the brass and the metal disintegrates, over very many years of course. The more expensive gunmetal or a new special brass just becoming available were both acceptable.

This peculiarity of the water supply left palatability unaffected, it had excellent sparkle and taste, certainly forming no detriment to health – the very opposite if the number of locals living to over ninety was anything to go by. Perhaps it contained a special unknown long-life ingredient? Or was that the clear air? Or even the easier pace of life?

"I wish!" he thought.

No lime-scale ever grew fur inside the kettle, and being accustomed to hard water the family had at first found difficulty remembering to use less soap, creating an excess of hard to rinse lather.

Gordon broke off plumbing to nail soffit boards under the roof eaves, driving the nails in with a small punch and filling over the heads with putty. These soffits and the already fixed fascia board where the guttering would later hang, were soon given their first protective coat of paint, although even these timbers had been preservative treated.

Work had really moved on; lighting was next. Having no electricity the toilets would of necessity be lit by Calor gas lamps; less powerful than florescent tubes but the softer light likely to attract fewer moths.

"However," Jan thought, "someone must light the lamps each night and turn them out in the morning. Never mind, one of us will be cleaning early every day in any case, well before most visitors are awake."

Even had electricity been available she knew they would always rise early except perhaps in winter.

* * *

"Don't be ridiculous, of course they must be the same height!"

Points of discussion connected with site and buildings ran into hundreds. Windows, door frames, ceilings, paint, roads, grass, the list was endless – but what else could they talk about? Gordon, at least, was totally absorbed by work and almost never left the site. In general, Jan listened, deferring to his greater expertise, asking odd questions and making comments, well aware she was being used as a sounding board to develop his own ideas. Partly too, these consultations arose from the sheer pleasure in chatting to each other, often with hands clasped together across the table. Nevertheless, occasionally Jan dug in her heels and insisted. In this particular case she was adamant. The dispute concerned basins.

Gordon maintained that as people were unfortunately manufactured in different sizes, the row of basins and mirrors should be staggered in height. Jan disagreed. His fatuous suggestion of adopting the method used in the Greek legend by the robber Procrustes, stretching short visitors on the rack and lopping bits off taller ones, met with little approval. Jan, chopping wild mint with a large knife, countered by suggesting they try taking a few inches off the taller ones at home first. She moved close, flipped off her shoes and standing very flat, looked up into his eyes with a questioning expression, gently swinging the knife from the fingertips of her right hand.

They looked at each other smiling; undoubtedly Jan had won the point! Gordon nodded acquiescence, giving way to her insistence concerning both basins and mirrors.

"They must be better level, you never see them staggered anywhere else; that would just look silly." She said it contemptuously, clearly implying that only a complete imbecile would contemplate such a thing.

The basins then, would all be a touch low for tall people and a little higher than ideal for short ones.

"Those in the Ladies" she stipulated, "must be two inches lower than the Gents."

"She's laying the law down a bit!" Gordon thought. She might be right but having lost the earlier point and not prepared to be dictated to in his own domain, he automatically voiced an objection.

"What about sexual discrimination? You could get me into trouble."

Jan turned, a look of exasperation on her face, searching for a suitably scathing reply, one foot tapping the ground, a sure sign she was not about to concede.

"After having your three children I should feel quite proud to get you into trouble for a change." She drew a deep breath, pleased with her own quick response, smiling as she waited, looking to see if he could find an answer. Then a further idea formed in her mind.

"If you can't have anything different in the Ladies, do tell me, how many urinals will you install there?"

Game, set and match to Jan!

Low wooden footstools would solve the problem for children, short adults might also occasionally stand on them. The basins could not be fixed until after wall painting, but one held at the agreed height with concrete blocks in front served as a test. Two blocks were high for Christopher, one block a touch low for Stephen. A few five or six-inch high footstool should work fine, Gordon would make them in odd moments here and there.

Preparations showed daily improvement. A textured tyrolean finish had been applied to all outside walls with a little gadget something like a miniature barrel organ. It splattered the surface with a special cement mixture in silver grey. Both toilet buildings were now structurally complete and nearing a functioning state, but January had gone with February well on its way.

A useful area of ground lay prepared and ready for occupation; insufficient to cope with the hoped-for midseason rush, but encouraging nevertheless. Most was grassed but some retained a hard finish, stone roughly levelled but otherwise just as it had come from the heaps – a few areas were bare earth, with soil already spread and now awaiting seed. The entire family worked relentlessly. Jan painted busily, hurrying to finish the first building's inside walls, a job she estimated would require two more days. This incomplete decoration continued to delay the fixing of basins, toilet pans, mirrors and doors.

Jim, having finished knocking holes, insisted on helping paint. A style, much more vigorous than careful, made advisable the use of several old sheets to prevent paint splashes coating the floor. Audrey supplied these sheets; she also looked after Stephen for much of the time and cooked most midday meals. Sharon helped by preparing tea when arriving home from school – it all allowed Jan more painting time.

No one escaped; Christopher was busy too, stacking leftover blocks in one tidy pile, Stephen carrying broken pieces. Together they cleared up after building operations, collecting cracked tiles, timber offcuts, strips of roofing felt, and sorted them for burning or burying.

Activity was constant and unceasing, every day saw improvements; a feeling of unstoppable momentum affected everyone. In addition the drawing-board no longer sat in the Mini van. It, together with other tools and equipment, now lay in the roof space.

Delayed on internal plumbing until Jan finished painting the wall surfaces, Gordon used the two days spreading grass seed on already topsoiled areas. Though early for germination, another chance might not quickly arise and it needed doing by mid-March. Raked well in, the seed should come to little harm for a few weeks while the soil warmed sufficiently.

More physical than plumbing, it nevertheless made a change, thus being in a strange way, simultaneously both energetic and restful. He wondered briefly if the choice of job had really been from logic or just the chance to daydream. Was it essential, or escapism? With soil, unlike pipework, nothing had to be exact!

As always, Robin and Blackbird, both found him as soon as he started disturbing the surface, their presence pleasing, he had missed them while working inside.

Why just these two? Chaffinches, yellow hammers, the ubiquitous tits, linnets and a host of others abounded; mainly stout-beaked seed-eaters attracted by gorse and other seeding plants in the valley. None had the rapport that developed between man, robin and blackbird. It was not so surprising. Though many would pass by in their search for food, few species associate with humans for preference. Robins and blackbirds however, habitually did just that, as generations of gardeners well know.

Since the first time Gordon thought he had heard Robin speak, the bird had not chipped in to his thoughts again. It had been, he realised, a figment of imagination, a lonely mind inventing answers. During the building work, constantly in contact with others, much saner thoughts prevailed. But on the second day working alone again? Ah well, things didn't seem quite so clear. Long solitary hours of previous association and familiarity so easily slipped back into place.

Jan was born at St Thomas's Hospital in London, within the sound of Bow Bells, qualifying her as a cockney. Gordon thought of Robin as a cocky cockney too. Its habits and its stance held that typical earthy brashness, the same flavour passing to comments he attributed to the bird. Blackbird on the other hand, appeared reserved and thoughtful, the black suit giving a reverend aspect. A vicar? No, that needed a white collar like the dipper they had seen only once on a rock in the stream; perhaps a philosopher then, or maybe an undertaker?

Resting against the handle, taking a short breather following a spell of heavy raking towards the end of the second day, the job almost complete, he chatted quietly, tired but contented, to the birds. Had he used the right type of seed? More rye perhaps for a quicker start? Or more fescue for that finer finish? He looked over to Robin questioningly.

"You're covering the ground with entirely the wrong thing."

"What then?"

"Customers! Cover it with customers. Forget the grass, anything will grow. Worry about people and how to lure them in. Tourists mean easy food!"

* * *

Jan, with some help from Jim, still painted in the Ladies, but the Gents paintwork had dried. Gordon pushed on, erecting sinks, all level at the agreed height, then toilet cisterns and pans. Connection of water and waste pipes took a further day, by which time the painters had cleared the Ladies and moved to the second building.

Finishing the Ladies basins and pans the following day, he immediately commenced hanging internal doors, all flush finished in Sapele wood veneer and hung as with the outer doors, on rustless nylon hinges. A first varnish coat was quickly applied but the little internal bolts must wait until a second coat had hardened.

Development continued apace, jobs ticked steadily off the list but the days ran even faster. March had blown in and was rushing by, new grass seed should soon be sprouting – the season almost arrived. There remained now the septic tank to be dug, a job taking precedence over the remaining plumbing in the second building where Jan had almost finished painting.

Septic systems were designed to contain 24 hours' volume of waste water, giving heavier solids time to settle on the bottom while lighter particles rose to the surface. Here floated a living scum, bacteria working busily away decomposing the organic matter. Water in the tank centre was thus fairly clear, suspended solids having sunk or risen by the time it reached the outlet. This almost clean liquid overflowed into a soakaway system. Action by the ground through which the effluent percolated would complete the purification process.

The main work therefore, was a large holding tank, the size of a small house but much quicker to build; just a solid base, then thick heavy walls with no fiddly openings and all covered by a concrete top. However, a water problem existed. The base needed to be eighteen inches below the natural water level. Unavoidably, a three-inch diesel diaphragm pump had to be hired, the sort that chug, chug, chug, a sound to be heard day and night for the next week.

Excavation commenced easily enough, using Max, the digger. Trimming by hand to the required finished surface proved much more difficult. The bottom sloped, assisting water to drain to a hole in one corner. Here the pump's suction pipe rested in a bucket to prevent silt clogging the strainer. Gordon was attempting to dig a little channel round the outside to drain off the water, so the base could be concreted without cement being washed away near the edges; but the soft sides kept falling in. It took much of the day wallowing in mud to shovel out the correct profile.

The ready-mix concrete lorry's arrival early the following morning made a welcome sight. To avoid trapping pockets of water the concrete was discharged in one great grey pile, placed centrally in the excavated hole. Both Gordon and Jan immediately started working the stodgy mixture evenly towards the outside, pushing surplus water before it. With shovels and rakes the concrete was drawn outwards to where a double line of building blocks formed a clean edge preventing concrete from slipping into that carefully prepared water channel.

To avoid treading on the previously levelled base leaning over to fill shovels at full stretch was unavoid-able, making the work more strenuous. The lorry had arrived at 9.30, they toiled on without a break, completing the task before lunch – they had to, the concrete was beginning to set!

Stephen, who had watched with interest as the lorry discharged, was being looked after and having lunch with Jim and Audrey. He had paddled over at intervals all morning, not very interested in the slow progress, but as usual, not quite prepared to stay away entirely, for fear of missing something.

Gordon worked alone for the last half hour while Jan prepared a meal. Having finished levelling and smoothing the base, he washed off his shovel and boots in the expanding pond the pump was creating in front of Jim's caravan and plodded off to climb heavily through their own doorway, totally spent. Relaxing into a bench seat beside the small table, he sighed, stretched his arms to relieve aching shoulders and watched Jan serving up.

"Nice timing," he thought, but faced the meal without relish. His hand shook slightly as it rested limply on the table between bites. He toyed with the food, eating with an effort, without enthusiasm, not clearing his plate, not rushing as he usually did to return to work.

Jan watched. She had seen him like this before, not often but once or twice when near to exhaustion, hardly raising the strength to eat. He would recover later, given time she thought, knowing from experience, leaning back and making no move to clear away. She too felt weary though she knew he had done three-quarters of the work. Second courses were not normal but she had gone to the trouble of making one, anticipating that for once he would be in no hurry, would be in no condition to hurry!

"Let him sit another ten minutes before I produce it," she nodded to herself.

By the time dessert appeared, Gordon could begin to feel an appetite returning and looked with pleasure at the steaming bowl of stewed apple and custard before him. Jan sat again on the other bench seat – between them the collapsible table hinged to the wall at one end, with a single folding leg at the other. The whole assembly changed into the double bed at night, just like the table in the little tourer had, a common arrangement in caravans. They looked at each other, he took a deep breath letting the air sail from his lungs, almost a heavy sigh, gave Jan a slightly weary smile, and both knew it was a job well done.

Lifting his spoon, he dug deeply into the custard. Chug, chug, chug... chug... Silence! The pump!

He shot from the seat banging a knee on the table leg, closely followed by Jan, and even more closely by the plate of apple as it catapulted through the air, describing a gentle arc to land with a significant splat, upside down on the thin, badly worn carpet. The table collapsed at the same time but neither gave it a second glance as they charged through the door, splashing their way to the pump. They had perhaps ten minutes at the outside to save the concrete base!

First job, check the diesel tank. Blast! Empty! Gordon silently cursed himself for having forgotten to fill it in the hurry to clear overnight falls of soil, struggling to be ready for the early morning concrete lorry.

Grabbing the empty can, he rushed to the large oil storage tank and vigorously worked the lever that always took twenty strokes before anything issued forth. With urgent energy, energy entirely absent seconds before, stimulated only by the crisis, the can was filled and hurriedly transferred to the empty fuel tank. Frantically he reached for the pump's handle and swung it hard, simultaneously trying to bleed the air from filters and injectors, a process that involved loosening various nuts until bubbles stopped emerging.

The water level was rising at an alarming rate. He swung with a force born of mad desperation and at last the engine fired, hesitated, then picked up.

A little whirlpool appeared over the suction pipe.

Fifteen minutes later the level was back to normal. They returned to the caravan to look sadly down at the gooey mess of custard on the floor, then at each other. A little shrug, a big hug, and the laughter of relief. Whatever else life might be, it was certainly never dull!

CHAPTER 13

The Buzzard

Sharon eased herself from the sleeping-bench, withdrawing legs slowly from alongside her young brother and crept stealthily towards the door. Surprisingly, although the grey of dawn now penetrated the caravan, no one else had risen. Why was Dad not working? She reached the door, levered the handle gently downward, silently slipping outside. Glancing up and down the riverbank, checking for but not expecting any passing stranger, she ran, placing bare feet with some care, towards the toilet, nightdress blowing in a cool pre-sunrise breeze.

Her exit had not entirely escaped detection. Jan moved as the door closed, rising to dress in privacy while the others slept. Today nothing could be done on the septic tank; the concrete needed to harden. The pump's dull chug continued, sounding clearly through the thin walls like a constant heartbeat. Was it that which made them all oversleep? She doubted it. The sound had already become a part of life. More likely their tiredness came from the previous day's exertions.

Today she would finish painting the Ladies inside walls in the second building, a task temporarily forgotten while concreting the tank base.

"A job brushed to one side," she thought wryly.

The first coat had been hardest to apply, all moisture

sucked from the bristles as they touched the absorbent and slightly rough cement render, making brushing the most wrist-aching work. The second coat was always so much easier. Once the surface had been sealed, paint slid on with relative ease, though the finish remained textured rather than smooth.

Jan picked up a flannel, reaching to turn the tap on, but glancing round at the two sleeping children and hearing Gordon's heavy regular breathing, changed her mind. He would hang the internal doors in the Gents today, maybe the Ladies too if the paintwork was finished in time. Taking a towel, she left quietly, pausing on the bank to stretch, the bracing air many degrees lower than inside. Though burning low by morning, the boiler combined with heat from five bodies, usually maintained comfortable temperatures within.

Easing carefully down the grassy slope, grass still wet and slippery with dew, she knelt dipping her flannel in the stream. Raising it, realising the soap was missing, she washed in clear water, droplets from loose corners splashing to disturb the smoothly flowing surface below. The water felt good. She repeated the operation for that cool freshness it imparted to her skin, then rose to return, breakfast already on her mind

Halfway up the bank, Sharon approached from the other direction. Jan signalled, finger to lips, beckoning her away from the caravan.

"The men still sleep, let's wake them with the smell of bacon for once. Wash in the river." Understanding Sharon's glance toward the caravan door, she passed the flannel and towel. "Use mine. I forgot the soap."

A smell of hot fat greeted the young girl minutes later as she re-entered, but still the men slept. Dropping towel and flannel lightly over Stephen's hidden feet at her own end of the sleeping-bench, she moved quietly to her mother's side as the first slice of bacon landed in the pan to sizzle loudly in the silence. No one awoke.

More slices were quickly added as Sharon carefully filled the kettle, lighting the gas under it before extracting plates from the cupboard, then looked at Jan in dismay.

"Where can I lay them?" she whispered.

It was a problem. Gordon still slept and the table lay beneath him forming the double bed. Jan leaned closer.

"They can eat in bed. Stack them on the draining board."

Lifting the hot pan, from which a strong smell of frying bacon now rose, she held it close to each bed in turn, wrist moving backwards and forwards, wafting its odour to the sleeping males. Returning pan to gas and adding slices of bread to fry in the remaining fat, mother and daughter leaned towards the double bed. Gordon's breathing changed, became irregular, almost sniffing the air. Lids fluttered blearily, to jerk back in surprise as they confronted two other pairs of eyes, crinkling with amusement, staring back from not three feet away.

Minutes later all five sat propped against walls and cupboards, eating happily, wondering how they slept so late as the sun's first rays broke across hills to the east.

In spite of a late start, the day went well, with most doors hung and the wall decoration finished. The effect of all that white paint, as had been clearly seen in the first building, made the interior very light. Although it would show the dirt, any grubbiness should be easy to locate and clean off, or if stubborn, just be painted over. For the urinal they had a special coating called chlorinated rubber, similar to white gloss but more chemical resistant, though the solvents were powerful in the confined space.

Towards evening when the children came home, the entire family carried concrete blocks from a newly arrived load, making stacks around the hole where the pump still chugged happily away. Stephen, too small to lift a complete block, carried broken pieces saved from earlier work, struggling without protest to keep up with his older siblings. Big and small, all sizes of block could be used up in the thick septic tank walls.

The pump still chugged steadily away. Creeping gradually forward, the lake being formed by its discharge now threatened to surround Jim's caravan. To Audrey's vigorous protests, Christopher and Sharon carried more blocks for stepping stones leading to higher ground.

"He'll fall off!" Audrey warned, as Jim, stick in one hand and grinning broadly, shakily descended the caravan steps. She should have known better than to expect much sympathy. Splashing past in his Wellies, Christopher paused, grinning as he glanced at Jim.

"Can we watch?"

"Hope we're not at school." Sharon gasped eagerly, clapping her hands together in an involuntary expression of pleasurable expectation.

Audrey looked at them sharply having seen nothing amusing about the situation, but a tight smile fluttered at the corners of her mouth as she waved a warning finger. "You would too, little devils! Just be sure you set them solid, so they don't rock!"

Only Audrey was worried, Jim standing behind her, pulled a face, winking at the children.

Christopher carried another block to the deepest part of the little causeway; it disappeared, a thin layer of water already covering the surface.

By the following morning four more had submerged

below the rising tide, but Gordon promised to lay the first two blockwork courses round the tank tomorrow, when the concrete base reached three days old. It should be sufficient to allow turning the pump off a day later.

Blocklaying proved a messy business, standing not on the newly constructed base, but in the drainage channel round the edge, mud climbing ever higher up his boots, sucking at them every time a foot moved. He finished before lunch but by then three more of Jim's stepping-stones had submerged and little waves lapped at his caravan steps. This however, was almost high-water mark for the artificial lake. True to that promise, early the following morning before the children left for school, a little group gathered near the pump.

Jim and Audrey still slept, or at least had not yet drawn their curtains. Jan stood, arms around the children looking down into the crater as Gordon moved to turn off the engine then stepped back by her side.

The effect was unexpected. Watching to see the water level rise, their attention was somehow diverted. A silence descended; eerie, disturbing – as if the world had stopped. They looked at each other, puzzled. Jan thought back to the silence of that day when they had first seen the valley. The sound of the pump, its constant chug throbbing in their ears for more than a week, had become part of the background, an extra heartbeat no longer heard; but its absence registered!

"Look!" Christopher pointed. "The water's rising."

Sure enough, the little sump, bucket and extraction pipe, were already covered. They pulled up the pipe, rescued the bucket and went about their various tasks.

Adding only three courses a day for the next few days to avoid fully loading the base too soon, left time between to hang the final internal doors in the Ladies, and screw the little bolts on those loo doors already fully varnished. Most of the second building's unfinished plumbing also received attention.

Less than a week later the septic tank walls were complete. Charles had popped back for a day to help. The enormous tank lay gaping and empty as the family stood looking in.

"Can we use the toilets now?" Sharon asked. She hated the old chemical bucket currently standing in the second building's service passage, and looked regularly at the twenty white porcelain toilet pans in their neat little white cubicles, a shining polished wood veneer door offering complete privacy to each one.

"Not yet, somehow we must find a cheap way to make the concrete roof." Gordon waved a hand at the tank but saw her disappointment. "Don't worry, we're nearly there, not long now."

It was true. Preparations were primitive but quickly made. Old corrugated iron sheets were used as shuttering to hold up the concrete, with piles of blocks supporting heavy cross timbers below – second-hand railway sleepers in fact, and wooden wedges so these supports could be taken out easily when the concrete set. Access holes to be covered later with concrete lids, were left in the top, and also a small four-inch circular inlet hole for air to replace the lighter methane gas produced by bacteria inside the tank. This gas, being so light, would rise of its own accord up through pipework and out via vents already installed above the toilet roofs.

Concreting the top proved comparatively simple. With the gap around the walls now filled, the Readymix lorry could reverse close enough to spread the concrete evenly. It needed less than a full load and all went surprisingly easily; hardly enough work to raise a good sweat, complete within the hour, including making sure the steel reinforcing remained correctly positioned. It was now a matter of waiting; the slab must set and strengthen.

Spring had arrived, not just on the calendar but in signs of new life. April was fast approaching, buds were fattening, some bursting, the grass beginning to grow. Pussy willow, little white blobs only a few weeks earlier, now hung in large yellow fluffy clusters, buzzing in the midday sun with bees expanding their colonies for the summer to come. Days were lengthening, deep winter had passed; it had been cold sometimes but fortunately with no frost to interrupt any work using cement. Jan understood from chatting in the local shop that this was quite normal for the area.

Thanks to the boiler, the caravan had remained warm and cosy throughout, and although none too roomy with everyone present, it was never as cramped as the small tourer had been. In the darker winter evenings they had talked a lot together and still tended to do so, in spite of extending daylight and warmer weather. Following completion of the septic tank Gordon was explaining to Christopher, with the others half listening, about the methane gas.

"Bacteria produce it as they decompose the floating surface scum. Pure methane is odourless, but the smell of rotting matter mixes with it inside the tank. People sometimes enter a tank or sewer then pass out and die, overcome by this gas."

Children are gruesome. Sharon and Stephen, not in the slightest interested in methane, suddenly turned, all attention! Microbes turning sludge to gas was boring,

273

but gas killing someone – that was different!

Gordon looked at Jan, shaking his head slightly before turning back to the children. So! To hold their interest required something drastic, let's try.

"Good job they never struck a match!"

He waited, the watching faces full of attention now. The pause lengthened. Seeing a question form on Sharon's lips, he continued before she could speak.

"That's the trouble with methane." His hands held loosely apart, flew violently together, the loud report dramatically emphasising the next words. "It explodes!"

Stephen's eyes lit up; there was absolutely no doubt he would strike a match just to see the bang. Sharon jerked backwards in alarm, then looked apprehensively over her shoulder to where the tank would have been visible except for the darkness outside.

"Don't worry. That's what the pipes sticking above the toilet roofs are for, to disperse the methane. Pity we can't collect and burn it instead of bottled gas. It would be free."

Living as they did, self-sufficiency held a special interest. During the evenings of the following week Gordon read up on sludge digesters, as methane gas plants are known, discussing them with the family. Digesters had been used on some farms, why not on a caravan park?

Had anyone asked, "What do you talk about over meals?", few people would believe the answer. "The merits of pig manure as against human waste for the production of a good quality sludge." However, it would have been the absolute truth. At lunch one Saturday, while eating fried sausages and mash they had indeed been chatting about the consistency of sludge and how to extract a sufficiently thick mixture from the site's septic tank. How ecologically sound, to provide hot water for people to use in showers, all produced from their own by-products.

Gordon explained how a primitive set-up could be made from a forty-gallon drum with no bottom, placed inside another slightly larger drum with no top, just like a miniature gasometer, the bottom vessel containing decomposing sludge. No air must mingle with the methane, such mixtures were very explosive. The upper drum should start with its top level with the sludge surface, with definitely no air at all inside. As methane formed, it would begin to fill this drum, which would rise gradually just as the old gasometers did.

An outlet pipe near the top would lead gas off to a cooker or other appliance, and the pressure could be altered simply placing weights on top of the drum.

It sounded feasible.

Studied in greater detail, certain difficulties emerged. The sludge needed stirring regularly, and at intervals spent sludge must be discarded and replaced with a charge of fresh material. Neither of these smelly operations appeared at all likely to enhance customer satisfaction with the site. The clinching point however, remained that initial warning. Should any air leak in with the methane, the resulting mixture would be extremely explosive!

Jan pointed out that if it did blow up, showering all the caravans and tents with decomposing human sludge might not be the very best method of advertising the site, though it would certainly get them into the national news. She attempted to mimic a male newsreader.

"Today a sludge digester exploded at River Valley. Foul play is suspected."

The children blinked in amusement, not at the pun which they missed, but at the deep voice.

275

"Perhaps we could get the caravans quarantined to stay for six months?" Gordon suggested.

Having finished the septic tank they worked together to connect drains and the soakaway system, then fitted guttering to all the buildings. Jim wanted to paint the window frames but Jan and Audrey, both aware of his tendency to slosh paint liberally around, looked at each other in alarm. Audrey spoke up persuasively.

"Jim, I'd like some air, I'll do the windows. Young Stephen needs a man's touch for a day or two, take him with you and collect all those bits of cement bag that are blowing around. He can do the bending, you carry a plastic sack to put them in. You could set fire to them too."

Jan heaved a small sigh, then smiled to herself. Her mother handled the situation well. She had never really noticed before, and tried to remember other occasions when her father had been manipulated.

"Is that where I learned it?" she wondered. "I hope Sharon develops the same sense. I don't think Jim even realised, but Gordon does – sometimes, at any rate. I can tell by the way he smiles, mostly I get away with it though."

Her mother enjoyed painting and did it well. If she undertook the more delicate brushwork needed to decorate those lower windows, the glass would remain transparent; with Jim that would be highly unlikely. Someone else could paint the higher ones later, from a ladder. Neither of the grandparents were able to work long or quickly, but they worked steadily. Just having them around helped.

* * *

Water dribbled slowly through the pipework and up into tanks in the roof space. Trickling sounds emanated from every side, from all the complex network of pipes and joints extending to every part of the building. Jan dashed from Ladies to Gents and back again, constantly scanning for drips. Above, Gordon climbed into and out of loft spaces, crouching and crawling on the ceiling joists with a torch. Filling the system slowly to minimise possible damage from any leak, took over half an hour. Out of some five hundred joints, only two were not watertight and needed resoldering.

Triumphantly revealing this result to the children at tea, Dad proudly expressed the view that a little praise might be due.

Shaking her head, Jan pulled a long face, winking, encouraging them to disagree. How disgusting. Leaks! Not just one; two leaks no less. Disgraceful! The three youngsters totally ignored their father sitting in the corner, a game they had played before, making their criticisms as if in his absence.

"Plumbing classes, that's what he needs, don't you agree?" Jan suggested.

They nodded eagerly, glancing furtively sideways to gauge Dad's reaction, feeling reasonably confident. Plumbing seldom left him very tired. Only when exhausted did his sense of humour suffer, and even then usually not unless something threatened to cause more work.

The showers were heated by large instantaneous gas burners. It was better, they thought, than storing hot water in a big cylinder, since instant hot water would never run out. Any time, day or night, even in peak season when showers would be in almost constant use, a good shower would always be available.

Having waited so long, the children were keenly anxious for this first trial. Each building had four showers; two for ladies, two for men. Jan ushered the whole family towards the Gents.

"Mum, it's the wrong side!" Sharon protested, hesitating on the threshold.

Ignoring the reluctance, Jan pushed her bodily through the doorway. "Make the most of it, this may be the last chance you ever get. It's not every girl who can shower in the Gents."

The choice was made with good reason. Being in adjoining cubicles enabled discussion of the shower's performance, turning one shower on and off, noting its affect on temperature and flow of the other. Jan and Sharon entered one compartment, Gordon took Stephen and Christopher into the other.

"Aah!" Sharon's shriek echoed through the building as a fierce spray of cold water drenched her hair and shoulders before she jumped clear, pressing back tightly against the wall. Jan, realising the gas would take some seconds to ignite had stood to one side, reaching over at arm's length to turn on. As the spray warmed she stepped forward, adjusting the taps.

Sharon held out an arm suspiciously, expression turning to delight at the feel of hot water. Quickly, she moved forward. Steam clouded the cubicle as warm droplets rained down drenching her skin. Jan looked at her daughter, face uplifted to the spray, eyes closed, small hands clenching and unclenching as she shrugged young shoulders in ecstasy, turning this way and that, extending fingers fully, reaching up towards the shower head, eyes still tightly shut, constantly moving to ensure every inch of her body was covered. A toss of the head flipped long hair, shiny black when wet, first one side then the other, to be held finally in a bun on top, exposing the nape of her neck to the falling water. The temperature fluttered marginally as the boys' shower started, but returned rapidly to its former state.

Such luxury! Piping hot and lots of it. They may not have liked baths in the river, but they loved this! The boys shouted over the partition wall, splashing, playing, letting steaming water run over them, elevating arms in the air, making absolutely no attempt at proper washing. Jan spoke without leaving the spray.

"It's lovely, the way it's all warm and runs through your hair. We've made them too good, no one will ever come out." Then after a minute, "You'll have to make somewhere to put the soap."

Eventually she insisted they actually wash, instead of playing, instructing the boys to do the same. A further time passed, including a short period turning each shower on and off to check its effect on the other, before Gordon shouted above the noise.

"That's enough, rinse away the soap!" and shortly after turned the water off.

Jan did the same, both parents ignoring a barrage of protest, including assertions that the system needed much more testing and Sharon's claim to have over a hundred proper baths to catch up with.

"One giant stride for... No, let's not get carried away, just a little leap in our standard of living." Jan thought, as they walked back to the caravan.

There could be no cleaner family in the land.

Jan remained alone in the caravan, Gordon working as always and the two older children at school. Stephen was missing too, Jim and Audrey had taken him in their car to Truro for some shopping.

"See you later. We'll be back for a very late lunch," Audrey had called as she waved goodbye.

Painting now finished, Jan sat close to the window where the light fell strongest, mending small rips and reinforcing button threads. A small bundle of children's clothes partially covered the table before her. When they first arrived she had tried to sew in the evenings but the gas lights made seeing stitches too difficult. Intensity of outside work over the past weeks had left a backlog of such repairs.

Movement to the far side of the area adjoining the caravan drew her eye. A large brown bird hopped along the fence line, not thrush-sized, more a chicken with a racy look.

"I believe it's a buzzard!" she thought, watching for several minutes, expecting the bird to fly away.

The pile of garments gradually diminished until, not wanting to leave her good vantage point, more were hunted from the cupboard, ones not originally intended for repair that day. Two hours later, just before eleven with the bird still nearby, she slipped silently out and hidden by the caravan, walked the long way round to where Gordon operated the digger. He stopped the engine, expecting refreshments.

Jan moved close to the cab to avoid shouting.

"Come back for coffee today, I've something to show you. Come the riverbank way."

Without explanation, she hurried off back to the caravan, boiled the kettle and prepared cups, putting coffee on the table, correctly guessing that curiosity would allow little delay. He appeared shortly after.

There were always buzzards wheeling in the sky above the valley, flying effortlessly with seldom a wing flap, issuing an occasional mewing cry.

"What would it be like to skim above the land, turning, diving, riding the thermals at will?" Jan had asked the first time they watched a pair majestically soaring, then twisting to swoop in mock aerial combat. Any such grace was completely missing from the one they now watched.

"It must be a *he*," Gordon claimed. "Look at that superb plumage."

Jan uttered a "Hmm" of ridicule in return, but the words were idle conversation, their interest focused on the bird's unsteady wanderings.

Still on the field not fifty yards away, it moved erratically, periodically taking three hops and a jump with wings extended, ending in an undignified nose-dive – obviously a failed attempt at take-off. It ranged first nearer then farther away then nearer again, resting at times, staying mainly in the large, recently cleared, grassy area, seeming to avoid the surrounding tangled vegetation.

"Do you think," Jan asked, "it could be a young bird in spite of its size? If it is, why don't the parents come with food?"

They relaxed together watching. Because of the angle, both sat close on the same side of the table, leaning partly back into the cushions, partly against each other, slowly sipping coffee as they gazed through the main window. Young or old, the buzzard was obviously in trouble. They wondered what to do, and found themselves quietly holding hands, snuggled together, deeply aroused by shared emotions. This impressive bird in its proper surroundings brought home their closeness to nature, stirring a deep feeling of their own luck at being here in this Cornish valley, at having their family around them, and most of all at having each other. They didn't want to interfere with nature, but even more than that, they did *not* want this buzzard to die!

Eventually Gordon dragged himself off to do some quiet seeding, not restarting the digger to avoid the noise. He knew that wild creatures normally ignored engines, but preferred to avoid the risk.

The buzzard was still in sight at lunch, but its movements were definitely weaker. While eating, they discussed the options; let it fend for itself or try to catch and feed it for maybe a week, until strong enough to fly again. The latter was more tempting; so special to be able to handle and help such a magnificent creature. It also seemed safest. A non-flying bird would be very vulnerable, even one this size.

The big bird looked slightly smaller than some buzzards, that and its present weakness inclined them to think it could be a fledgling in spite of the fully formed feathers. The young are always most vulnerable. If this really was a youngster, then a very slim chance existed that the parent birds might return, but after so long and with strength failing, it appeared unlikely in the extreme.

"I don't think it can find food in that condition," Gordon said sadly. "It's too weak. No one else is likely to pass through the valley, so the decision is down to us. Once out of sight, it will almost certainly weaken and die in some inaccessible spot, with no one aware of its plight."

Birds of prey, fortunately, accept almost any type of meat, though hair or fur should be mixed in to enable pellet regurgitation in the normal way. The problem would not be keeping the bird alive, but judging the correct time to release it back to the wild.

Leaving the caravan, he approached slowly. The big bird withdrew under a bush, more or less trapped against the dense foliage, but in a strongly defensive position. As his hand reached slowly forward beneath the bush, the buzzard cowered back with a rasping hiss, mouth agape, wings half spread and fanned in the most intimidating stance its weakened state could muster.

Stooping lower Gordon looked into the unblinking eyes, took in the fine but subtle pattern of the feathers, then reached carefully farther forward. With a sudden movement the buzzard grabbed at the extended hand driving strong talons deeply into the flesh of his wrist.

"How ungrateful!" The thought came involuntarily, for he knew it was alarm, not belligerence. "Never mind, faint heart never won a fair maid, as they say."

Now lying flat on the ground, he reached forward again, easing his free right hand towards the bird's left side. Dark talons of the brightly yellow left foot remained deeply embedded in his left wrist. As they faced each other, the big bird could not grab the approaching hand without crossing its legs or releasing the existing grip. It hesitated a fraction too long; his free hand was on the feathered back, compressing body and legs so the other foot could no longer be freely moved.

Pulling the buzzard towards him in a steady unhurried movement generated pressure and some pain from the embedded talons. Taking care to keep his face beyond striking distance, he rose to one knee, carefully stood, then took a deep breath. Proudly walking back to the caravan holding it close to the chest with his free right hand, he could see Jan watching their approach from the window. The bird's right foot now gripped a fold in the sleeve of his working jacket. Once inside, sitting quietly down, he rested the arm with the buzzard across his knee.

Jan started with alarm, noticing blood dripping from

his wrist. Bending closer, she saw the claws sunk deeply into flesh.

"You're bleeding! Can't you get it off?"

"Not without damaging the bird. Trying to force those talons out will only make him clench harder. If we both sit quietly for a few minutes I think he'll let go. He's only gripping from fear." Seeing her continuing frown of anxiety, he attempted to make light of the injury. "I'm only dripping slowly, there must be enough in the system for a while. Don't worry it's falling on my knee not your carpet."

She smiled at the idea of being worried over an already threadbare carpet. It relieved her concern. She moved to far end of the caravan and sat down.

"Read a book, or do something that gives a little movement but not too much. Absolute stillness may seem threatening. Avoid staring, act natural."

In less than five minutes of quietness and restricted movement, with Jan feigning unconcern still in her far seat, the leg began to relax. Gordon's hand, still rested easily on the back, gently stroking and ruffling the feathers in a continuous movement, not dissimilar to the way birds groom each other, looking for flies and other vermin. Shortly the talons withdrew, the bird moving a few inches up the arm onto the thick jacket sleeve that it seemed to prefer. Blood continued to drip, and at a slightly faster rate now the fleshy holes lay exposed. The condition of his trousers later showed it had done so rather more freely than either had thought at the time, although in the excitement the loss was scarcely noticed.

After spending an hour in the caravan gaining their new companion's confidence, Jan patched Gordon's wrist with two plasters and they took the bird to the second toilet building. Taking turns to be with it, they swapped places at intervals, one leaving and the other immediately returning, each time offering morsels of food. After a few changeovers the young buzzard reacted less to movements and would come onto Gordon's bare wrist without making holes, but not straight away, only if he spent time gradually moving closer, talking quietly as he went. Jan made no attempt to persuade the bird onto her arm, but sat close by, patiently offering small tit-bits of food on her upturned palm.

Returning from one visit, she found Gordon working outside the caravan putting footstools together. Seeing her arrive, he laid the screwdriver aside, preparing to head for the buzzard but she reached out a hand detaining him. He stopped as she stepped in closer, holding on, letting the other hand fall casually about his waist, fingers moving gently as she looked up from under fluttering eyelids with a hint of mischief.

"Yes?" he asked, waiting, expression questioning.

"Just wondering what it would take for this bird to get some attention. You never find time to take an afternoon off for me!"

He leaned forward, pulling her closer, bending to kiss her lips softly and tenderly, then whispered in her ear, "But don't you think the other bird is so much more attractive?" Two could make mischief. He stepped smartly aside and sprinted for the building.

Having heard the vehicle approach, both parents stood waiting as Jim's car crossed the bridge and drew to a halt. Stephen had been away most of the day, he jumped out, stumbled and fell in the dust, then rising, dashed across towards Jan. Audrey was already watching over the car roof but Jim still struggled to stand up.

Jan knelt to hug the lad, calling across to her mother, "We've something to show you. A bird, a big one."

Audrey shook her head, she had a phobic fear of big birds and hated being close to them. Neither she nor Jim would visit, but Stephen did, and very much took to it. A photo was taken with the bird perched on his outstretched arm, the arm well wrapped in a towel and resting on a recently erected basin, almost level with his shoulder. Bird and boy stared at each other in fascination. Had its wings opened, they would have spanned almost as long tip to tip as he stood in height.

Stephen waited with impatience for Christopher and Sharon's arrival home from school, then signalled them to follow. They declined until Mum, appearing in the caravan doorway, indicated with her hand that they should. He led them off, a broad grin of pride and satisfaction across his face. Reaching the toilet building entrance, he pushed a way in, struggling against the force of the closer, and stood holding the door open in triumph. Dad was sitting at the far end, the buzzard perched on his arm.

Feeling the bird jerk nervously and its talons tense slightly, he looked up, smiling at the children. Stephen stood confident and proud, the other two still outside the doorway, hesitant, their expressions a mixture of surprise and apprehension. Christopher leaned, his arm stretched out still helping support the door, Sharon hung slightly behind, half ready to bolt. Gordon spoke softly to them, using the same unhurried monotone in which he had for the past fifteen of so minutes been talking intermittently to the bird.

"Approach very slowly, don't make any sudden movements or you'll frighten it. Let Stephen come first, it knows him. There's a towel on the basin, bring it with you for rolling round your hand and arm. You can talk one at a time, but softly like I'm doing."

In all, half an hour passed before the bird had rested on everyone's arm. Even Sharon held it, with some trepidation at first. She was good with animals but preferred them small and cuddly, not sharply dangerous. It was Christopher who displayed the real talent, putting the bird at ease, quietly confident, firm and steady without fuss.

"He'd make a good bird handler." Gordon thought, "I wonder how much he'll exaggerate the wing span when telling all his friends at school tomorrow?" He placed the buzzard back on the old saw-bench carried in earlier to make a roost, and they all left, still moving slowly and talking in quiet tones.

At tea Jan recited the events leading to the young buzzard's capture.

"Was it capture or rescue?" Gordon asked, when she paused from a lurid description of his stooping to reach under the bush, a story that had held the children almost spellbound in anticipation. "Usually those words are opposites, here they could mean exactly the same."

It was an interesting point, well above Stephen's head, but created a breathing space before Jan resumed her narrative.

"Those talons were buried deep into his flesh," she spoke in a low sinister voice, making a claw with bent fingers, extending a hand towards the children like some witch from Macbeth. They all but stopped breathing, eyes wide; a pin drop could have been heard. "Then the blood seeped slowly from his wrist, drip, drip, drip..." She said the words slowly, voice dropping still lower.

Suddenly, her pace changed to a rapid staccato.

"Show them your arm!" she ordered, simultaneously

reaching out, pulling Dad's hand quickly forward to reveal the band of plasters. Though there was now little to see, the sudden movement following that macabre narrative, and maybe the unexpected width of the plaster patch, drew little gasps of indrawn breath. Lowering the arm again, she looked at them seriously.

"Dad will tell you what to do."

Their eyes turned.

Not expecting to be thrown into the limelight so quickly, he hesitated, momentarily collecting his thoughts.

"Every time you enter, it will be nervous. If you approach slowly and offer food, and are very patient it will usually take what you offer. It may prefer to remain on the perch, that doesn't matter. If it does come on your arm, hold it away from your face and always wrap a towel round yourself first – Mum's getting short of plasters!"

Later that evening with the children asleep, the parents sat discussing how their new charge would affect the work program. Gordon looked earnestly at Jan.

"It mustn't," he insisted. "I've lost half a day now, must push on again tomorrow. You and the children can do the feeding. It's very strange, you know, our buzzard. The plumage is fully grown, it ought to be able to fly. Perhaps, on the point of leaving the nest something happened to the parent birds. If the fledgling waited and waited until hunger forced its first flight, those big wings could have glided for maybe a mile before coming to earth and it just lacked the energy to get airborne again. But I still think it might be a last year's bird one weakened by hunger; the feathers are so full and it's early for that. Either way, if we can build up its condition with plenty of food, it could go again in just a day or two."

CHAPTER 14

Flushed with Success

Christopher rose early, dressed with hardly a sound, to disappear, creeping through the doorway. Jan, always a light sleeper, rolled over in bed, prodding the prostrate figure lying next to her.

"He's gone already." she whispered.

Gordon grunted, felt a renewed attack on his ribs and reached out to pull the bedclothes back around himself but they had disappeared. He rolled over to find Jan already sitting on the edge of the bed. She leaned over and whispered again urgently.

"He's gone! He never got up this early in his life. Sharon sometimes but never Christopher. You know where, don't you?" It wasn't really a question, she continued almost without waiting, "He's gone to the buzzard."

Still sitting, she slipped the nightdress over her head, tossing it to one side and reached for clothes piled on the floor nearby. A roughened hand snaked out, dragging her back onto the bed. She turned, he was pulling her waist with one hand, the other reaching, trying to recover blankets from where she had thrown them to the bottom end of the bed. Instead of trying to escape as he had expected, she went willingly to him, their still warm bodies pressed together as they kissed, forgetting the bedclothes. As she anticipated, he eased round to lean above, looking down at her. Lightly with tender hands she encouraged him, then at one critical unbalanced moment as he moved to cover her, she shoved with all her strength against his left shoulder. Simultaneous pressure from her right thigh added irresistibly to his momentum, rolling him straight over to land with a heavy thump on the caravan floor.

The two children began to murmur and move in their bed, a sure signal they were on the point of waking. The parents dressed hastily, a little smile lingering on Jan's face as it often did when she scored a success.

An hour later Christopher returned for breakfast, unwashed, hair uncombed, but with a certain peaceful glow not normally associated with young boys. Reluctantly separated from his bird, he ate with haste and in silence, far outstripping the rest of the family, then made to slip off again but was detained – Jan's insistence that he must wash and tidy up thwarting his real intention. Walking off along the track with Sharon to school, he several times looked back, gazing towards the buzzard's temporary home.

Later that morning Gordon became feverish, his temperature rising. Certain private parts were swollen and extremely tender. Unable to continue working, he lay in pain, resting on the bench seat that was normally Christopher's bed, his skin a shade lighter under the deep suntan. As the pain worsened, deep surges of agony coated his body with sweat and Jan called Dr Blewett on his first ever visit to the caravan.

Whatever the cause, the antibiotics prescribed shifted it in two days and he quickly resumed working, but Jan warned the children again to wrap their arms well when handling the buzzard.

The Easter weather was sunny, not the burning warmth of late May and June, but sufficient to sit outdoors in shirtsleeves for coffee break, drinking and looking at the river. There were only fixed bench seats in the caravan, no removable chairs, so outside they sat on the ground, on pillows laid over old plastic bags.

"Pity we're not ready for visitors yet, there might be a few about this week." Jan shaded her eyes, glancing up at the cloudless sky, then scanned along the river. "Look. There's a couple walking upstream."

A man and wife perhaps, both about retirement age, approached. Chatting to each other while walking they paused in front of the caravan. The man said "Hello," and the couple fell naturally into conversation, probably pleased enough to find someone to talk with after two miles walking alone. He was a retired schoolmaster and local historian, Gordon and Jan's first encounter with anyone who understood the Cornish language.

Talk turned naturally to the valley. The visitors, having slaked their own curiosity with enquiries as to current ambitions for the site, chatted freely on the river's history. The man, shortish, ordinary of stature and appearance, spoke with a pleasant voice, quiet but in some way commanding attention.

"Relubbus has the meaning *Village by the ford*, from the old word *Res*, a ford – in some books the old spelling starts Res. How long since the ford existed? Who can tell? A bridge has been there from at least the early fourteenth century, that much is certain, verified from old documents. No one knows exactly when the first bridge was built but it was the main route from London to St Michael's Mount at one time."

"Six hundred years ago! But surely the present one is not so old, not dating back to the time of the ford?

Must have been rebuilt more than once, mustn't it?" Gordon asked.

He had looked closely at the existing bridge, made entirely of Cornish granite. Underneath it consisted of a dozen huge stone lintels laid side by side, their span restricting the river's flow to no more than five feet in both width and height. A smaller arch, some three feet wide at a slightly higher level might be for flood relief, but at the moment little more than eighteen inches of water rushed under the main span. Further along the village close to the chapel, another granite bridge spanned what might be called a tributary but was so small as to look more like a drainage ditch. A date plaque high on the chapel gable proclaimed 1875, this second bridge was surely much older, but again no one knew. Nearby stood another disused but valued relic, the old village pump.

Their visitor shook his head. He could not say if both bridges were of similar age, his historical revelations relating more to the stream.

At St Erth, a larger village some two miles downstream, the river many centuries earlier flowed wide enough to be crossed by ferry. Small sailing ships were said to have come up to that point, and small boats up to Porthcullum, a mile downstream from where they sat.

When looking at the River Hayle today, it was difficult for the listeners to envisage these ancient boats, fully rigged, with a minimum of sail set, making slow majestic progress up the river even as far as St Erth. At Relubbus it was perhaps ten feet wide, in places less, and seldom ran more than eighteen inches in depth, though here and there deeper pools existed. Many points shallowed to below a foot in summer. A man would have trouble finding depth to swim, let alone sail a galleon, or more probably a trading packet.

Of course it could have been just rowing boats, tales handed down tend to suffer from exaggeration, though the river was said to be tidal as far as Relubbus at one time. Looking back further, say two million years ago, the very tip of Cornwall may even have been an island, or so fossil remains indicated.

The family had always believed that the river would never flood, a notion reinforced by talking to local people. Apparently it did at one time, before cleaning and straightening took place in the nineteen-fifties or sixties. Certainly very little rise had occurred in the past winter. Waving goodbye, Jan watched the elderly couple depart, then gazed back at the river lost in thought.

"We're very lucky," she took another sip from the now cold coffee and reached for Gordon's hand. "There can't be too many dwellings in the country situated right on the edge of a river where you have the pleasure of sitting in your home or just outside, watching the water flow by, little ripples on the surface, seeing the fish jump and yet never be in danger of a flood." Putting down the empty cup she leaned over, resting her head on his shoulder, knowing he would dash off to work again any moment.

The children too, liked the river, especially close to the bridge. She felt happy for them to play along the edge or even in the water – it was shallow and looked so clear and pure.

* * *

Jan gazed at the headless body, full length on the ground at her feet.

"Must tell him how much more attractive he is

without a face." She smiled at this impish thought, as Stephen ran up and simultaneously Gordon's head re-emerged from peering down the inspection hole into the septic tank.

"The bottom is covered in water, it's dark down there but I can see it glinting. Can't tell how deep. It's from trying out the showers, we forgot about removing these supports!" He eased a pair of steps through the hole, struggling to open the legs below before lowering himself down and disappearing into the blackness.

Stepping off the ladder into water, he dropped one foot gingerly until it touched down on the floor below. No feeling of wetness. Good! But how high had water come up the boot? – impossible to see in the tank's dank, murky, gloom. Reaching over, feeling the Wellington top, he slid a hand downward until it touched water; about halfway, not too bad. Wiping fingers against his old trousers, the rubber glove was slipped back on.

"Good thing we've not used the toilets. The smell's not too bad, don't think there's any methane yet." He grinned wryly, muttering to himself in the shadows, remembering his own dire warning to the children that people could die entering tanks like this, and now he did it himself. But surely this water remained too fresh to produce gas? After a while his eyes adjusted to the restricted light entering from the small hole above, absorbed quickly by darkly wet surfaces. From the first blackness, dim shapes now emerged, but no more than vague outlines. The work must be done by feel.

With a hammer the task commenced, driving out wedges from one column of blocks supporting the tank roof. Reaching for the second one, a mesh of wetness touched then clung to his face. Removing the glove again, he groped at the web, scraping it free with his fingers, then flicked the hand in an attempt to dislodge sticky filaments, finally rubbing them off on his trouser seat and wiping his face again with one sleeve. Before moving he focused closely striving to see, but no sign of the remaining web or its occupant could be discerned. Not surprising, a tarantula could go undetected down here. Never mind, the intention was only to move the spider safely to one corner.

A rustle in the water over at the far side drew his attention. A rat? If so this would be the first. But what else? Remembering his trousers were tucked well into Wellington tops rather than open at the bottom, brought a small sigh of satisfaction.

Moving the first block, he passed it up through the opening into Jan's waiting hands, closing eyes against the light to preserve the little vision available below. Removing several more blocks loosened the old railway sleepers used for main supports. Single-handed in this dark confined space and barely able to see either end, manoeuvring these heavy timbers up into position then heaving them bodily through the small exit hole, proved difficult. However, combined efforts, pushing from below and pulling from above, hoisted the sleepers out.

The tedious business of passing up each block that formed the supporting columns took longer. The bottom two from each pile were submerged! Lifting these, the dirty, slightly smelly water trickled out continuously, thoroughly wetting Gordon as each was offered up overhead and through the narrow opening. Jan could hear the trickling streams falling as hollow splashes on the liquid surface beneath. Stephen, who from time to time lay on the new concrete roof to peer down into the darkness, gurgled with delight.

Well before lunch everything easily removable had

been cleared. Those corrugated iron sheets on which the concrete had actually rested and to which it had well and truly stuck, were left in position. Corrosion in the constantly damp atmosphere would disintegrate them eventually. Gordon emerged from the pit, laying down to reach back in, hauling the steps out into sunlight and passed them to Jan.

She stepped back, screwing up her nose in protest.

"No thank you! I'm not touching them, they're all smelly."

"Nonsense, they're cleaner than before." He took a pace towards her with the steps.

"They're covered in sewage, of course they're smelly. So are you!" She stepped back again quickly as he made to move closer. "Don't you come near me! Go and shower – take clean clothes with you."

He replaced the tank lid, took a shower, had lunch and spent the afternoon levelling topsoil. Postponing tea until darkness to make maximum use of daylight hours was no longer practical with the extending evenings. It made more sense now, to stop and eat then return to work afterwards; so when Christopher and Sharon arrived home from school, the family gathered for the meal.

"Dad was smelly!" Stephen said just before they sat down. He moved backward several paces, copying Jan's motion at the time, adding his own touch for emphasis, lifting index finger and thumb to hold his nose. That was it. No detail, no follow up. Just the three words and the little mime.

Christopher and Sharon looked at each other, then turned from Stephen to Dad and back to Stephen again, their curiosity piqued. Stephen said nothing. A happy grin sat comfortably on his face, he was satisfied. They wanted to know, he wouldn't tell them. The seconds passed. He bent down, then straightened up with a little jump, a characteristic sign of his pleasure, and clambered into the bench seat opposite Jan, the grin broadening in devilment, mischievous rather than evil.

Gordon, standing watching with interest, moved to join Jan, but she shrank back in mock alarm.

"Are you *sure* you're not still smelly?"

"Mum!" Sharon was beyond herself. There was something going on here, something others understood while she did not. What was being kept from her? She stood indignant, annoyed and just a little bit lost.

Jan looked at her daughter, lips pursed in understanding and beckoned.

"Come, sit next to Dad and I'll explain."

Sharon moved forward uncertainly.

"Next to Dad? He's not...? I'll sit next to Stephen, I can hear you better." She slipped into the opposite bench, looking expectantly towards Jan but eyeing her father with suspicion. Christopher joined her, equally curious but wisely saying nothing.

Jan's narrative tended to comedy rather than the dramatic. Seen from above in full daylight, events had offered a different aspect. To the older children's great amusement she described in detail the smelly water trickling from concrete blocks over Dad's head and shoulders as he hoisted them up through the small opening.

When Jan asked a question, Gordon, taking up the narrative, portrayed the dark, musty, dimly lit inside. Watching their merriment change to round-eyed interest, he continued, disclosing the incident when a web had stuck to his face, something not mentioned at the time. Interest changed to concern as, with graphic actions, he indicated how the sticky mass had clung to his skin,

297

resisting removal in the darkness.

On hearing of the attempt and failure to find the spider, Sharon's eyes looked him up and down with alarm, as if expecting the creature to reappear at any moment. She eased back in her seat with a grimace of distaste, creating maximum space between herself and her father. Christopher asked, could he go down, but looked relieved rather than disappointed at Jan's flat refusal. Only Stephen, who had seen inside from above, looked entirely keen. Jan knew he would attempt to climb down if the steps had not been removed. As it was the young lad satisfied himself by following his sister's example, leaning back away from Dad, once more pointedly holding his nose.

The following morning, Saturday, the toilets finally came into use. Sharon could hardly believe her luck. Each compartment had a polished door, with a proper bolt on the inside and a chain that flushed, as she kept telling the rest of the family on each of the many times she returned from the building that day!

At tea Gordon whispered, loud enough for everyone to hear, "There'll be no coffee for Sharon. If she goes to that Ladies any more, they may wear out before we get a single visitor!"

Rising to the bait as usual, Sharon drew herself up and took a deep breath, ready to protest – but she stopped suddenly. With a schoolmarm expression and a stance obviously copied from Jan, she faced her father.

"Be careful, Dad. I'm the one who makes all the coffee at weekends. If I can't have any, some other folk may go without."

The two boys looked quickly across at her, a new respect in their eyes. One up on Dad was good!

After several days of plentiful feeding, the buzzard appeared much better. Christopher noticed first.

"Buzz is getting harder to feed, it takes longer before he'll let me approach, I think he's stronger?" It was part question, part assertion.

Gordon went with him to look. They returned to the caravan shortly afterwards, announcing their opinion that the bird was now strong enough to fly.

The old saw-bench placed in the toilet building had become the bird's favourite roost. Carrying this bench, Dad led the way. Christopher walked slightly behind and to one side, the buzzard on his left arm at roughly waist level, his right hand resting lightly on the bird's back. With the family tailing on behind, the little band proceeded slowly to the corner of the field below two large oaks.

Christopher knelt down, carefully extending his arm. The buzzard, unaware it was now free, stepped back onto its familiar perch now positioned a little distance from the trees. Father and son moved steadily backwards, the entire family standing together to watch.

Some time elapsed before the young predator spread its great wings and lifted off into the nearest oak. There it remained for over an hour. Only Christopher stayed long enough to see the big bird, to which he had become so attached, glide off over the brow of the hill. He raced back with the news.

"It took an enormous jump from the tree, swooping down gathering speed, almost hitting the ground, then soared upwards, gliding across the sky incredibly fast!" He spoke urgently, breathlessly, eyes alive with pride and excitement, right hand moving, mimicking the motions. "It only flapped three times, but travelled miles!"

They all felt pleased but a little sad.

It was natural of course, that Sharon should notice the problem first, but testing soon confirmed she was right. The toilet cisterns took ages to fill. Not just longer than usual but a totally unacceptable five minutes plus! That could create havoc in the summer.

A little research revealed that every cistern had a high pressure valve. OK. The pressure in the mains was high, very high, almost enough to blow your head off! That's the effect of living in a valley. However, water by-laws forbade connecting toilet cisterns direct to the main. They must flow from large tanks in the roof. Because the toilet buildings were single-storey, there was not much head; that is to say, water level in those tanks was not very far above the toilet cisterns, which therefore tended to fill slowly.

Although changing the valves to low pressure only needed plastic inserts with bigger holes, they seemed difficult to obtain. Jan pestered the suppliers for nearly two weeks – ridiculous for so small a part; a hundred in a paper bag would take less room than a tin of baked beans and weigh less too. Using baked beans as a comparison came naturally; they were cheap, nourishing and the family lived on them quite a lot. Eventually new valves arrived, curing the slow filling completely, every cistern refilling in less than two minutes.

One remaining essential job entailed laying land drains to disperse clear water that would trickle from the septic tank. Although use of the toilets had already commenced, the tank itself would take months to fill with only one family using it, but the soakaway system must be completed before customers started arriving.

Part of this work entailed removal of a low soil bank. In doing so two young rabbits were exposed. The small size of the family was a surprise, usually there were at least four, but it was still early in the season. Although the children, home for the weekend, searched long and carefully, no further babies appeared. They did not expect to see the doe, for she does not keep her brood in the warren but digs a short burrow elsewhere, blocking them in. Only at intervals does she return, digging out the entrance to feed her young. Rabbits, they knew, were present here and there around the site, but seemed not to be numerous.

Small, cuddly, totally vulnerable and defenceless, Sharon immediately wanted to mother them. Kneeling down she held both on her lap, one supported by each hand. As she bent far forward until a cheek rested snugly against each small bunny, one turned towards her, rubbing her face with its tiny nose. She sighed, her young body giving a little shudder of pleasure.

An outside cage was not so much constructed as thrown together from odd bits and pieces, and sited close to the small remaining pile of building blocks for shelter. A hydrometer used for testing the excavator batteries was thoroughly cleaned to provide a feeder. Sharon filled it with milk and holding the babies on an old towel on her lap, put the end to one small mouth; squeezing the rubber bulb gently made the milk flow. A white blob appeared on the muzzle, running down to drip slowly off fur under its chin. A little tongue protruded, licking outside the mouth and soon locating the milk source; natural instinct probably, to look for something hanging and suck at it. Another little mouth pushed its way forward searching for a share.

The rest of the family looked on intrigued, but no one, not even Stephen, tried to help. They just watched, enjoying but not interfering. By some mysterious tacit consent, these rabbit babies were Sharon's. How everyone accepted it without a single spoken word was a puzzle to which no one knew or sought an answer. Gordon and Jan looked at each other and shrugged; they were hers, a substitute for absent dolls perhaps but treated with infinite care, love and patience.

After a while they no longer tried to run and hide as they had at first. She handled them inside the caravan for long periods each evening over several weeks, mostly on her lap. They liked to hop around on the floor, occasionally giving a sudden vertical jump to face in almost the opposite direction. The motion was comical, even the young rabbits appeared bemused at times to find themselves facing a different wall, but Jan tended to discourage such play for their little droppings could be a nuisance. Sharon proved a good substitute mum, they seemed to trust her, she had a gentle way with them and later played with both rabbits in the yard and on the grass. They nibbled at various foliage, quite free and unrestrained. It was several more weeks before they finally decided to run off into the hedge, and even then they would come out if Sharon offered a drink of milk. She also discovered they loved to lick honey from a finger, finding that an even greater temptation.

The final drainage task now loomed. Convince the building inspector that the soakaway system worked satisfactorily! The local council was fortunately staffed mainly by practical men of some experience, a definite advantage since they knew when something worked without needing constant reference to a book of rules.

Just over 180 feet of porous land-drain pipes had been laid in several lines, to carry away clear effluent from the septic tank. As a test for the inspector, Mr Atherton on this occasion, it was proposed to fill many dustbins with water and empty these directly into an inspection chamber leading to the outlet system. This simulated several hours peak flow in a couple of minutes.

The test was ridiculously severe, but Gordon had suggested it to display confidence that the deep stony bed of tailings would take virtually anything. He did not expose the last pipe, but extracted one only five pipes down from the tank outlet. It proved impossible to tip dustbins as fast as the water ran away, and no liquid reached even that fifth pipe, the ultimate in convincing tests. It was immediately passed.

"Almost there!" Jan handed Gordon a coffee, easing herself onto cushions opposite, her skin still glowing from a recent shower. "I know there's years of work ahead, but for now, just one or two more vital jobs. We *are* going to be ready on time!" She smiled, but for all her confidence, there remained a hint of doubt. She turned, eyebrows raised questioningly, seeking confirmation.

"Yes, we should. Barring accidents! Only the road surface and signs are essential. More pitches would help, depends how well we do."

The original temporary name-sign painted soon after their arrival, rough letters on an old wooden board, had sufficed only to direct lorry loads of building materials. Left in place, its attractiveness to visitors would compare unfavourably with the effect of a fluttering skull and crossbones on treasure-laden galleons, as Gordon put it during one discussion.

"That expression," Jan agreed, "is very apt. Visitors

303

arriving in their caravans will indeed be *treasure-laden galleons* to us. We do need the plunder! I feel quite piratical already."

The present sign rested haphazardly on a pole right next to the little box where the postman had once left their mail. How many people have had a letterbox half a mile from their front door, but neither mail van nor bicycle could have been expected to negotiate the road regularly in its original condition.

Planning consent for permanent signs, one on each side of the entrance, came with the original building permission. Both boards were already cut to shape in marine plywood, the white background carefully painted and repainted; primer, undercoats, gloss coats, five in all. Now only the wording was missing.

A local signwriter, another small but unavoidable expense, produced superb professionally polished black letters offering visitors the prospect of quality. Gordon mounted the boards on short sections of second-hand telegraph pole on both sides of the entrance, hoping they would entice customers to enter rather than pass on to other sites.

From time to time, record photographs were taken showing site progress. One set had even been sent to the solicitors for date stamping to prove various works had been started and properly executed.

"Record everything," Gordon said, "never mind if it doesn't seem necessary; you never know what proof may be needed in the future!" It would be some time before they realised how profoundly true these words were to become and how useful a suspicious nature could be! Any surplus exposures were used for family snaps, money not being available to buy films solely for that purpose, which they regretted as the children grew up. After one session, five frames remained to complete a roll. Christopher, apparently driving the digger, was photographed from a slightly off-centre angle, concealing the fact that his legs were still too short to reach the pedals. For the second, Jan snapped the three children hoisted high in the front bucket.

Jim, nearby at the time, tried but failed to climb into the machine, his bad leg making the ascent too difficult. Arranging a special shot, the front bucket was forced downward, raising the forward end of the excavator. As it rose the machine took on a slope until the rear bucket, the one used for digging trenches, touched the stony surface preventing further movement. It was sufficient. The front wheels dangled well clear of the ground. Jim and Audrey stood each side of one raised front wheel, gripping the tyre as if lifting it with their own hands. By ensuring the front bucket lay out of shot, it would appear as an act of great strength.

Another shot showed Christopher lifting with Jim, and finally Jan was persuaded to sit on the rear bucket which now rested on the ground. Again the picture was taken to exclude the machine's front end. He didn't tell her, and neither she nor the others realised this shot would give the impression of her weight tipping up the machine.

When the snaps were collected, she saw the proof! Fortunately Gordon's leg was not stiff like Jim's. He took two steps away when she came to the photo, and as she turned and lunged, he leapt headlong through the open doorway to land nearly ten feet away, well beyond the steps. Acting so quickly, he missed her ill-concealed smile, though she had undoubtedly intended to thump him soundly.

Catching his balance as she reached the doorway, he turned, holding up a hand and signalling her to stop, his look of concern easy to feign.

She halted, hesitating, unable to see what was wrong, watching the waving hand that urged her backwards.

"Move back! Stand nearer the centre of the caravan, we don't want *that* falling over too!"

Having spoken, he took a series of rapid backward paces, expecting pursuit.

"Wait till you come back for lunch." She threatened quietly from the doorway.

"I think Jim's invited me to eat with him today."

"Coward!"

An abundance of clearing and filling still awaited attention, but the pressure had gone. The site would be ready; that now looked assured. One more heavy and unavoidable job remained – the entrance road.

This task involved most of the family. Gordon loaded a trailer, towing it with Max, the excavator to the next piece of road. Here it was emptied in a long line, tipping and creeping forward at the same time in an effort to achieve a covering of stone nine to twelve inches deep over half the road width.

While he returned for further loads, Jan picked out stones too big to be levelled, helped occasionally by Audrey, or Christopher and Sharon when not at school, but often on her own. These over-sized chunks were carried or in some cases rolled, to either side where they reinforced the road edges.

It was Gordon's job to rake by hand these uneven tippings into a smooth finish. Jan unhitched the trailer then drove Max up and down over the new surface, compacting it while he continued raking and levelling as pits and hollows appeared under the pressure of those large knobbly tyres.

In this manner they toiled, sweating, moving ever towards the village, gradually, gradually, eating up each yard of the half mile track to the entrance. It was now well into spring, some days extremely hot, the minimum amount of clothing worn, any exposed skin becoming distinctly African. Despite drinking prodigious amounts of water to prevent dehydration, many pounds were lost over this period, but at last the village was reached. The road surface lay smooth, even, and wide enough for two vehicles to pass. The narrow entrance had been enlarged substantially, not just to give a sweep in, but an additional area allowing easy turning when their visitors drove up to make purchases at the village shop or for the telephone kiosk. A sign was erected to keep it private and prevent casual parking.

The final essential task was now complete! Smart signs pointed the way along a track looking wide and smooth when viewed at a distance by any customer debating whether to enter, and the toilet facilities were not only functioning, but clean and inviting. In addition several grassy areas lay attractively waiting.

May was passing, the bank holiday approached and now at last, after the rush, the sweat and the sheer hard work, River Valley was open!

At times it had seemed impossible that all the vital jobs could be completed in time. How had they done it, how had they stood up to that first year, to all the hard labour, to a lack of any food but the cheapest? What had sustained them through the pressure and tension of not knowing if the work could be completed, not knowing if the money would last?

What indeed? They had made it – but neither could

truthfully say how. Strangest of all, they had really enjoyed it, had revelled in pitting themselves against the challenge.

Though moments of doubt had arisen, belief in success had always dominated. Life in the valley had been, and very much still was, superb. Far from causing friction, the difficulties had only brought them closer. Not just the parents, the children were happy too.

"But," Jan thought, "I wouldn't want to meet such a challenge again. Although we've triumphed on this occasion, there must be a limit to stamina somewhere!"

Everything was working, all ready and waiting to receive the first paying customers, they were elated. Not much money remained, but now that all the main expenses had been met, what was left would last many weeks living cheaply.

Jan decided to make a small celebration party and spent lavishly, at least by her own standards it was lavish. A whole chicken, fresh vegetables, fresh fruit to make a strawberry-topped pavlova with real cream – that was lavish! Sharon helped with the preparations, especially the chicken roasted in Audrey's oven. For her, this was part of the fun. Although still learning, her cooking skills were really good. Lunch, the briefest of cold snacks at which Stephen protested, merely sharpened appetites for the evening. That night they sat down to a banquet, celebrating the opening, and impending arrival of their first paying visitor.

The festive spirit evaporated somewhat over the next days, deepening first into gloom, and then depression as weeks passed. Not a customer to be seen. The big six-foot signs in the village had been polished at least half a dozen times, but any idea that this would result in an influx of tourers was crushed as empty day followed empty day.

June arrived, but still not a single customer. Gordon worked on but in a desultory fashion, without zest, his whole spirit consumed by a certain lethargy. Jan had been restless for weeks, she couldn't believe how many times she had polished the taps and toilet seats. The basins gleamed so much, visitors were going to need sunglasses!

They would sit together for long periods discussing the situation over the table in the caravan before Gordon suddenly rose, disappearing again to immerse himself in clearing work like an ostrich digging its head in the sand.

So it was that Jan sat disconsolate and alone when from the corner of her eye she spied the top of a caravan approaching down the road. A great surge of emotion, a mixture of relief, elation and panic, hit her. For a minute she froze, unable to move. The word *mirage* came unbidden to mind, then anxiety.

"Let them stay, don't let them turn round and go away."

To be continued

details on back page - but the story changes!
How strangely visitors behave! Can the family cope with their odd sometimes embarrassing ways? There is laughter in the valley, a touch of intrigue and some danger! And how do you keep milk fresh? Buy a goat!

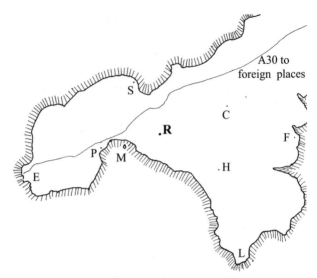

R = Relubbus

M = St Michael's Mount   P = Penzance   S = St.Ives
H = Helston   C = Camborne   E = Land's End
F = Falmouth   L = Lizard point

Relubbus is by a very long way the smallest place on the map, just a handful of houses, no more, and even these are not within sight of that tiny caravan hidden away downstream in the wild deserted valley.

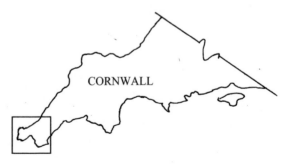

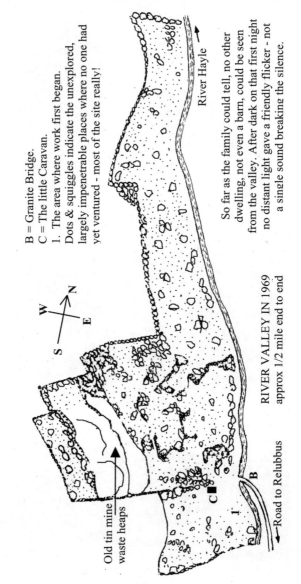

B = Granite Bridge.
C = The little Caravan.
1. The area where work first began.
Dots & squiggles indicate the unexplored, largely impenetrable places where no one had yet ventured - most of the site really!

So far as the family could tell, no other dwelling, not even a barn, could be seen from the valley. After dark on that first night no distant light gave a friendly flicker - not a single sound breaking the silence.

River Hayle →

↑ N
W ← → E
S

RIVER VALLEY IN 1969
approx 1/2 mile end to end

Old tin mine waste heaps

→ Road to Relubbus

Stephen and the Buzzard

Max - and everyone!